Pra~e for Lacey Weatherford's

The Demon Kiss

"The Demon Kiss is truly a story that will tug on your heart strings whether you're 16 or 36. I am highly anticipating the next chapter in this magical romance!"

~Lori A. Arcelay, Romancing the Darkside

"Not only does The Demon Kiss have an abundance of romance and passion, it has plenty of humor, suspense, and adventure as well. This book just goes non-stop and when you get to the end, you'll be begging for more."

~Tishia Mackey, Paranormal Opinion

"The Demon Kiss book left me begging for more and frantically searching the computer looking for the release date of the 3rd book. Lacey Weatherford is a genius. She has written the book in a way that engages both the mind and heart of the reader, taking them on a ride that they won't easily forget."

~ Belinda Boring, The Bookish Snob

"The Demon Kiss is a fast-paced, tragic, triumphant, romantic, inspirational, emotionally loaded, powerful story. It grabs you from the first sentence and doesn't let you go! This is a "cover to cover, hope you downloaded book three on the same day" read."

~ Beverly Sharp, The Wormhole

"The Demon Kiss is as action-packed as the first in the series, and just as engrossing. And once again, Lacey Weatherford was the Queen of the Cliffhanger! She gets to that edge, and just stops, leaving you wanting MORE, somehow without allowing the reader to feel unsatisfied. A-MA-ZING!"

~ Kim Deister, The Caffeinated Diva

Of Witches and Warlocks

The Demon Kiss

Book Two

By Lacey Weatherford

Moonstruck Media

Arizona

DEDICATION

For all of my readers, who love "LOVE" just as much as I do. May dreams of Vance and Portia continue to dance in your heads!

ACKNOWLEDGEMENTS

I would be remiss if I didn't take the time to thank the many people who proof read and reviewed this story for me. Your input and opinions were invaluable and always right on the money! You all know who you are and I want to thank you for putting up with me from the start and listening to my hours of rambling on the subject.

To Connie, Larissa, and James, you all truly influenced the plot line in this book and for that I will be forever grateful!

Thank you to everyone who has continued to support me in this little adventure. It's been a blast rubbing shoulders with all of you!

Chapter 1

I had tasted a love stronger than any emotion I'd ever felt in my life.

It was a bold statement for a sixteen-year-old girl to make, but it was the truth.

I thought back to the first day I realized our school's resident bad boy, Vance Mangum, had an interest in me. My connection with him was instantaneous. There had never been any question he was the one for me, even after I found out he was a powerful warlock who was running from his past.

My mind began to run over everything that happened in the last few months of my life with him.

I found out on my sixteenth birthday I was a witch, descended from a long line of witches and warlocks. I learned my grandmother and father were leaders of a magical coven. And I discovered the coven was protecting the person I loved most in this world from a horrible danger—his own father.

I'd fallen in love with Vance Mangum, almost sacrificing my own life to save him from what should have been a certain death. But when I awoke from all the trauma, it was to find him gone from my life, set on a collision course with the very evil which almost destroyed him once before.

I took a deep sigh and looked back into the eyes of the

young man who faced me now in my living room. Disbelief and deep confusion were etched upon his face.

"This is a lot to comprehend." Brad let out a deep breath as he leaned back into the chair, clearly finding it difficult to believe anything I'd been saying to him for the past hour now.

"Show him something, Portia," Shelly suggested, sitting down next to me, urging me to be a little more forceful in my demonstration.

Figuring she was probably right, and knowing I needed to get things moving along, I did as she suggested. I sighed as I lifted my hand into the air and motioned for the magazine on the table next to Brad to come toward me.

It lifted easily, floating, and was soon settled into my outstretched palm.

"Whoa!" Brad jumped from his chair to his feet. He shook his head in disbelief. "That's intense!" After a short pause he grinned at me and added, "Do something else."

"Brad," I complained, walking over to drop the magazine back onto the table. "I really don't have time to do a magic show for you. Every second is of the essence right now. I need to know if you're in or out. What's the verdict?"

He pondered this carefully for a few moments before he answered.

"I'm in," he said with a bigger grin, nodding between Shelly and me. "But we're going to need to come up with something to tell my parents."

"That's all taken care of," Shelly replied. "We had to tell my parents everything. They're going to cook something up about sending us on a vacation to recover from our traumatic event, which in a sense will be somewhat true."

The traumatic event she was referring to was an explosion that happened at Sedona High School a couple of weeks prior. Several of our classmates had been killed in the disaster. As a matter of fact, I was the only one to survive the blast in the classroom where the incident occurred, thanks to a magical shield that protected me.

It turned out the explosion had been orchestrated by an evil coven in order to capture my boyfriend, Vance. Vance's mother, Krista, had taken him, but it was his father, Damien Cummings, who'd been behind the scenes planning everything.

While Vance had nearly been changed into a demon, he had actually been the one to destroy his mother in a last ditch attempt to save my life. I, in turn, healed him, but woke to discover he'd left me to go find his father.

I was very angry that he'd gone off on his own. His dad would be way more powerful than his mother. He had no protection of any kind. He was reacting to some misguided thought that he needed to do this to protect me, so we could have a real life together.

My best friend, Shelly, had inadvertently been placed in the middle of all this when Vance's mother cast an evil spell over her and used her as a puppet. Shelly and I were now trying to explain to her boyfriend, Brad, all the things that happened over the last little while. He, up until this time, had been in the dark about everything going on in our lives.

We were going after Vance, and we were asking Brad if he wanted to come with us.

"It's all set," I said to my dad, Sean, as he walked into the room. "Shelly's going to take us in her car. Brad's coming too."

"Portia, I'm very apprehensive about sending the three of you out alone." My dad shook his head slightly. "What if something were to happen? You're the only witch in this group. If you were to somehow come upon this demon coven, it could be disastrous. You can't fight off a whole coven by yourself, you know."

I let out a big sigh before I spoke, feeling a little overwhelmed.

"We've been all through this, Dad. We won't get involved with the demon coven in any way. As soon as we locate them, or Vance, I promise you the very first call I make will be to you." I placed my hand gently on his arm, trying to reassure him.

"Make sure you do. I don't want you getting remotely close to that coven," he replied, looking very concerned for my well-being.

"They aren't looking for me anyway. It's Vance they're after. If they find him alone out there ...." I trailed off as I sighed again in frustration over the whole matter. "Why did you let him go, Dad? It's like he's serving himself right up to them."

"I didn't have anything to do with that," my dad said, lifting his hands slightly before dropping them dejectedly back to his side. "He left without consulting any of us. I would've tried to counsel him differently had he come to me."

"It's my fault," Shelly piped up, looking sadly at me. "He came to me with this. I should have talked him out of it. I just didn't know what to say."

"Would all of you just stop?" Brad piped in, glancing around at us with an irritated look. "It isn't anyone's fault. Vance is eighteen and an adult. He made this choice, and whether or not it was right or wrong lies solely with him. We just need to find him before something else happens. He shouldn't have to face what he's looking for alone."

"You're right," I agreed, feeling more than grateful to hear Brad was taking things in stride and on my side of the issue. "Take Shelly to get things squared away with your parents. If they're cool with everything, you can meet me

4

back here in an hour. I'll be packed and ready to go by then."

After walking them to the door, I opened it to let them out and closed it behind them. I slid down to the floor in exhaustion, a sudden wave of dizziness threatening to overwhelm me.

"You're still so weak, Portia. Do you think this is wise?" my dad asked, squatting down next to me with a concerned look. "Why don't you stay here and rest for a few more days?"

I was weak because I'd given almost every drop of blood in my body to feed Vance, in a desperate attempt to keep him alive after his near demon conversion. I shuddered realizing how close I'd come to losing him completely. I felt the unease moving down my spine when I thought of how near he had been to killing me in return.

"I'll be fine, Dad," I replied, pushing the unwelcome thoughts from my head, trying to concentrate on the present situation. "It gets better with every passing hour. Just give me a minute, okay?"

He nodded and sat with me for a few moments, never taking his eyes off me, before offering a hand out to pull me up. He walked with me up the stairs to my bedroom, placing an arm gently around my waist to give me support along the way.

An empty suitcase was lying on the bed, and I slowly moved around the room, packing it with a few items I might need. Conserving energy, I didn't use any magic.

The final thing I placed in my suitcase was the last thing Vance had given me—a letter. It explained he had decided to leave me and why he was doing so. Folded inside were pictures the two of us took on an outing together. I had looked at them so many times the edges were beginning to look worn. They were my most precious worldly possession.

"What direction do you think you'll head?" Dad asked, pulling me from my reverie. I placed the letter and pictures into a safe spot in my purse, where they wouldn't get crumpled.

"I'm thinking east, toward Albuquerque. That was the last area where you tracked his father's coven to. I'm thinking he probably would've gone there. I'll just have to follow my instincts and see if I can feel him, using my senses."

Vance and I had performed a binding ritual together early in our relationship in an effort to make a more permanent commitment to each other. The binding spell was so intense we now felt a strong physical pull toward each other. When we were together, everything was great. When we were apart, it was like being physically sick with an ache that actually caused us pain.

I used the power of that pull to help me find him the last time he disappeared. I was banking on the same thing to help me out this time.

Because of our link we also discovered we had an excellent mental connection, too. When the distances between us weren't more than a few miles, we could actually communicate by thought.

This didn't always help me, though, because Vance had extreme control over his mind—a control I hadn't mastered. Whenever he deemed something to be too dangerous for me to know, he would close up like a steel trap against me. After that, I could no longer hear him, and reaching him was almost impossible.

I planned on giving him an earful about this the next time I saw him. I was sick to death of him always shutting me out for my own protection. I felt I'd proven on several occasions I didn't need to be treated like something that was going to break, seeing how he was currently alive because of me.

At my dressing table, I paused to check my appearance in the mirror. I looked pitiful. I picked up a hairbrush and combed through my black hair, deciding to pull it back into a ponytail.

There was nothing I was going to be able to do about the deep dark circles under both of my eyes. My skin was even more pale than usual after Vance had taken so much blood from me. The large purple bruise with several puncture marks on my neck was a constant reminder. I ran my hand absently over the damaged tissue, which would most assuredly carry a permanent scar.

I didn't hate the mark, though. It was proof he'd been there, that he was alive now.

"Can I carry your suitcase downstairs for you?" my dad asked.

I dropped my hand and moved away from the mirror. "Sure," I said, nodding as I faced him, trying to muster up a smile. "Thanks."

"No problem," he replied as he picked up the luggage and carried it out of the room.

I dropped my brush back on my dressing table, grabbed my bag, and rechecked it for my proper identification. When I was finished, I proceeded downstairs toward the living room. I heard a knock on the door just as I entered.

I opened it and was surprised to find Grandma Milly standing there, a small box in her hands.

"Hi, Grandma. Come in," I said, stepping aside to let her in.

"I've brought you some things to take," she explained, her hands gripping a box.

"Okay," I replied, and followed her over to the sofa, sitting down next to her.

"As I'm sure you're aware, your dad and I have been

very leery about letting you go off on your own to search for Vance ... especially after everything that's happened lately. You'll be the only source of magical protection for the three of you, which doesn't give you very good odds if you run into some sort of problem. So we put our heads together, and I think we may have found a way to help out with that a little."

She opened the box and pulled out a red ruby amulet on a gold chain. She then opened two smaller boxes.

One box contained a flat silver ring that held an onyx stone in the center. The other held a similar ring in gold, with the same red-colored stone in the middle of it that was in the amulet hanging from the chain.

"These are for Shelly, Brad and Vance. The one for Vance has been charmed with spells of protection. I don't know how helpful those will be, seeing how the demon coven has gotten around protection spells we've had on him in the past, but I figured something is better than nothing."

She held up the second ring and amulet so I could see them better.

"These other two items are a little unorthodox. They were made specifically for Shelly and Brad. These are not made from regular stones, but magical stones that carry some serious power in them. The wearer of these will actually be able to use the magic as their own to some extent. While the jewelry will never make them as powerful as a real witch, of course, it will significantly enhance their ability to be magical."

"How do they work?" I was deeply interested in the whole idea a charmed item could be used this way.

"These particular ones work on a purposeful action. The ring has to be twisted in a half turn for the magic to work," she said, making a motion with her hand in demonstration. "The necklace's power is released by placing one hand over the stone. They're both easy actions, but Brad and Shelly will probably have to practice to get the feel of them before it becomes natural."

"Does the magic ever wear off?" I asked, as she placed the amulet in my hands so I could examine it.

"Not as long as the wearer doesn't remove it," she replied while I dangled it close to my face, taking in the beautiful shimmer of the stone before I handed it back.

"So what kind of powers will they be able to perform?" I asked, curious about how much magic these things would actually be able to wield.

"Anything the person wearing it asks, to a certain extent. For instance, if the wearer asked for something to levitate, it would, albeit it might be a bit shaky compared to you commanding something to levitate. Also, if the individual has any kind of natural ability, the amulet will enhance that power."

"Like what exactly?" I wasn't really following what she meant.

She shrugged. "Let's say if someone were to have psychic abilities, the charm would enhance the power greatly, even if they aren't a witch," she explained.

"Oh, I see. That's kind of cool." Brad and Shelly were probably going to eat this stuff up.

"Yes, well, there are a lot of things I need to teach you, but they're just going to have to wait for another day," she said, with a look of regret.

"Well, I thank you for these. Hopefully we won't ever have to use them, but I'm sure they'll come in handy if we do." I smiled, reaching over to pat her hand.

"Portia, I'm sorry if I've failed you in any way. Your powers are so different from anything else I've ever encountered before. I'm just not wise enough to instruct you. In some ways you're the teacher—you just don't know what you're doing or why you're doing it."

"Grandma, you've been a wonderful teacher. We're all learning from this experience. You know the old saying: That which doesn't kill us makes us stronger."

"I never intended for that verse to apply so literally to you, though," she said sadly.

"Hey! I'm not dead! That means I'm stronger, right?" I smiled softly at her, wanting to cheer her up. "Besides, it wasn't like I wasn't warned or anything. Vance has always been afraid he might do something someday that would end up hurting me."

"He still could," Grandma stated, looking at me with an expression of warning on her face. "He had to fight his attraction to the darkness even before he was nearly changed into a demon. It could be even worse for him now, something like an addict going through withdrawals I'd imagine."

"But I healed him," I said, thinking her comment didn't make any sense.

"As far as we know, you did. He was quick to leave, though, without consulting any of us. Plus healing someone from a demon conversion has never been heard of before. We've entered uncharted territory with this. Only time will tell if everything has truly been stopped."

I realized she was right, and I wondered if perhaps this might be another reason he left me. The thought of it scared me even more. If he had such a strong attraction now, how could he possibly stave off the very thing he was craving long enough to fight his father?

I had to find him, and soon. He couldn't do this alone.

There was another knock on the door, interrupting our conversation. Grandma waved her hand slightly, and the door opened allowing Shelly and Brad to enter the room together.

"We're all set," Shelly said with a smile. "Are you ready to go?"

I nodded. "Grandma has something for the two of you before we go, though," I said, gesturing to the items in her hands.

They sat down next to her and she explained it all to them as she had just done for me.

Dad came into the room and picked up my suitcase again to carry it out to the car. I followed after him. He loaded my things in the trunk before turning to face me, a serious expression full of concern written across his face.

"I can come with you, Portia," he said.

I shook my head in denial. "No, Dad. The coven is weak right now, and you're needed here to get things back in order. I want you and Grandma to get everything back to full strength. We may be in for a big fight in the near future. It's time to pull all your resources together."

"Just promise me you'll be careful, Pumpkin. I can't lose you." He pulled me into his arms, wrapping me in a tender embrace.

"I love you," I said, hugging him, squeezing really hard. I didn't know when I would see him again.

"You'd better go in and tell your mom goodbye." He gave a nod back toward the house.

I followed him, going into the family room where my mom sat curled up on the sofa, staring absently at the television.

"Stacey, the kids are getting ready to leave now."

She looked at me and sighed before coming to me.

"I know you don't agree with all this, Mom, but it will all work out somehow."

"I'm just wondering how many times you'll nearly die for this boy before you decide he isn't worth it," she said, shaking her head. I could still feel her anger over Vance's previous attack on me.

I stood there for a moment trying to control my emotions before I spoke, not wanting my last words to be in anger toward her.

"I'll never stop, Mom—even if it means death. I wish I could make you understand how I feel." I swallowed hard. "I can't live without him. He is my life, and he's worth it."

She wrapped her arms around me then, hugging me tightly. "I'm trying to understand, Portia. I really am," she whispered in my ear. "I'm just greedy when it comes to you. You're my only child, after all."

"I'll be careful. I promise. Just keep praying for us, okay?" I smiled at her. "Those prayers have worked miracles for us in the past."

"There'll be one on my lips every second you're gone," she replied looking a little bit choked up at my request.

"Thanks, Mom."

We walked arm in arm into the living room. Brad and Shelly were now practicing their new magical powers on levitating some small objects there.

"This is so sick!" Brad said with a big smile as he made the same magazine I had used earlier float into the air beside him.

"Just use them wisely," Grandma cautioned them. "And help protect my lollipop while you're at it."

"We'll do everything in our power to keep her safe, Mrs. Mullins. I promise," he said solemnly, setting the magazine back on the table beside him.

We all walked out to Shelly's Mustang. It was still painted black with its little skull and crossbones detailed on it. She hadn't had time to change it back to the pink color she loved before.

I actually preferred the car this way. It made us a little more inconspicuous, I felt. People don't tend to miss a really pink Mustang as it drives down the road.

We gave hugs all around once more. Then we piled into the car and left the driveway.

I didn't glance back at the worried faces behind us.

The Demon Kiss

Chapter 2

We drove out of Sedona and headed up the canyon toward Flagstaff. We stopped at a truck stop to get some gas and a few snack items for our trip, before heading east on Interstate 40.

I watched the tall Ponderosa pine trees zip past my window as I listened loosely to Brad and Shelly's excited discussion about things they would like to try out with their magic.

I didn't realize I had dozed off until I awoke a little while later to find myself staring at the flat plains that surrounded the small town of Winslow, Arizona. We drove through without stopping until we reached Holbrook, about thirty miles down the road. We stopped for some fast food before moving on.

The sun was setting as we passed through the outer edge of the Petrified Forest National Park and the Painted Desert. It was very beautiful with its reflecting whites, reds, and purples layered in the mounds of dirt.

We traveled on for a couple more hours before we finally crossed the state line into New Mexico. We ended up stopping for the night at a sleepy little hotel on the far edge of town in Gallup.

My dad had sent a whole wad of cash with me, as well as one of his platinum credit cards. Shelly's parents had also sent a lot of money with her to help cover our expenses.

As we were checking into our room at the front office, I pulled one of my pictures of Vance from the envelope and asked the night desk clerk if she had seen him before.

"Sorry," she said, taking the picture from me to look it over. "I'm positive I'd remember that face. He's a handsome devil, isn't he?" She laughed. "Too bad I'm too old for someone like him."

She handed the picture back to me and gave us the keys to our room.

"It's number 18, way down in the corner there, right next to the ice machine." She pointed in the direction we should go.

Earlier, we decided it was best to just get one room with two beds. Even though I didn't anticipate anything going wrong at this point, I didn't want to risk us separating and having something bad happen.

Shelly and I took one of the queen-sized beds, and Brad took the other. I was so exhausted from our trip and trying to recuperate from my ordeal with Vance, I fell right on top of the bed as soon as we entered, falling asleep without even taking my shoes off.

I felt much better when I woke in the early morning hours of the following day. It was amazing what a good night of sleep could do to rejuvenate the body. I got up and went to sit at the window, watching the sunrise crest over the rolling hills around us.

Taking advantage of the quiet time, I proceeded to center all my thoughts and energies, concentrating only on Vance, hoping against hope I might be able to sense him somehow. I was slightly disappointed when I couldn't hear anything, even though it was what I expected. But the physical pull wasn't any worse, so I decided to just keep heading in the direction we had been going.

Brad and Shelly woke up shortly after I was done getting

showered and dressed for the day. I sat on the bed and watched television while the two of them took turns getting ready in the bathroom, after which we went to the small lobby where a continental breakfast was being served.

We stocked up on orange juice and doughnuts before going back to the room to load our things up so we could head out again.

The majority of the traffic on the road at this time of the morning was semi-trucks hauling their freight down the interstate. I watched them absently for a while, wondering where they were all heading, before reaching over into my bag and pulling out the letter from Vance which contained the photos he left for me.

I couldn't stop looking at him. I found my favorite one and stared intently at it, lightly running my finger over it, tracing the lines of his face. He had been propped up on his elbow looking at me intently, the love shining in his eyes. I sighed as I wished for those happier times … the days before everything had turned completely berserk.

"Are you doing okay, Portia?" Shelly asked, looking in her rearview mirror at me. "You seem really down this morning."

"I actually feel quite a bit better," I replied, looking up at her. "I'm just feeling frustrated today. Sorry. I don't mean to be a drag."

"You aren't," she replied with a soft smile and a compassionate look into the mirror. "I know things have been hard on you. I just wish there was something I could do to help you feel better."

"You're already doing it. Taking me to find Vance is exactly what I need."

"So where are we going when we get to Albuquerque?" Brad asked, changing the subject.

"I have some addresses my dad collected when he was

trying to keep track of Vance's father and his coven. Damien and his group are long gone from there, but I figured Vance would try to track them the same way."

"So where do we start looking?" Brad turned to glance at me over his shoulder.

"Well, I thought Vance might have started with the closest address and worked his way outward. I plan on working our way from the farthest addresses back in, on the off chance he might be around still, and we might meet up with him. It's a long shot, though, since he has a full day head start on us."

"What are we going to do when we show up and he doesn't want us there?" Shelly asked. "I'm afraid he'll be angry when he finds out we brought you here. The whole reason he left was to protect you from being exposed to this, after all," she added, concerned clouding her features.

"He will just have to deal with it!" I snapped back at her, my anger at him flashing to the surface once more.

"Sorry," Shelly said, sending me an apologetic glance in the mirror. "I didn't mean to upset you."

"No. I'm sorry," I replied back to her and ran a frustrated hand through my hair. "I love him so much, but right now I'm just furious with that addled brain of his. He's driving me crazy!"

"He loves you, too," Brad interjected. "I can't imagine he wouldn't be happy to see you again. He has to be feeling about the same way you are right now."

I didn't answer, and the conversation drifted off.

We listened to lots of music as we covered the miles. I took the opportunity to nap and let my body regenerate itself some more. A couple of hours later we were in Albuquerque.

We checked into a nicer hotel this time, and actually unpacked our things since we planned on being the area for a couple of days at least.

Physically, I was having a very confident feeling. I was definitely closer to Vance. He was either here, or had been not too long ago. The ache in my body had lessened considerably. I tried reaching out to him with my mind again, but the connection was still firmly severed in my head, proving that, if he was indeed here, he was locked down tighter than a drum.

When we were done unpacking, we decided to go right out to check on one of the addresses from my dad as I was feeling very antsy and agitated, wanting to get on with things.

The three of us were walking out to the car in the parking lot, when suddenly a little boy, about the age of three, darted out of the lobby doors and straight into the path of an oncoming vehicle.

Instinctively, I reacted.

I tossed my hand out toward the car just as Brad twisted his ring and thrust his hand toward the child also.

My magic threw the vehicle slightly off course, and the child fell backward in the direction Brad had motioned with his hand. The car screeched to a halt a few feet past the boy, and the driver jumped out, just as the youngster's parents broke through the door at a run.

"Tyler!" the woman shouted and rushed over to her son.

"Is he all right?" the young man from the car asked.

"He fell. The car didn't hit him," I said as we hurried over to the frantic group.

"What have I told you about running away from us like that?" Tyler's dad chastened him. "You could have been killed!"

The little boy wrapped his arms around his mother's neck and cried into her shoulder.

We stood there for several moments, until the parents assured us that everything was all right, before going to the Mustang. "That was *awesome!*" Brad said, a giant grin spreading across his face, as soon as we were out of earshot.

"Great reflexes, Brad," I said, congratulating him. "It was like you were a natural at the whole magic thing."

Shelly frowned at this comment. "Yeah, and I sat there like a dumb idiot without a clue."

I laughed. "Don't feel bad. You reacted the way you normally would have, with shock and horror. Brad has always had fast reflexes, as he has proven many times in sports. The magic is enhancing his natural ability to react quickly to things. Grandma said that could happen."

"So what are my natural abilities?" Shelly asked sarcastically. "Will I be able to match an outfit together in the dark with my eyes closed?"

I was still laughing, and it felt good. I hadn't done it in a while. "You'll do fine. Just do what feels natural to you, and let the magic work through it," I said, trying to cheer her up.

She didn't look too pleased as she glanced at me in the rearview mirror while starting the car.

We drove across town to look for the first address I wanted to check out. It was in the warehouse district, and we exited the freeway at the appropriate spot.

The neighborhood became more and more shabby the closer we got to our destination. Graffiti, trash, and general abandonment were obviously commonplace around here.

"This area gives me the creeps. It looks like something underhanded would be going on," Shelly commented.

"Dad said he followed several interactions between these buildings which I have addresses for. They were shipping something in long crates," I explained as we rounded a corner. "This is it," I added, pointing to the large building located on our right.

Shelly parked the car, and the three of us climbed out and shut the doors. Immediately, the car's alarm activated.

"What?" Shelly said as Brad and I gave her a quizzical look. "Just because we don't see anyone around here doesn't mean someone isn't lurking, waiting for the chance to pounce. Besides, I love my car."

We made our way around the building, looking for an entrance which didn't include one of the large bay doors, hoping to be a little more discreet. We finally found a small side door that was locked.

"Open it," I said to Shelly, nodding toward the knob, figuring I could give her the opportunity to try out her magic.

She stepped forward hesitantly, placing her hand over the stone hanging at her chest, and reached out to twist the doorknob. The door swung open easily. Shelly turned, grinning from ear to ear.

"Let me go in first," I said and stepped past her, wanting to make sure there was nothing which would harm either of them.

I walked into the entryway and stopped to look around. We were standing in a long, narrow hall that appeared to lead out into a larger holding area.

The two of them followed after me, looking in a couple of offices that led off the hallway. In one of them, I rifled through a stack of abandoned papers on a desk.

"What are we looking for?" Shelly asked in a whisper.

"Anything. Everything," I replied, examining a shipping invoice that had been left behind. "Something that would show what Vance's dad has been up to or where he might have gone from here."

We dug through stacks of papers left behind in filing cabinets, finding only shipping receipts from all over the world. I read through several of them.

"I have no idea what he was receiving, but there sure is a lot of it and from all over too."

"Maybe he deals in antiquities or something," Shelly offered. Brad gave her a questionable look, followed by a small snort. "What?" she asked looking annoyed at him.

"I was just wondering why a demon warlock would feel the need to deal in antiques, that's all," he said with a shrug.

"It could happen," Shelly said defending herself with a little sniff, turning away from him. "Just because someone is a demon warlock doesn't mean he has to lose his taste for the finer things of life."

I smiled at the remark and continued digging through the drawer. Shelly was a piece of work, but I loved the way she honestly spoke her mind, never caring what anyone thought about it.

After we were done with the offices, we made our way out into the bay area. There were some long, empty wooden crates piled around on the top of each other which we took a moment to check out, but we didn't find anything helpful.

"I think this place is a bust," Brad said, sliding his hands into his pockets.

I agreed with him. "I don't think Vance has been here either," I replied, a disappointed feeling washing over me.

"How do you know?" Shelly asked me.

"I don't. Not for sure anyway, but everything left behind here was still pretty neat and organized. Look at the mess we've made going through all of it. I don't think if Vance had been here, he would've put it all back in nice and proper order."

"That makes sense," Shelly said, as we headed back out to the car.

"So where do we go next?" Brad asked.

"The next address is about ten miles from here," I replied, giving Shelly the coordinates.

We wove our way through the city traffic, as I watched every single vehicle that passed by us, looking down every alley I could, hoping I would be lucky enough to spy Vance out there somewhere. He never appeared.

When we finally reached our next destination, we all crawled out of the car, Shelly locking it behind us once again.

I didn't have to prompt Shelly to open the door for us this time—she was excited to do it.

Once we were inside, we spent the next hour doing more of the same that we'd done at the last place, finding all this searching was indeed growing very old, very fast.

"Receipts, receipts, receipts. That's all I'm finding," Shelly said in exasperation, tossing another handful of invoices onto the ever-growing pile.

We soon called this place finished, too, after failing to uncover anything of significance, and headed to a nearby drive-through to grab some lunch and take a much needed break from shoveling though dusty papers.

"I just thought of something interesting," I said, while we waited for our order.

"What's that?" Brad asked, staring out at the busy street next to us.

"All those receipts and shipping orders. They were all for orders received. There was nothing for an outgoing shipment," I explained.

"Now that I think about it, you're right," Brad agreed, nodding his head thoughtfully.

"And all those crates were just left there, too," Shelly added. "Whatever was shipped in them was taken, but the crates were left behind."

The restaurant server opened the window to hand us

our food. Shelly paid and pulled to the side of the parking lot so she could hand us our items.

"Where to now, Captain?" she asked with a small smile and a wink, right before she took a big bite of her hamburger.

"Hang a right and drive straight for about five miles," I replied and took a sip of my soda.

We drove the distance quickly, turning into another warehouse district that was even worse than the other two had been.

Damien must have really been slumming it here, I thought.

We pulled up to a very large, old building. We quickly finished up the last couple bites of our food and climbed out of the car once again.

Brad stepped forward to open the door to this building, stating it was "his turn" now. Following our previously established ritual, I stepped ahead of them and entered the building first.

The emotions hit me all at once, and suddenly everything was spinning out of control. I took off running down a narrow hallway and into a large shipping area, looking frantically around the enormous room the second I entered it.

There he was, standing across the huge space in front of me, rifling through an old filing cabinet. His back was to me, but I knew his leather and jean clad physique anywhere.

My breath caught, and I could feel my pulse racing in my neck at my reaction to seeing him.

He straightened suddenly, stopping what he was doing. Slowly, he turned to face me with a puzzled look on his face.

Our eyes connected instantly across the room.

"Portia?" he breathed out softly, looking at me in confusion, as if he couldn't believe what his eyes were showing him.

"Hello, Vance," I replied, trying to sound calm and collected, but I couldn't keep out the tiny tremor that crept into my voice.

I couldn't judge his reaction to tell whether or not he was happy to see me standing there in front of him.

He hesitated for a moment, before he started moving toward me, quickly then, and my heart began pounding hard in my chest.

The Demon Kiss

Chapter 3

I matched his pace, crossing the room toward him, meeting in the middle with all sorts of thoughts tumbling in my mind—relief and anger being the foremost.

"What are you doing here?" he asked, stopping just short of me as if he were afraid to touch me. I saw the uncertainty flash over his face.

"I came to do this," I said, my emotions threatening to boil over the surface in that very moment.

I swung back and punched him in the jaw as hard as I could.

He fell back a step, his eyes widened in surprise, and his hand reached up to rub his jaw while he worked his mouth out for a second.

"What was that for?" He looked at me completely confused, as if I had suddenly sprouted two heads or something.

"That was for leaving me and going off on your own, you stupid jerk!" I yelled at him, my eyes flashing in anger.

"Portia, I was trying to protect ...," he started to explain, but I didn't let him finish.

"Don't you *dare* try to feed me that 'protect you' line of bull again! I have had it with you, Vance! I think I've proven, on several occasions, I'm not the one who's been needing protection!"

He watched me, his eyes growing wide in amazement

over my little emotional display.

"Wow! You're really angry!" he said, and it took me a second to realize he said it into my mind.

"Get out of my head!" I continued, shouting back to him out loud. "You've lost the right to be there! You cut me off without any warning whenever you feel like it, only to step right back in whenever you want!"

I turned away from him and started walking in a huff toward Brad and Shelly, who were both looking very uncomfortable at the moment.

Vance grabbed me before I could take two steps away from him and swung me back around to face him. He pulled me into his embrace with one arm while grabbing my hair in his other hand, tilting my head back as he lowered his face and started kissing me.

"I love you," he said, his words penetrating my mind as his lips ravaged mine, obviously not caring one bit that I had just told him to get out of my head.

I tried staying stiff in his arms, but I was having trouble resisting him. I missed him so badly.

"I'm sorry. I wasn't trying to hurt you. Really," he spoke through our link, and I felt his tongue trace lightly over my closed lips. "I just wanted to keep you from any danger."

I stood still for only a moment before I was unable to fight him any longer. I felt my arms wrap around his neck and I really kissed him back.

We held each other tightly, our reunion becoming heated very quickly. I kissed him like I hadn't seen him in years, instead of just days. I ran my hands through his hair, over his face and down his neck, forgetting completely about Shelly and Brad standing in the doorway behind us.

His mouth moved away from mine, and he began kissing across my cheek. I found I instinctively leaned my head over to the side to give him better access, and his lips traveled down my neck. His tongue snaked out to lick seductively over the spot where he had bitten into me before.

I flinched involuntarily.

Suddenly he released me, pushing me away from him and taking several steps backward.

We just stood there staring at each other, our breathing ragged from our encounter, and I could feel the sparks flying between us.

"I need you to leave now, Portia," he said, his teeth clenched as he spoke. "You aren't safe here."

"Why? I'm not afraid of your ...."

"Because of this," he said, cutting me off and stepping closer to me, but making sure not to touch me.

I felt a streak of terror pass through me as I watched his eyes flash a dim shade of red, not wanting to believe what I was seeing.

"No. I'm not leaving," I said flatly, standing my ground against him.

"Don't you get it?" he replied in frustration, his voice getting louder. "I still taste you! I still want you! I could kill you right now!"

He reached out to grab me to him, but was suddenly stopped by some sort of magical force field which had popped up between us.

"That's what I'm here for," Brad said, and I noticed his hand was between us, creating the barrier which had stopped Vance.

"What the heck?" Vance said, stepping back from Brad, looking at him incredulously.

"Let's you and me take a little walk," Brad said, nodding his head in the opposite direction.

Vance looked in amazement between Brad and me, as if

searching for an explanation, before he turned to walk with him away from me.

"Are you okay?" Shelly asked softly from behind me, placing a hand lightly on my shoulder.

I sighed deeply. "I'll be fine," I said softly and glanced back at her before returning my gaze to the two young men across the room.

"All I can say is … wow! The two of you are intense! I seriously thought I could break the two of you up?"

"Apparently." I gave her a small smile.

"Well, I'm an idiot!" She laughed.

"You weren't exactly yourself at the time," I reminded her.

"That's true." She moved past me slightly. "What do you think they're talking about?"

"Beats me," I said turning away from the scene in a huff. "He still isn't letting me listen."

I left the room and wandered back out into the hallway we'd come through previously. Leaning up against the wall, I was suddenly very tired, so I slid down the surface until I was sitting on the floor and held my head in my hands.

I knew the exact moment when Vance came to stand next to me because all of a sudden his mind was completely open and unfettered.

"If there is any chance of us making this little reunion work, then I'm going to have to be completely honest with you," his voice spoke into my head.

Sighing, I looked up into his eyes, not replying. Brad and Shelly tried to sneak past us to go outside.

Vance crouched down to my level, resting his arms against his knees, and his gaze bore into mine. At that moment, everything he'd been holding back began to slam into me like bricks hitting a wall.

His memories raced through my mind, starting at the

moment the explosion happened at the high school. I could feel his terror and pain as he rushed through the panic-stricken halls, trying to reach me.

Then suddenly his mom was standing in front of him. He only had a second to register the shock before he felt a sharp stick from behind. The needle stabbed into his neck knocked him out instantly.

He awakened later to find himself magically restrained in the room I discovered him in at the bar. Krista taunted him for hours with stories of her life since she had left him. He kept his mind closed to protect me, even though he didn't know where I was or how badly I was injured.

His mother had begun to feed on him regularly, as well as taking a lot of blood from him to store up for his father. She hadn't been quick about it either, enjoying the torture, though she made it clear she intended to change him first and then take him to be reunited with his dad.

She had to push him to drink her blood in the beginning, literally pouring it down his mouth and forcing him to swallow. After a while, he began craving the blood as the change in him started, even though it made him sick.

He lost consciousness frequently during the process and was often overcome with horrible spasms and vomiting. Krista would clean him up when he was finished and start the process all over again, all while he suffered in silence, never speaking a word.

I felt his horror when he realized I had found him and he knew I wasn't safe. Then his emotions changed to terror when he realized he wanted nothing more than to kill me as he'd been instructed to do.

He had no intention of letting me live until he heard me say I loved him before he bit me. Those words were the only thing that broke through the confusion in his mind. I realized he felt something that must have been close to ecstasy for him as he tasted me for the first time, the fresh blood, laden with all that uncontaminated power. It took everything he had to hang onto the one moment of sanity that allowed him to destroy his mother, even though his heart ached by doing so.

It was the thirst which awakened him for the first time, after I brought him back with me, thirst that was all-consuming, above anything he had ever experienced. I saw he only thirsted for my pure blood, not the demon blood that belonged to his mother.

His anger and hatred overwhelmed me as I continued to refuse him the one thing he most wanted. He knew he had to have a drink or it would mean death, and I felt his crestfallen spirit finally accept defeat when he knew he was going to die.

And then I fed him. He wanted to consume every drop at any cost. I reached him once again by telling him I loved him.

His feelings turned, and desire began to course through his body. He lost all sense of his moral compass. He would let me live, but he was determined to have me physically, one craving being traded for another of equal power.

I felt the pain coursing through his veins when I started speaking the words of our binding spell to him, as if fire were racing though his very body, melting everything inside. The pain had been so bad he wanted to scream out, but he had been frozen by the power, unable to move. The change had happened as the white light that consumed us began to stop his demon transformation.

He held me for only a moment after I passed out, laying me gently on the floor and scooting back against the wall. He sobbed in anguish, racked with guilt over what he'd done.

He watched without moving as my dad and my grandma

rushed back in to pull me out of the cell and then sealed him back in again.

They left with my body, and he waited in agony for word on how I was doing. When they finally returned to speak with him, he had to work hard to convince them he had truly changed.

They were reluctant to let him out of the chamber. After a day, they finally believed him and set him free. He had come directly to my room and crawled onto the bed, lying down next to me, entering into my unconscious state.

He held me in my dream, in the field of flowers, and was explaining to me how everything worked. While he held me, he felt the first stirrings, the cravings threatening to raise their evil heads once again. He knew then that I had stopped the conversion, but the desire was still there. He had to leave, to see if he could put an end to this once and for all. He refused to risk being so close to me, afraid he would harm me once again, knowing he would never be able to live with himself if he did.

He went back to his home to find all his things had been taken, so he went to my house and got some of his stuff from there. That was when he had seen the camera I had given him. He took it with him and developed the pictures at a one-hour photo place, while he wrote me the letter he left for me.

Even while he was away from me, preparing to leave, he still felt the cravings at regular intervals. He knew he was going through withdrawal. He had to get away. He had to protect me, that thought being first and foremost in his mind.

It had been difficult for him to part from me, in fact, excruciatingly painful. He tried to concentrate on the job in front of him, though he had to stop several times during his searches, overcome with the need for blood, and wait for the attacks to pass. He knew he had been right to leave when he realized it was specifically my blood he craved, though he wished desperately it wasn't so.

In spite of all that, I experienced the first surge of joy he felt when he realized I was standing behind him today, followed by the second surge of fear that he would lose control.

He was truly surprised when I hit him, but he wasn't angry. He felt like he deserved it. If it were up to him, he would have let me beat him to a pulp.

When he grabbed me and kissed me it had been with good intentions, but the force of his emotions had quickly changed everything. Without realizing it he began to crave another drink of blood, the sound of it racing through my veins calling out to him in the heat of passion.

"Don't you get it?" he asked me softly, his blue eyes streaked with shots of red in them staring deep into my soul. "I want all of you. I crave all of you. My body is demanding to have all of you, and my emotions are always right behind them. I'm always teetering on the brink of disaster. One second, I just want to sink my teeth into you— the next, I want to throw you down and have my way with you. It hurts to be away from you, but I think it might hurt more to be with you. If I slipped, just once, and did something bad to you I'd never be able to forgive myself. I've gone too far already. That is why we're in this mess."

He stood up and paced away from me over to the opposite wall, which he slammed hard with his fist, causing me to jump as cracks appeared in the thick block, and I wondered if he had broken every bone in his hand.

"What do I do, Portia?" he asked quietly, without turning, hanging his head in frustration. "I'm completely out of control."

I stood and walked over next to him, reaching out to

place my hand on his shoulder.

He flinched away from me as soon as I touched him, leaving my hand in midair. I slowly pulled it back and lowered it to my side.

I turned to walk across the hall from him, leaning against the wall and folding my arms over my stomach, trying to keep all the quivering emotions in there and out of my voice.

"So what do you want me to do, Vance?" I stared at his back. "If you really want me to be completely out of your life, then just say so. I'll leave and never come back. I don't want to do that, but I love you. I'll do whatever you need me to do."

I felt like my heart was being shredded by my own words and I held my breath waiting for him to answer, hoping against hope that he would tell me everything was fine and we would be okay.

There was a very long pause before he spoke. I could feel him trying to shutter his emotions from me as he struggled over them.

"Please. Just leave, Portia," he said in a tight voice, never turning to look at me. "We are no good together anymore. Things have changed, and the feelings we've had for each other are being affected differently now. I think this would be the best thing for us to do."

I felt my insides grow cold at his words, as if they were turning to ice then breaking into a million pieces. I had to search hard for my voice.

"Fine," I said, pushing away from the wall, trying to maintain my composure. I walked over, reaching into my jacket pocket to pull out the box which held the ring my grandma had sent to him, placing it on the floor next to his feet. I turned and walked down the hall toward the exit. Over my shoulder I said, "By the way, please keep in contact with the coven at least. They're waiting to hear from you so they can come help you with your father. They sent that to you." I gestured toward the box. "Don't be stupid and try to do it alone."

He didn't look at me or even say anything more as I left the building and walked out into the bright sunshine.

I passed Brad and Shelly, who were standing outside the door, and walked over to get into the Mustang. They exchanged puzzled glances before they joined me.

"What's going on?" Shelly asked with a worried look.

"Let's go back to the hotel," I replied and leaned back against the seat, closing my eyes to signal the end of the conversation. They climbed into the car after me.

I managed to keep things together until we reached our room.

"Do you two mind if I have a minute alone?" I asked them, trying to control the slight tremor in my voice.

"Not at all," Shelly said, eyeing me with another concerned gaze. "We'll go down to the restaurant and get some tea. Can we get you anything?"

I shook my head.

They whispered together as they went down the hall, while I fumbled with opening the door. I walked inside and went over to the desk to place the room keycard on it.

I peered at my stricken face in the mirror. It was pale and tight. My whole body started shaking, and I turned, stumbling over to the bed and fell onto it.

"He left me!" I cried out, the sobs racking my entire being. "He left me!"

I grabbed a pillow, burying my face into it and cried. My grief took complete hold of me. My body convulsed, and tears streamed down my face.

I didn't want to live. There was no way I could go on. I wished for death right there on the spot. I wished he had killed me. Death had to be easier than this.

I had no idea how long I lay there, but I didn't move when Shelly and Brad came back to the room. Shelly took one look at me and rushed to my side.

"Tell me," she demanded. She sat next to me and lifted my head, putting it in her lap.

"He left me!" was all I could say, and the fresh sobs came even harder.

I cried for hours, Shelly holding me, stroking my hair into the darkness of the night. I hoped numbness would finally overtake me, but it never came. I couldn't stop.

Brad sat in one of the chairs, occasionally jumping up to pace the room back and forth.

"Sit down!" Shelly finally snapped at him. "You're just making her more nervous!"

"I can't," he said and grabbed for his jacket and put it on. "I'm going to go out to find that jerk, and then I am going to beat the crap out of him!"

"Don't go!" I pleaded with him, sitting up a little. "He made it very clear that he needs me out of his life."

"Well, then after I kill him, he'll have his wish," Brad said through clenched teeth, his hand on the doorknob.

I was still crying when he opened the door to step out. I blinked my swollen eyes in confusion for a moment before I realized my brain wasn't playing tricks on me, and Vance was actually standing on the other side of the door.

Brad's reflexes acted quickly: He cocked his arm back and threw his punch.

Vance was quicker. He grabbed Brad's fist in midair with his hand, stopping it completely.

"I need to talk to Portia," he said, with a deadly look. "Alone."

The Demon Kiss

Chapter 4

"Don't you think she's had enough already?" Brad yelled at Vance and yanked his fist away from him. "She can't take anymore!" he added angrily. He stood square in the doorway, trying to block the entrance.

"Let him in," I said softly as crying hiccups overtook me.

Brad glared back and forth between the two of us before he stepped out of the way and allowed Vance to enter the room.

"Come on, Shelly," Brad said, nodding toward the door, not acting too happy about the situation.

Shelly turned to me, her face full of concern. "Are you sure you want me to go?" she asked gently.

I nodded. "I'll be fine," I said, swallowing the large lump in the middle of my throat, feeling thankful to have friends who cared about my well-being so much.

Shelly grabbed her coat on the way out and paused in front of Vance.

"Don't you dare hurt her anymore," she commanded, staring him in the eye. "Do you understand me?" she added when he didn't respond.

Vance still said nothing, flatly returning her gaze, not acknowledging he heard her in any way.

Finally, she just pushed past him and out the door.

When they were gone, Vance locked the deadbolt and the latch behind them. He stood there for a moment, staring at the door before he turned around and walked over to sit on the other bed, across from me.

I didn't say anything, watching him as he rubbed his palms together, moving them back and forth slowly. He didn't look at me, appearing to be lost in thought, just staring at his hands. I sat patiently, waiting for him to speak to me when he was ready.

We sat in silence for several long moments, only the sound of my hiccups filling the air, and I was beginning to think he wasn't ever going to say anything when he finally lifted his head and gazed intently at me.

"Portia," was the only thing he said, and he shook his head slightly from side to side, giving a deep sigh.

He thrust a hand through his hair, before standing up and shrugging out of his leather jacket. He placed it on the bed and sat back down.

I watched his muscles rippling under the tight t-shirt which did little to hide the ripped physique beneath. My physical reaction to him would never change, I realized as I felt my pulse leap up in tempo.

"I can't do it," he said, looking into my eyes.

"Do what?" I asked, trying to follow.

"Leave you," he answered. "It's tearing me up inside, and it's obviously doing the same thing to you."

"Listen, Vance," I said pushing myself up to sit cross-legged on the bed. I moved my disheveled hair back from my tearstained face. "I can't do this anymore. You have some decisions to make right now. I will not play this game with you. Do you understand me?"

"Anything you want. Just tell me what to do," he replied with a dejected sigh.

I looked at him hard, trying to gauge his emotions, knowing he had never been one to handle ultimatums well in the past.

"You have to make a choice right now, this minute. You either commit to me here and now, or you leave. I know you're in pain, but I need to know I can trust you."

"I understand," he said, his gaze not moving from my face.

I paused for a second, feeling more than a little melodramatic at the moment, along with also experiencing a need to let him know how badly I really felt about all this.

"And if you think you can't abide by that and you need to leave me, then I have one request."

"Which is?" he asked, confusion lighting his face.

"I would rather you just kill me next time, if you decide to go. Drink every single drop of my blood please and let me die, because this hurts too badly." I pointed to my chest and my eyes welled up with tears again.

He was instantly over to my bed and kneeling on the floor in front of me, softly placing his head in my lap.

"Portia, stop. Don't talk like this. I don't want to hurt you—ever," he said, reaching his arms around me.

"You already have," I replied, and ran my fingers lightly through his hair, unable to help myself. "I just want you to understand if you need me so badly that you're willing to leave me for my protection, then don't. I'm offering myself up as a gift to you. I'll even be with you physically if it's what you truly desire, and I'll give you every drop of blood I have. Just please let me know it's the end so I can savor each and every moment I have left with you. The choice is yours. Whenever you want it, all you have to do is ask. I will give it to you freely—just don't leave me behind again." I knew I sounded crazy, almost hysterical.

"Portia, stop it!" he said, and grabbed me by the arms, shaking me slightly. "I'm not going to take your virginity and then drink you dry."

He was exasperated with me now. I could feel it

coursing through him before he released me. He rose to his feet and paced the room.

My eyes never left him.

"I wouldn't have come here tonight if I thought I wouldn't be able to control myself. When you walked out the door, and out of my life, I thought I was going to die. I could feel the pain I caused you, and I felt horrible." He sat back down on the edge of the bed. "I realized then that your life and your happiness mean more to me than anything else. I thought I was doing the right thing by sending you away. Don't get me wrong. I second-guessed myself a lot. I've had to do quite a bit of soul searching over the last few hours, and it was brutal. All I could hear was your crying."

"You were still listening?" I was surprised to hear this.

"I'm sorry. I couldn't help myself. Your grief was overwhelming me," he said, looking at me with sad eyes.

"Why did you wait so long to come to me?" I asked, thinking of the torment he put me through.

"I had to be sure. I had to know it was the right thing for me to do, the right thing for you." He looked away from me for a moment, taking in a slow breath, and moved his gaze back to me. "I'm being totally selfish here. You'd be much better off without me."

"Vance. That's not possible." I lifted my hands to the sides of his face. "I'll take you any way I can. Even if it means you become a raving demon lunatic. I just have to be with you."

He stood up and walked around the bed so he could crawl up behind me. He wrapped his arms around my waist, pulling me up against him, leaning back on the pillows behind us.

We sat there in silence for several moments, and I reveled in the feel of being back in his arms.

"I'm sorry," he whispered into my ear.

"I love you," I said, rolling from my back to my stomach so I could look at him closer.

"I love you, too," he replied, reaching out to run his fingers through my hair.

"Then kiss me."

I knew I was tempting fate with this request, but I had to know how he would react.

He hesitated for a moment before he finally pulled me to him and kissed me gently.

I didn't close my eyes. I wanted to see his reaction, and I found he didn't close his eyes either, instead choosing to look deep into my mine.

He rolled me over suddenly, so I was on my back and he was leaning over me. He just looked at me for a minute, stroking my hair, and then he brought his mouth down to mine and kissed me like he was starving to death.

I felt the passion between us heat up quickly, but still I didn't take my eyes off him. I saw the red color flash through his irises, signaling that his desires could be getting out of control.

He didn't move from me, though, continuing to kiss me. As his fervor began to grow his eyes became redder still.

I watched him until he left my face to trail his kisses down my throat to the purple mark that was so clearly visible on my neck. I closed my eyes and let him nibble slightly at the spot before he moved back up to my lips.

I reopened my eyes to stare into his flaming ones.

"You're playing with fire you know," he commented casually, brushing his lips against mine.

"Yes, I know." I stared up at him.

"Why tempt fate? Or me, for that matter?" He pulled back a little so he could look at me.

"Because, if you were going to lose it and do something

awful, you'd have done it by now. You have more control over yourself than you think."

"So you're testing me then?"

"Yes."

He started kissing me again. This time a little more roughly, passionately. His hands tangled in my hair, occasionally leaving to run up and down my arms, stroking them.

I wrapped my arms around him, pulling him down against me tightly, kissing him back with everything I had.

I heard him let out a small groan, and he pulled back away from my mouth so he could kiss my cheek.

"We need to stop this," he said as moved back down my neck to suck on that same spot again.

"No. I don't want to." I held him against me even harder. I knew I was supposed to be just testing him, but I could feel that control slipping as he sucked at my throat.

"Don't stop," I said, breathless.

He sighed, and it was over. He quickly got off the bed and walked to the window where he stood staring out at the night sky.

I really was sad to see him go, but as my senses cooled I felt a moment of triumph. I'd been right. He loved me too much to take me. He could control it. He just had to know he was the one in control.

"Did I pass?" he asked, offering me a small smile in the dim light.

My heart did little flip-flops at the sight. "You did." I smiled back. "I might have failed however." My smile turned to a small frown.

I heard the latch on the door begin to jiggle. Shelly and Brad were trying to get back into the room with their key.

"Portia?" Shelly's voice called through the door.

Vance walked past me, picking up his jacket and slinging

it over his shoulder, before opening the door for them.

Brad and Shelly both careened their heads around it, looking into the room, trying to check on me.

"I'm fine, you two. Come in." I smiled reassuringly.

"So, Brad. How about you and I see what it would take to get checked into the room next door?" Vance said with a small grin.

Brad gave him a puzzled look before looking over to me.

I just smiled and nodded.

"Okay," he answered, with a shrug of his shoulders, and turned to follow Vance out the door and down the hall.

"So, what happened?" Shelly asked, coming in and closing the door.

"Nothing—and everything," I replied, my smile growing soft with the memory of it all.

"Are the two of you good then?"

"We're good," I said with a nod. "Now let's go to sleep."

In the morning I called my dad to let him know we found Vance and the four of us would be continuing to search for any information that might lead us to his father's current location.

Afterward, Shelly and I met up with Brad and Vance, and we decided to go to a local pancake house for breakfast.

I hardly tasted my food. Vance held my hand every second he possibly could, and I loved every minute of the simple connection with him. Never again would I take such a sweet gesture for granted.

We chatted over breakfast, and I informed everyone I had called home to catch the family up to speed. I also told them my dad had been in contact with some other covens and they pledged to help in any way they possibly could, if we should need it.

After we were finished eating, we set a plan for the rest of the morning. There was still one warehouse that hadn't been searched. We would go there to see if anything turned up.

We decided to leave Vance's motorcycle at the hotel and piled into the Mustang together. It wasn't exactly the most comfortable way to travel since Mustangs aren't really built to be a passenger car, but we made do. Brad scooted up his seat as far as he could so Vance could have a little leg room, and I sat sideways in the seat next to him with my legs slung over his lap.

Shelly, being a cautious driver, insisted we all have our seatbelts on, and once the buckling up was done, we were on our way.

I noticed Vance kept absently patting one of my legs as we drove through town, visiting with one another. I enjoyed the familiar contact, happy that he seemed to have really missed me, too.

Shelly soon turned off the road and drove down a smaller street until she pulled into an empty parking lot.

When we drove up to this address, I was surprised to find it was a much smaller building than the others we had visited. Upon entry we discovered the reason why.

It wasn't a warehouse at all, but an office building. There were two floors in the building, so Shelly and Brad said they'd look through the bottom floor if the two of us wanted to take the top.

We split up, and Vance grabbed my hand as we made our way to the second story. Most of the offices looked abandoned on this floor, wiped pretty clean actually. There was the odd piece of office furniture here and there—the occasional metal desk, along with some empty filing cabinets with the drawers still open, as if someone had emptied them in a hurry.

"I don't think we're going to find much here," Vance said in a discouraged voice as he magically popped open each door on the floor before we went inside.

"It's kind of looking that way," I agreed. I brushed past him to study the last room.

I was turning to leave when something that seemed a bit odd caught my eye, back behind Vance.

"What is it?" he asked, turning to follow my gaze.

"It's this wall sconce," I said, walking up to look at the fixture. "I didn't see anything else like it in the building. Why would it be left here, in this odd place by itself?"

I reached out to run a finger over it. It was then I noticed the slight scuff marks next to the light. I placed my hand firmly on the lamp and pushed on it, surprised to find that it turned to the right with my hand.

Slowly, a panel in the wall slid to the left, revealing a secret closet behind it. The inside was piled high with box after box.

"I think you found something," Vance said with an arched eyebrow, stepping forward to pull several files from the box on the top.

Shelly and Brad entered the room. "The downstairs looks like it's pretty empty ...," Shelly started before trailing off. Her eyes rested on our find.

"Grab a box," Vance said to them and handed one down from the top of the pile to me.

He passed one along to each of us, and soon we were all seated on the carpet going through mountains of paper, which appeared to be more of the same stuff we had seen before ... receipts, invoices, and the like.

Vance pulled another box down for himself and opened it.

"Hey, look at this," he said after a moment, handing the paper he was looking at over to me.

Shelly and Brad looked over my shoulder.

"It's a shipping invoice," I exclaimed, after I examined it a little closer, realizing what Vance had seen.

"We have a thousand of those," Shelly complained. "What makes this one so special?"

"It's a shipping invoice from here to a different location. All the rest have been invoices shipping into Albuquerque," I explained. "It says the entire contents of one of the warehouses were shipped to a place in Puerto Peñasco."

"Puerto Peñasco? Where's that?" Shelly asked, a perplexed look on her face.

"You know it as Rocky Point," Brad explained absently as he looked the paper over.

"It looks like we're going to Mexico!" Vance said with a grin, winking at me. "Do you have a passport with you?"

"I do," I replied, and we turned to look at Shelly and Brad, wondering if they were carrying theirs also.

"I'm a world traveler!" Shelly giggled. "Do you really have to ask? And Brad and his family came with us on our last vacation, so he has one, too."

"Yeah, but I left mine at home," Brad replied giving an apologetic shrug. "I didn't anticipate a trip out of the country."

"So what should we do?" Shelly frowned.

"I think we should go back to Sedona. We can drop off Vance's motorcycle and get a bigger car. That way Brad can pick up his passport," I suggested. "Then we can travel to Phoenix."

"We can go through Ajo to Lukeville and cross the border there. Rocky Point will be much closer from that direction," Brad said.

"That's a good idea," Vance agreed. "Then we can check in with the coven and see how things are going."

We heard a car door slam outside, and Vance leaned

over to look out the window.

"We have company," he said. "Let's move."

We hurriedly restacked the boxes and closed the wall tightly, then quickly ran down the hall to the stairs, just in time to hear a couple of male voices float up the stairwell toward us.

"They're coming up the stairs!" Vance whispered and ushered us through the door of the nearest empty office.

The four of us leaned our backs up against the wall to hide ourselves from view until the men passed. Then we hurried out the door one by one, tiptoeing down the staircase.

Slinking as silently as possible, we went out the back door and over to where we parked the Mustang. Shelly started the engine just as one of the men came running out the back door after us.

"Gas it, Shelly!" Vance yelled, and suddenly we were pealing out in reverse, the tires scrabbling and spewing gravel everywhere.

Shelly slammed on the brakes to change directions, throwing us forward.

We raced past the front of the building, seeing the other man jumping into a dark-colored sedan. He pulled out in pursuit.

We spun out onto the main road, and Shelly gunned the GT 500, its motor roaring loudly.

Vance watched the car behind us. "You take care of the obstacles in front, and I'll cover the rear," he shouted out to me and nodded ahead.

I faced forward to look at the traffic which was moving much slower on the double-lane road ahead of us.

"They're slowing for the light," Shelly yelled, sounding panicked. "What should I do?"

Immediately I flicked my hand toward the light, and it

turned green again. The first few cars started to move, but the ones behind were too slow.

"Don't slow down, Shelly," I said.

I leaned forward and thrust both of my hands out, using magic to make the cars slide to the side, clearing the way.

Vance used his powers to wave the cars back onto the road behind us.

The black sedan tried weaving madly through the vehicles which were being thrown in its path. It avoided several before Vance finally just threw his hand up in a stop signal. The car's front end screeched to a halt, and the back end of it flipped up high into the air, landing upside down in the road with a loud crunch.

"That ought to do it," he said, with a grin.

I could feel the adrenaline coursing through him as he reached a hand out behind my head and pulled me in for a kiss. When we separated, I noticed Shelly hadn't slowed down at all, and I started to laugh.

"What's so funny?" she asked, sending me a piercing stare in the rearview mirror.

"Not a thing," I said, nodding my head slightly and gesturing for Vance to look at Brad.

Brad was hanging onto the door handle with one hand and the emergency brake with the other, his mouth gaping wide open in shock.

He slowly turned his head to look back at me. "That *rocked!*" he exclaimed and flashed a giant, boyish grin.

We all busted up laughing.

Chapter 5

We arrived back in Sedona to the waiting arms of our family and coven. Everyone was so happy to see Vance again, and he received lots of hugs as well as a chastening from my dad for leaving on his own—which he took rather well, I thought.

Jinx, who acted as if she hadn't seen me in a year, personally mauled me. She purred like a motorboat on my lap, while we explained our findings to my family and told them of our plan to go to Mexico.

We ended up trading Shelly's car for Marsha's, which Vance had inherited after she had been killed. It was a silver-colored Audi S8. Vance loved driving it because of all the power it had. I figured it was a guy thing, as I reflected back on my little green scooter. I felt like I hadn't driven it in ages.

We packed up and left Sedona the next morning and headed down the I-17 toward Phoenix. It was a sunny December day. The closer we got to the valley, the warmer it became.

We stopped to stretch our legs and get some lunch at a Cracker Barrel restaurant just off the I-10. Afterward, we continued on to Maricopa and then over to Gila Bend, where we turned to head down to Ajo.

In Ajo, we got some ice cream before continuing on to

Lukeville, where we purchased gas at a station right before we crossed over the border into Sonoyta, Mexico.

We drove through the town until we reached the turn that would head us toward Puerto Peñasco.

The drive took about an hour through the beautiful Sonoran Desert. Watching the hilled scenery pass by, I could tell when we started getting closer to the ocean because the soil quickly turned sandy, becoming ever thicker, until there were rolling hills of it surrounding us.

We reached the outer edges of Rocky Point when we came to the turn that would lead us out to the oceanfront resorts of Sandy Beach.

The colorful hotels loomed over us on our drive along the winding, palm tree lined street until we came to the gates, which led us into the parking lot.

My dad had reserved us a room at the Sonoran Sea Resort. He said he felt better about us staying someplace with on-site security. We pulled up at the towering ten-story hotel and checked in.

Our condo was a spacious three bedroom deluxe suite on the sixth floor and was lavishly decorated in a palm tree theme. There was a sage green down sectional at one end of the room with a large custom made entertainment center along with an entire wall of windows that led out to the balcony.

At the other end of the room was the kitchen, complete with granite countertops and furnished with all the necessary appliances. The adjoining dining room had a beautiful glass-topped table with plush dining chairs.

The master bedroom was gorgeous—with a tall, four-poster, king-sized canopy bed. It was so high that a stool was placed next to it to use to climb up on the bed. The room came with its own master bath complete with a Jacuzzi tub.

The secondary bedrooms also had king beds and shared a bathroom. It was decided that Vance and Brad would take those rooms, while the two of us girls would share the master suite.

We put our luggage away and headed out onto the huge patio that overlooked the immaculate grounds of the resort below us and then out into the beautiful Sea of Cortez.

"This is great!" I said, placing my hands on the wrought iron rails and taking in the view.

"I agree," Vance said, wrapping his arms around my waist and leaning his head against mine.

Brad and Shelly joined us at the railing, and we watched the people playing on the private beach beneath.

"Isn't the water cold this time of year?" Shelly asked as several young teenagers ran squealing into the light surf.

"Probably, a bit," Brad replied. "The water temperatures stay pretty good year round. However, in the summer it's extremely warm. I imagine the water would be fairly cool right now, but not as bad as say California would be. It can get chilly in the evenings, though."

"When was the last time you were here?" she asked.

"A couple of years ago. Our family used to come in July, but it was just too hot, plus there were a lot of jellyfish. We started coming in October, and that was more fun. The temperatures were better and no jellyfish! I've never been here in December before, though."

My stomach chose this time to start growling loudly, causing the others around me to chuckle.

"Well, I'm hungry," I said turning to Vance. "What do you want to do? You're technically the leader of this little coven." I laughed.

"I can't let you starve now, can I?" he said with a smile. "Let's get some dinner, and then we can plan." To Brad he said, "Do you know any good places to eat?"

"There's a sweet little place down by the marina called the Friendly Dolphin."

"Sounds great!" Vance said. "Let's go there."

We were soon back in the car and on our way down the road toward the marina. We found the restaurant easily with Brad's help, and soon we were inside seated at a table on the ground floor.

The place was rich with atmosphere. Spanish tile covered the floors, and the walls were painted with bright colors and decorated with all sorts of Mexican and seafaring artifacts. A talented mariachi band wandered about the room, singing for the patrons sitting at the tables, who would in turn tip them generously.

While we waited for our food, another man came by the table selling long-stemmed roses.

"Flowers for your pretty ladies?" the man asked in slightly broken English.

"Absolutely," Vance replied and fished out his wallet, Brad doing the same. "I'll take twelve," he added with a smile.

The man's face lit up into a thousand watts as he realized he hit a jackpot. He handed Vance a dozen roses wrapped in clear cellophane.

"For my beautiful lady," Vance said in a whisper close to my ear as he handed me the roses.

"Thank you. They're wonderful." I accepted them with a smile, and he placed a kiss on my cheek.

"Yes, but they pale in comparison to you." He reached over to hold my hand, softly chuckling over the blush that was now spreading across my face.

The food arrived and was delicious. Vance and I both ordered a couple of the Mexican food dishes, while Shelly and Brad had seafood.

The flavors were much different than what we were used to in the States, but very good nonetheless. We enjoyed every bite while we visited together.

After dinner, we returned to the hotel where Vance invited me to go for a walk on the beach and enjoy the last rays of the sunset.

We walked hand in hand, barefoot next to the water's edge, letting the cool waves rush over our feet. The light reflected beautifully over the water as the sun dipped low on the horizon.

"It's really nice here," I said, enjoying sharing this moment with him.

"It is." He gazed out into the distance over the water.

"Too bad it just can't be a vacation."

"I agree. Maybe someday we can come back here—just the two of us."

"You think my mom and dad will let us come back here alone, together?" I said laughing.

"They would if it was for our honeymoon," he said softly.

I stopped and faced him. "You want to come here for our honeymoon?" My heart beat a little harder at the unexpected change of subject.

"Maybe," he replied, his eyes moving slowly over my face as if gauging my reaction.

"That could be a long time from now."

"Actually, I've been pondering on that," he replied, searching my eyes closely. "If it's okay with you, I was thinking perhaps I could talk to your parents and see if they'd let us get married before you turn eighteen."

I was stunned. I knew we had planned to married eventually, but I had no idea he wanted to do it so soon.

"I'm only a junior in high school," I replied, realizing I was feeling a little bit blindsided. "I still need to finish my senior year."

"I know," he said nodding his head. "I thought after I graduate this year, I'd look for a good job in Flagstaff. I could go to N.A.U. there. We could get a little place to live, and you'd still be close enough to finish your year at Sedona High School."

He had really put a lot of thought into this, and while I was feeling a little nervous about what he was saying, it made my heart sing that he wanted to be with me.

"So what do you think?" he asked after several moments passed, his eyes never leaving me.

"I think I love you," I said taking a step closer to him, the wind blowing several strands of my hair across my face.

"I *know* I love you," he replied, smiling as he reached out to tuck the wayward strands behind my ear. "But you aren't answering the question I'm asking."

"Which question was that?" I asked, toying with him.

"Never mind," he said suddenly and looked away from me toward the condo. "Wait here," he added.

He took off and ran up the beach toward the hotel.

"Wait! Where are you going?" I shouted after him.

"I'll be right back," he called over his shoulder. "Don't move!"

I stood looking after him, perplexed, before turning to look back out over the water. I was soon absorbed in the beauty of the waves crashing against the shore.

It had only been a couple of minutes when I heard him call my name softly from behind me.

"Where did you go?" I asked, facing him.

"I had to get something." He was panting a little from his quick run.

"And what was that?"

"This." He slowly retrieved a small velvet box from his pocket.

"Is that what I think it is?" I asked in shock, my eyes growing wide.

He slowly lifted the lid to reveal a sparkling princess-cut diamond ring.

I couldn't speak as I looked at him in amazement, wondering where he had come up with the beautiful gem.

"When you and I first got together, I already knew you were the one I wanted to spend the rest of my life with," he explained, his eyes deepening with some hidden emotion. "I had secretly been in love with you for two long years, though you barely knew me.

"I was so excited when things finally started working out for us, and to find out you felt the same way about me, I started thinking crazy, fantasizing about our future together. I actually bought this ring with the intention of giving it to you when we did our binding spell, but then I changed my mind.   I was worried I was rushing you too fast, that too many new things were being thrust upon you at once, so I decided to wait.

"I've carried it with me every day, hoping for a day when I felt it was the right time to give it to you." He started laughing. "Isn't it ironic that the one time I don't have it on my actual person is when the moment presented itself."

He sank to one knee on the sand in front of me, and I felt my pulse shoot up to an incalculable level.

"Marry me, Portia," he said softly, smiling. "I will spend the rest of my life trying to make you the happiest person on earth."

I stood over him for a moment, my emotions racing through my body, my head spinning.

"Now? But don't you think I'm a little too young?"

"I know you're young, but humor me here. I've never wanted anything in my life more than I want you. I love you, and I want to shout it from the rooftops. I don't care who hears me. I'll talk to your parents about the timing, but even if we have to wait, I just want to see the ring on your finger, letting the world know that you're mine." He paused for a moment, and I could see the love in his eyes as he spoke to me again. "I love you. Please, Portia, if you feel even remotely the same way about me, would you do me the honor of becoming my wife?"

I stared at him, my heart racing, thinking his proposal was like something out of a movie, only I was the star. I let my gaze wander over the handsome planes of his face and his muscled physique, faintly wondering how I had become so lucky, before letting a huge smile cross my face.

"Yes," I whispered, nodding my head, "I will."

He stood suddenly, grabbing me around the hips, lifting me into the air and twirling around in the sand, laughing.

"Yes!" he shouted triumphantly, as my laughter joined his.

He let me slowly slide back down his body until my feet touched the sand again.

"I love you," he said breathlessly, his blue eyes sparkling in the fading sunlight.

"I love you, too." I reached up to place my hand against the side of his face.

Then he kissed me. It was a soft, sweet kiss, but it conveyed all his tender emotions to me. He pulled me closer to him in a strong embrace, and I could hear his heart beating in his chest at the same frantic pace of my own. I didn't ever want this moment to end.

When it did, he stepped back from me and pulled the ring out of the box. He reached out and lifted my hand toward him, took the ring and slid it up my finger. Then he leaned over and kissed the ring on my hand.

"Thank you, Portia," he said, with a smile. "You have no idea how happy you've made me."

I heard a squeal of delight, and then clapping filled the air. I turned to look over at the resort. Shelly and Brad were standing on the balcony watching us excitedly.

Vance laughed as he pulled me close and wrapped his arm around my shoulders.

"I told them what I was doing when I ran in to get the ring out of my suitcase," he explained.

I laughed, and waved.

"I guess we should go up so you can show Shelly the ring, before she dies of a heart attack," he added, dropping his arm and reaching for my hand.

"In a minute," I said, pulling him back toward me.

I kissed him thoroughly this time, letting all my passionate feelings for him flow freely into his head. I kissed him until neither of us could breathe properly and his grip had tightened almost painfully around my waist pulling me tighter to him. I didn't care who was watching or who could see us, I just wanted to really let him know how I felt about him. When we finally released each other, I could see the blue eyes were gone and the irises were lined with red again.

"Now we can go back," I said. "It'll give you some time to cool down."

"You don't play fair, do you?" he asked, reaching over to intertwine his fingers in mine before lifting the back of my hand to his mouth for a kiss.

"Never," I said and smiled.

He slipped a pair of sunglasses from his pocket and placed them on his face, even though the light was too dim for him to justify needing them.

"Are you okay?" I asked looking up at him, worried I may have pushed him too far.

"I'm fine." He gave my hand a squeeze before leading me back up to the room.

We spent the rest of the evening in the condo with Brad and Shelly, visiting on the comfy couch and watching television, which thankfully was mostly in English since none of us spoke a lick of Spanish except for Brad.

I would occasionally lift my hand to look at the ring on my finger and let it sparkle in the light. While it was extremely beautiful, it was the meaning behind it that made my heart leap with excitement every time I saw it.

Vance sat next to me the entire night, holding my hand, often whispering sweet nothings into my ear, never leaving my side.

When we finally decided to retire to bed, he walked me to the doorway of my bedroom.

"See you in your dreams," he whispered, lifting my hand to kiss it again.

"I could come lie by you in your room if you want," I suggested, remembering how he used to spend every night with me.

He shook his head, reading into my mind. "It was too hard before—it'll be way too hard for me now. I don't want to push my luck where you're concerned."

"I understand," I said with a sigh, as a wave of disappointment washed through me. "I've just missed lying next to you every night."

"Me, too," he said leaning in to give me a light peck on the lips. "Now get some rest ... and lock your door!"

"Like that would keep you out!" I was still laughing when I walked into the bedroom and closed the door behind me.

Shelly was already changed for bed and brushing her teeth at the sink when I passed through the bathroom to go into the large walk-in closet. She was still there when I emerged dressed in my bunny pajamas.

"What are you wearing?" she asked in horror, spraying

toothpaste out of her mouth, giving me the once over. I laughed at the expression on her face. "I'm wearing happy memories," I replied with a smile.

"Whatever that means," she said, rolling her eyes before turning to spit into the sink and rinse out her mouth. "Now let me have a better look at that ring."

She grabbed my hand and held it up into the light. "Mmm. Half carat, princess cut, set in fourteen-carat white gold. Good clarity it looks like. Nice choice. He paid a pretty penny for that."

I laughed at her and her spoiled little rich girl qualities that were coming to the surface.

"What?" she asked. "I'm not joking. That ring was well over a thousand dollars."

I stopped laughing and began choking. "What?" I brought a hand up to my throat.

"It's a really nice ring," she said, nonchalantly.

I strode out of the bedroom, marched down the hall to Vance's bedroom and knocked on the door.

He opened it, wearing only a pair of boxers.

I sucked in a breath as I tried not to let his body distract me, but I had to pause for a quick glance. I'd never seen him this undressed before.

I shook my head, trying to clear my mind. "A thousand dollars?" I questioned, holding up my hand so the ring was shoved in his face. "Where did you get that kind of cash?"

He paused for a moment with a look of subtle surprise before he answered. "About that …," he started, watching me carefully, "I may not have ever mentioned it to you before, but I happen to have quite a bit of money."

"What? From where?" I demanded, none of this making any sense.

"You remember when I told you my mom cleaned out her bank account when she ran with me?" he asked.

"Yeah."

"Well, she emptied my trust fund, too. All of it was signed over to Marsha. I received it on my eighteenth birthday."

"So, you're trying to tell me you have like a hundred thousand dollars or something stashed away in some bank account somewhere," I said, crossing my arms over my chest.

"No. It's more like a million."

Chapter 6

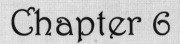

"A million dollars!" I shouted.

"A little over actually," he replied, laughing at my reaction. "Give or take a couple hundred thousand."

"What's all the commotion about?" Shelly asked coming up into the hall just as Brad opened his door.

"She just found out I'm a millionaire," Vance said with a smile, leaning against the doorjamb with his arms folded over his chest.

"That's awesome!" Shelly said smiling, as if finding out one was a millionaire was an everyday occurrence in her world.

"Where did you get that kind of money?" Brad asked casually, slightly lifting an eyebrow.

Vance shrugged a shoulder, almost as if the subject was boring him.

"My dad opened the account for me before I was born. I guess he used to deal in antiquities quite a bit. He made a bundle off it," he explained.

Brad looked at Shelly in amazement.

"Told you," she said, flipping her hair back behind her shoulder.

"Told you what?" Vance asked.

"It's nothing," I said, waving my hand in dismissal, as I

recalled their conversation about a demon dealing in antiquities. "It was a comment she made at one of the warehouses one day, which is proving to be surprisingly accurate."

"Can I speak to you privately?" he asked, gesturing for me to come into his room with a nod.

"Alright," I said, entering as he stepped backward, and closing the door softly behind me. I stood with my back up against it, and he leaned over me placing one hand on either side of my head.

"I want you to listen to me careful, Portia. I need you to understand that none of this changes who I am," he said, searching my eyes. "It is just money. Money is helpful, but it doesn't buy you happiness. It buys you things. Do you get what I'm telling you?"

"Yes, I think so. It's just I just had this image of you in my head. You know, the guy who couldn't afford a motorcycle, so he fixed one up, that kind of thing."

"I built the motorcycle because it's something I enjoy doing. I like working with my hands. There are times I could do things with magic even and I don't because I enjoy the work it gives me. I really am just a t-shirt and jeans kind of guy."

"Well, you aren't right now," I said, letting my eyes trail away from his face and down his rock hard body—over the sculpted chest, the six-pack abs, and the muscled legs, before traveling back up to his face.

His eyes were already glowing by the time my gaze returned to his. He dropped his arms to his sides, leaning back, away from me.

"You'd better leave this room right now if you intend on looking at me like that one more time," he said, deadly serious.

I turned quickly, being careful not to touch him, and

opened the door as he moved away from it. I stepped out and hurried down the hall, my face flaming at my brazen reaction to him.

"Hey," he called after me, and I turned to look over my shoulder. "I love the pajamas." He winked at me with one of his red eyes before closing the door.

I smiled to myself and went back to my room.

"So how does it feel to be rich?" Shelly asked, from her perch atop the huge bed, where she was watching television.

"I'm not rich," I replied, climbing up into the bed next to her.

"You will be."

"I don't care if I ever see a dime of that money. I just want *him*," I said, meaning every word of it.

"Well, you'd better get used to seeing more than just a dime of it, 'cause there's a thousand dollars of it flashing around on that finger of yours," she said flickering her gaze over to my hand.

I held my hand up and really looked at the ring, letting it sparkle in the dim lights.

"He wants to marry me," I said, with a small smile before biting at my lip.

"I know!" Shelly giggled, grabbing me into a girlish bear hug with a little squeal. "Are you excited?" she asked, when she pulled away.

"I can't think of anything I'd love better in my life." I replied as a grin spread wide across my face.

We moved at the same time, so we could curl up underneath the down comforter.

I sighed heavily, closing my eyes.

"Portia, it'll be okay," I heard Shelly say. "I believe we'll find a way to help him out."

"I hope so," I said, as a slow heaviness began to creep

back into my heart. "Just knowing he's still in danger makes everything else seem unreal. It's like none of this can really happen until we get him all squared away."

"I know. Just keep the faith," she replied with a yawn, and soon she was fast asleep.

For a long time afterward, I lay awake, thinking things over. So many thoughts were racing through my mind.

"You're doing it again." Vance's voice crept into my head.

"I know. Sorry," I replied back, feeling badly that I was keeping him awake.

"Just get some sleep now, baby. We'll talk over everything in the morning."

"All right."

I tried really hard to relax my mind, concentrate on breathing, and just let everything go. It wasn't working. My thoughts of him continued to race—worries and fears on his behalf.

"Portia, listen to me. I want you to repeat the words I tell you, okay?"

"Okay." I listened as he spoke.

"Let go thoughts and feelings,
"Let go now to dreaming.
"Let body relax into sleep,
"Let the rest be ever deep.
"Let me wake with morning light.
"Let me now enjoy this night."

I realized as I repeated that these were the words he quietly mumbled to me on other occasions when I couldn't rest. I'd never really known what he was saying before.

As soon as I was finished reciting the spell, I was asleep almost instantly.

When I awoke in the morning, I was refreshed and

ready for the new day. I was a little surprised I didn't remember dreaming anything at all.

"Good morning," I heard him say softly in my head.

"Back at you," I said, smiling as I stretched in the bed.

"Did you sleep well?"

"You know I did," I said, feeling apologetic. "Sorry I didn't see you in my dreams."

"It was my choice," he replied casually. "We both needed the rest."

I climbed out of the bed, padded down the hall to his room, and opened the door.

I gasped in surprised at what I saw.

He was sitting up on the edge of the bed, shaking violently. He lifted his head as I entered the room, and the flaming red eyes greeted me.

Instinctively I moved to go to his side, but he held up his hand to stop me.

"Stay there," he said through gritted teeth. "I don't want you to come any closer."

"What can I do?" I asked helplessly, knowing he was trying to protect me, but desperately wishing I could just hold him.

"I'll be okay. The withdrawal is always the worst in the morning when I wake up."

A tear escaped from one of my eyes, running down my face as I watched him struggle.

"Don't cry," he said, clenching his jaw. "Just give me a minute, all right?"

I nodded slightly and stepped backward through the door, closing it after me. I turned and found Brad was standing behind me.

"Is he tripping out again this morning?" he asked when he saw my face.

"Again?"

"He had a pretty bad episode of it at the hotel in Albuquerque," he explained, glancing down the hall.

"Why didn't you tell me?" I almost wanted to strike out at him for not telling me something so important.

"He told me not to. He didn't want you to be scared," Brad said, with a slight shrug of his shoulders.

"Yeah. Well, I am." I moved away from him to walk across the room, going over to sit on the overstuffed sectional with a plop. "I'd hoped he was cured of all this."

"You just stopped the demon conversion from progressing any further," Brad said, following after me. "He explained it all to me. It sounds like all this residual stuff sucks, though."

I ran my fingers through my hair and looked out the window at the peaceful morning outside, the ocean moving out with the tide.

"It's just so unfair." I sighed, turning back to look at Brad. "He's such a good person. He deserves to have that kind of life, too. I just don't know what to do to help him. I still don't really understand any of this."

"There may be nothing you can do, Portia," Brad said, a sorrowful look on his face.

"So then what? Does he just exist like this for the rest of forever? Or will the cravings eventually subside like they do for someone going through rehab?"

"Time will tell, I guess," Brad said giving me a sympathetic look.

Shelly walked into the room wearing her cute little tank top and shorts she had worn to bed.

"Hey," she said and wandered toward the kitchen. "I thought we could go to the little supermarket we passed last night on the way to dinner and pick up some groceries for the condo." She gave a slight yawn before really looking at us. "What's the matter?"

"Vance is having withdrawal this morning," Brad said.

"Again?" she asked.

I threw my hands up in the air in exasperation. "Does everybody know except for me?"

"Brad told me," she said, with a matter-of-fact air about her. "We're supposed to be helping to protect you. I needed to be informed."

"Really?" I asked, getting a little upset now. "Well, I just pledged to spend the rest of my life with the guy, so it might be nice if I actually knew what was going on around here when it comes to him!"

I stood up brusquely and went out onto the patio, shutting the sliding door behind me. I walked over and grabbed the railing tightly, my knuckles turning white as I stared out over the grounds below and into the sea.

This is so irritating! I hate it when people treat me like I'm too weak to handle anything of importance. Haven't I proven myself to anyone yet? I thought to myself. *I've been doing a pretty good job at holding my own lately, especially under the circumstances. Sure, I don't always know what the heck I'm doing, but at least I'm trying to help out … to make things work for the better.*

My thoughts continued to boil in my head for the next several minutes as I attempted to try and calm myself down. I took several deep breaths and listened to the soothing sounds of the ocean moving back and forth in its timeless rhythm.

"Hey. You aren't going to jump are you?" Vance's voice said from behind me.

I slowly turned around to face him. He appeared to be a little bit pale, but other than a slight bloodshot redness in his irises, he looked almost normal.

"Are you okay?" I asked, my concern for him almost overwhelming me.

"Nothing I can't handle," he said walking closer to me. He reached out to lift my left hand toward him. "You don't want to bail on me now, do you?" he asked, running his finger back and forth over my ring.

I shook my head. "Nope. I'm in this for the long haul."

"Well, I'm sorry I'm the baggage that you have to carry on this trip," he answered softly.

"You aren't baggage, Vance. I love you. I'll do anything I can to help you." I reached my hand up to cradle his face.

"You *are* helping me," he replied, lifting his hand to cover mine. "Just by being here, you're helping me more than you'll ever know."

"It isn't enough, though," I complained, removing my hand and turning away from him to stare back out toward the ocean.

"It's enough for me," he said, coming up to wrap his arms around my waist. He pressed his lips against my neck to kiss me lightly.

"You need to let me in on things that are happening with you," I said. "I don't like being left in the dark."

He lifted his head to stare out at the ocean. "I'm sorry about that, Portia," he apologized, hugging me tighter. "It's just in my nature to want to protect you. I never meant to hurt you. Sometimes I see you as this beautiful, fragile creature, one I can't believe is real. I'm afraid I'll wake up one morning and find out this was all a dream, one I created in my head, that you were never really here, or worse, to find I did something to make you disappear."

"I'll never disappear from you, Vance," I replied. "Not as long as there is breath in my body."

He didn't say anything back to me, only pulled me tighter into his embrace and we stood there in silence for a few moments before he suddenly pointed out across the railing.

"Look! Dolphins!" he exclaimed. I followed the direction of his pointing finger.

Sure enough, two dolphins were frolicking in the water, jumping through the air in a fascinating arcing pattern.

"They're so beautiful!" I said, calling for Brad and Shelly to join us outside.

They hurried out onto the balcony and looked where we showed them.

"This is so awesome!" Shelly spoke with excitement. "They really are amazing creatures!

We watched them for several minutes as they continued their play, before they disappeared from our sight.

"That is a good sign," Vance said softly.

"How so?"

"In magic, dolphins are believed to balance the energies of the planet through their harmonics. Maybe they're here to help balance our energies," he suggested with a smile.

"That would be nice," I agreed. We could truly use all the balance we could get.

The four of us headed though the large sliding doors into the living room.

"So what's the plan for today?" Brad asked.

"I thought we could get some breakfast and then see if we can get some help locating the address on the shipping invoice. I figured we could check it out. As far as after that, I'm out of ideas. Hopefully we can get some type of lead in our search which will give us a new direction to go," Vance said.

"We need to get some groceries for this place, too," Shelly added, going over toward the kitchen. "It's a pain to have to go out to eat every single time we're hungry when we have everything we need to cook with right here."

"That makes sense," I agreed with her. "Plus it will

make things easier. Let's go get cleaned up, and then we can leave to run our errands."

A short time later after we were all ready, we decided to eat breakfast at a restaurant on the pier near the shopping area downtown. A small boardwalk led out to the café, as well as forming a deck of sorts around the building. We sat at a table under an umbrella, watching the fishing boats make their way out into the harbor.

The morning air was cool and refreshing, and the food was delightful. We enjoyed pleasant conversation together while we observed the comings and goings of the locals and other tourists in the area.

When we were finished with our food, we paid and walked back down the boardwalk, crossing the street to go over to one of the colorful little shops that vendors were set up in at the plaza.

"Disculpe. Favor de dar me direcciones a este lugar?" Brad spoke in Spanish, stopping a man on the sidewalk and showing him the shipping invoice we brought with us from Albuquerque.

The man studied the paper for a moment and began speaking rapidly in his native tongue, while pointing off in another direction.

"Si. Si," Brad said nodding. "Gracias." He shook the man's hand, before returning to us.

"What did you say?" Shelly asked, tugging on Brad's arm.

"I asked him for directions to the address on the shipping invoice," he replied with a grin.

"Did he know where it was?" I asked.

"Yes, he did. He said to take the main road back to where Benito Juarez and Freemont Boulevard intersect, then turn right and drive for about a mile before turning off on a little unnamed street where the building is located."

"Great!" Vance said, and we walked back to where the car was parked.

We followed the directions we were given back into the main part of town, turning at the appropriate intersection, and easily found the warehouse building we were looking for.

It turned out to be a multi-unit building. There was a large gate at the property, with a security guard booth there also.

"Where are we going?" I asked feeling a little confused as Vance drove past the property without stopping.

"I don't think it would be wise to just waltz in there. We don't know what could be going on. I'm thinking we should come back tonight when it's dark and see if we can't stake the place out first," he explained.

"That sounds like a good plan to me," Brad agreed wholeheartedly. "Better safe than sorry."

Vance drove the car around the entire perimeter of the building, before heading out the way we had come, working our way back to the main intersection.

We waited at the light for a few moments before turning right on the street.

"Hey, look. It's an herbal shop like your grandma's," Brad said, pointing out the window toward a business in a little strip mall.

"Let's stop and walk around these shops," I suggested to Vance. "Maybe we can talk to some of the locals and ask questions to find out if anything strange has been going on in the area."

"That's a good idea," he agreed, and he slowed down to look for a place to park the car along the roadside.

We decided to check out the metaphysical shop first, though we stopped and visited with several shopkeepers who were displaying wares out on the sidewalks as we passed by them. Thankfully most of them spoke English. We slowly made our way down the block, toward the store we were interested in, trying to appear casual as we moved along. Vance even purchased a couple of Mexican artifacts from some of the displays we passed. Finally, we reached the entrance to the tiny shop.

As we entered the door there was a chime that rang, and a small Hispanic man came out from a back room. He took one look at all of us before he rushed over, waving his hands wildly in the air, speaking Spanish very quickly.

Brad stepped closer and tried to get him to slow down so he could understand him better. The man continued waving his hands, gesturing to us.

Brad turned to look at us.

"He wants us to follow him."

Chapter 7

We looked at each other briefly, before Vance spoke up.

"Lead the way," he said, with a shrug, motioning for Brad to follow the man.

The rest of us moved behind Brad, as the man led us through a beaded curtain near the rear, which went into a small room in the back of the store. The man walked over to a small closet and pulled out several folding chairs for us to sit on.

"I ... Juan," he said, pointing to his chest.

Brad made the introductions of our foursome, pointing at each of us in turn as the man nodded at us individually.

"I try speak English, yes?" Juan said as he looked at us.

We nodded in understanding.

"You ... um ... wishes?" he asked, looking us over, before his eyes rested on Vance in particular.

Vance shook his head, lifting his arm in a semi-helpless gesture. "I'm sorry. I don't understand," he said, apologetically.

Juan looked very frustrated for a moment before he turned and began speaking rapidly to Brad in Spanish once again.

When he was finished, Brad turned to Vance with a

surprised look on his face.

"I believe he wants to know if you're a witch," he explained.

This shocked all of us, and I watched Vance ponder this, several emotions passing over his face. Vance looked at Juan as if he were sizing him up. He finally pointed over to me.

"Portia's a witch," he said, before pointing at himself. "I'm a warlock."

"Si! Si!" Juan said excitedly, and then pointed to himself. "I ... warlock."

Vance sat up a little straighter and watched Juan closely. "You're a warlock?" he replied, leaning forward now in interest.

Juan spoke to Brad with what seemed like incredible speed, waving his hands in the air wildly and making strangling motions around his face. Then he pointed back at me, gesturing toward my talisman which hung around my neck.

Brad finally translated for the rest of us. "Juan says he's been a warlock since the age of sixteen. He said the magic has passed through his family for generations, though sometimes it skipped a generation or two. He's the first one in his family who's experienced these powers in over a hundred years.

"When we walked into the store he recognized the jewelry we were all wearing as having magical significance.

"He says several months ago a new warlock came into the area. He specifically calls him the demon warlock. Juan says one night when he was closing up his store, some men came and overpowered him. They took him to a nearby location where he was assaulted."

"They beat him?" Vance asked, his eyes moving between Brad and Juan.

"No. He says they removed his magic from him. They

stole it," Brad replied.

"They stole his magic?" Vance looked a bit confused. "How is that possible? The only way I know of taking another's powers is through drinking their blood, which is usually the result of a demon conversion, and even then, unless the witch is killed, they retain their own power. This man clearly isn't a demon."

Brad turned and asked Juan a few more questions before turning back to Vance.

"He says they performed something called the Demon Kiss on him," he explained.

"What the heck is a demon kiss?" I asked Vance, my eyes widening at the term I'd never heard of before.

He shook his head in bewilderment himself. "I have no idea. I've never heard of such a thing. Brad, can you please ask Juan to explain exactly what happened to him? Tell him we're unfamiliar with the term he's using."

Brad spoke briefly with Juan again.

"He says the demon warlock has to drink the blood of many witches or warlocks to make himself stronger. Once he has the strength he needs, he performed something like a kiss—only he didn't actually touch the mouth. Instead he leaned over and literally sucked the magic out of his prisoner, in effect leaving the person completely mortal, taking all the powers for himself.

"Juan says he had never heard of it either until it happened to him. Apparently this warlock bragged quite a bit about it. He also says no one can stand up to him because he's too strong. Juan says even the people who worked for him seemed afraid."

The pieces began clicking into place for me, as I looked at Vance in horror.

Damien must want Vance's powers to make him stronger so he could perform this demon kiss. He had always been after the power in Vance's blood. Or could it be worse? Perhaps he wanted to steal Vance's powers from him completely. Damien was way more powerful than any of us had imagined.

I could feel the tears come to the surface as I saw the shock registered on Vance's face. He was totally speechless.

Juan began speaking to Brad again, looking very upset.

"He says no one will listen to him. Everyone thinks he's crazy. The people here don't believe in magic. The police laughed him out of the building," Brad added.

"Why did the demon warlock let him go?" Vance asked, clearly overwhelmed with this information.

Brad relayed the question to Juan and waited for an answer, before replying back to Vance.

"He says he releases all of them after a kiss is performed. He says no one will believe them, and once the witch is completely human again, there's no way they can retaliate. He also threatened Juan's family if he tried to come after him. Then he told him if he got any other covens involved in this, he would take their powers, too. He just doesn't see anyone as a threat."

Juan spoke up again, and Brad relayed the message afterward.

"Juan says the only witches or warlocks he keeps are the ones he turns into demons. They become like slaves to him because he supplies them with the blood they crave so much."

At this comment, Vance's eyes suddenly flashed red.

Unfortunately, Juan saw this and jumped up, knocking his chair over and yelling frantically while pointing at Vance.

Brad stood and went to him trying to calm him down, while explaining what had happened to Vance. It took several long minutes before Juan calmed enough to pick up his chair and sit back down, though he scooted a little farther away from Vance, watching him warily.

"Tell him I'm no threat to him," Vance said to Brad, a sad look on his face.

"I did already," Brad replied with a sigh. "I gave him the short version of your story."

"Well, then tell him thank you for the information, and let him know we'll do everything possible to help in any way we can," Vance said, as he looked back at Juan with a nod.

Brad passed on the information and then Juan replied back.

"He says that he offers his services to you, and if there's anything he can do to help to please let him know."

Vance stood and nodded again toward Juan, being careful to stand back from the nervous man as Brad shook his hand.

The four of us went back through the beaded curtain and out of the store to the outside to the car.

Vance climbed inside and sat there for a second before he slammed his hand hard against the steering wheel.

"A demon kiss?" he growled, and I could feel the heat and anger rolling off him.

"I'm sorry," I said, placing my hand gently on his shoulder. He leaned his head back onto the headrest with his eyes closed.

He lifted his hands and started rubbing at his temples with his fingers.

"I'm starting to think I'm the spawn of Satan himself," he said with a sigh. "I didn't think it could get any worse."

"Let's go back to the hotel," I suggested. "We need to call Dad and figure out what to do from here."

Vance looked over at me for a moment, reaching out to pat me on the leg before he started the car. He pulled out, speeding through the slower moving traffic. I could tell by the set of his jaw he was very angry.

No one spoke for the entire trip back to the condo. We parked the car in the lot, and Vance came around to open my door, reaching a hand in to help me out. He didn't let go of my hand, but he didn't say anything either as we waited to board the elevator.

I followed him into the living room, where he led me to the couch, and we sat down together, Brad and Shelly joining us.

"I think you all need to go back home," he finally said, though he was looking directly at me. "Things are way worse than I could have ever anticipated. I don't want to place you in any kind of danger."

"Not a chance," Brad piped up. "Shelly and I are no threat to your dad. If he wants to take our magic away, all he has to do is take these amulets. Even then it won't give him any more magic since the charm will lose its power if it's removed."

"But what about Portia?" Shelly asked him, a concerned look on her face as she glanced over.

"That's my fear. I think he'd find her powers too desirable to pass up. He could use my power to help him perform a kiss on her," Vance said, continuing to look only at me.

"Or vice versa," I said, getting a little angry that they were talking over me like I didn't have a say. "Vance, I'm sorry, but there's nothing you can do or say to get me to leave, especially if you're still here."

"So, you'd bring the whole coven down here to possibly have this kiss thing performed on all of them? You heard what Juan said. No one can stand up to him. He's just too powerful!" Vance exclaimed.

"And what are you going to do about it? Are you just going to waltz in there and face him by yourself? How do you intend to accomplish that? Jedi mind tricks? 'I am not the warlock you are looking for.' How is that any better?" I asked, waving my arm in frustration.

"That's different," he replied, shaking his head. "I won't be risking anyone else if I go by myself."

"So you'll just become his 'little protégé' like he always intended?" I protested loudly, knowing my feelings about the situation were starting to get the better of me. "Think, Vance! If he turns you, where do you think the first place is that you'll go hunting? The whole coven will be sitting ducks, waiting for you to come and destroy them, just like you've always been afraid that you would do! No. We need to call Dad and start uniting some forces to see if we can come up with some sort of plan to stop your maniac father."

Everyone sat quietly for a few moments while my comments sank in. I tried hard to calm myself by taking a few deep breaths.

After a few minutes of no one speaking, Vance reached into his pocket and pulled out his cell phone, pressing a button. I heard the speed dial activate with a short series of beeps.

"Hey, Sean," he said after a moment, staring into my eyes. "We found my father, and it's a lot worse than we thought. I think you're all going to need to come down here."

The two talked back and forth for several minutes, my dad plaguing Vance with questions about the situation before he finally hung up.

"They'll be here tomorrow," he said still looking at me. He reached out to gently squeeze my hand.

"Okay," I replied, thinking of the date in my head. "Tomorrow is Christmas Eve!" I added in surprise, wondering where all the time had gone.

Vance nodded. "Your dad said we're not to go anywhere near my father or that warehouse again until they're here to help. He said to go buy a tree or something and decorate for Christmas. We'll celebrate with everyone and make a plan about what to do then."

Dad knew I loved Christmas more than any other holiday. He was trying to distract me, but I also knew I didn't want Vance out snooping around, possibly getting into some trouble while we waited for the others to get here.

"Well, let's go shopping then."

We spent the afternoon searching through several stores, purchasing decorative items, gifts for each other, and lots of groceries, before coming back to the condo.

I purchased a classical Christmas CD, and soon the sounds of holiday favorites were floating in the air. The music was very soothing to the somber, yet anxious mood we were all in.

That evening, Vance and Brad put together the artificial tree we had purchased, while Shelly and I wrapped up some presents we bought. When the guys were done getting the tree assembled, Shelly and I came in and shaped its branches.

It turned out to be a very Spanish-styled tree, complete with hanging red chili lights, little colorful sombrero hats, and maraca ornaments. There were gold-colored beads in strings and brightly striped ribbon which we carefully twisted to drape over the branches. The top of the tree was graced with a plain metal gold star.

Vance surprised me after I placed the star on the tree. He walked up to touch it with his finger, and it started to glow.

"Beautiful," I said. He stepped back and came to stand behind me, wrapping his arms around my waist.

We stayed that way for several minutes, with Shelly and

Brad doing the same next to us. The moment was magical. "I'm glad we're doing this," Vance said softly as he ran a hand gently through my hair. "I know your dad is just trying to keep us occupied, but this is nice, in light of everything that's going on."

"Christmas is my favorite holiday." I smiled as I leaned into his touch. "It's just a shame it has to be marred by all this crazy stuff that has been going on."

"Well, hopefully things will work out for all of us and this will be the first Christmas of many," he whispered into my ear, as he nuzzled at my neck with his nose.

"I hope so," I said, enjoying his touch. "How're you doing, by the way?"

He shook his head slightly. "I'm still reeling, just trying to take it all in," he said, as he ran his hands down my arms.

"Well, I hope you aren't comparing yourself to him," I replied, leaning my head against his chest. "You're nothing like him. You know that, right?"

"I hope that's true. It's just hard to believe since it turned out both of my parents were involved in this."

It was the first time he had even remotely mentioned his mother since the day he killed her.

"You did what you had to do," I said, knowing what he was thinking, and wanting him to not blame himself.

"I murdered my own mother," he stated softly, and I could feel the despair rippling through his voice.

"Krista wasn't your mother anymore," I replied, trying to comfort him. "She was just a pawn in your dad's little web of lies and deceit. It was because of his actions she died."

"It still hurts," he said, very softly, next to my ear. "I had hoped to find her safe again somewhere, someday. I wanted her to be a part of my life."

I turned in his arms and hugged him. "I know you did,

and I'm sorry things turned out the way they did—for you and her. You saved me, though," I reminded him tenderly. "So something good came from it, right?"

He gazed into my eyes. "I would do it exactly the same if we had it to do all over again," he said seriously, watching me intently.

"I know. I've never doubted that."

We continued to stare at each other, those looks passing many unsaid messages to one another.

"Hey!" Shelly piped up suddenly, breaking the intense mood between us and we remembered we weren't alone. "Let's make some holiday goodies now."

"That sounds fun!" I said, standing on my tiptoes to give Vance a quick peck on the lips. I had forgotten about all the groceries we purchased this afternoon.

The guys voted to have us bake some brownies first. Shelly and I had fun stirring up the ingredients together, and soon we were fighting over who got to lick the bowl.

I ended up winning, and I shared the leftover batter with Vance, spooning it into his mouth, while Shelly and Brad licked the beaters.

Afterward, while the brownies were cooking in the oven, we all cuddled up on the couch and watched 'It's A Wonderful Life' in Spanish.

Brad chuckled over the movie translations, while the rest of us had no idea what was being said, until Vance had the bright idea to turn on the English subtitles, which, of course, made the movie much more enjoyable.

When the program was over, we decided to call it a night. After a chaste hug and kiss goodnight with our significant others, the four of us headed to the directions of our beds.

This time, I found sleep claimed me quickly.

When I woke up in the morning I was surprised to find I was the last one to get up, despite the early hour. I crawled down from the enormous bed and made my way into the living room, finding Shelly curled up on the couch—a glass of juice in one hand and a fashion magazine in the other.

"Where did the guys go?" I asked, when I realized they weren't in the apartment.

"They're working out down in the weight room," she replied, taking a sip of her orange juice as she flipped her magazine shut. "Vance felt the need to work off some aggression after his withdrawal pangs this morning. They said for us to join them when you woke up."

"Oh. Sounds fun," I said, watching Shelly closely, trying to judge if she were hiding anything from me. "Is Vance doing okay?" I finally asked.

Shelly nodded. "He seemed perfectly fine to me when they left."

"That's good," I replied feeling relieved.

Soon we were both dressed in some workout-appropriate clothing and headed down to the gym. Shelly opened the glass door, and we walked in to find Vance spotting Brad at the weight bench. Brad was lifting what appeared to be a very heavy set of weights on the bar up over his chest. They were the only two people in the room.

"Three hundred and twenty!" Brad breathed out hard, dropping the bar with a loud clank back into the bracket above him. "Beat that!"

Vance traded places with Brad and easily lifted the weights, not even breaking a sweat, let alone allowing a tremble to pass through his body.

"You're cheating, aren't you?" Brad asked with a laugh, poking his finger into Vance's chest as he stood up. "You're using magic!"

Vance shook his head. "On my word, I'm not cheating."

"How much can you bench press then?" Brad asked, looking doubtful as he eyed Vance up and down.

"Four twenty-five," Vance said with a grin, as he adjusted a pair of fingerless gloves on his hands.

"Bull!" Brad challenged, shaking his head in denial. "That's the school record."

"I know," Vance replied, as his smile widened. "I'm the one who set it."

Brad shook his head again. "You're unbelievable," he muttered as he bent to pick up some more weights. He quickly loaded the bar up to four hundred twenty-five pounds. "Prove it." He stepped away from the bench and gestured for Vance to sit down.

Vance slid into the seat and leaned back. He placed his hands at even intervals and lifted the bar with a grunt, bringing it completely down to his chest before fully extending his arms and replacing the bar back in the brackets.

"You stink!" Brad said, grinning as he punched Vance in the shoulder.

Vance stood up and stepped away from the bench. He looked at the bar and slightly waved his fingers in an upward motion. The weight bar lifted easily by itself and floated into the air as if it weighed nothing at all.

"Now that one was magic," he said laughing, while Brad's eyes widened in awe.

"What a stud!" Shelly giggled, in a whisper next to my ear, as we watched the exchange.

"What a show off," I replied back to her with a smile, as we walked over to them, my insides quivering a little in pleasure at his awesome display.

"Hey!" Vance said when he saw me, dropping the levitating bar back into the brackets, without even looking. He came over and gave me a kiss on the cheek. "Sorry. I'm all sweaty," he apologized with a grin.

"No problem," I replied, smiling. "Shelly and I are going to run on the treadmill while the two of you finish your competition, uh ... workout."

He chuckled at my remark, and he winked at me before turning to walk back toward Brad.

Shelly and I enjoyed the view of the ocean as we ran in front of the floor-to-ceiling glass windows that stared out over the scene. We put in a good thirty minutes before the guys were done, and then we all headed back up to the room together.

The four of us got showered and dressed before we met back in the kitchen. We decided to make up more goodies before the coven was to arrive.

As it turned out we had piles of brownies, crispy rice treats, chocolate chip cookies, and coconut macaroons by the time my mom, dad, and grandma walked in.

"Everything looks so great and smells so good!" my mom exclaimed as she rushed up to give me a hug.

"Merry Christmas, Mom." I laughed as I wrapped my arms tightly around her.

"Hey, Pumpkin!" Dad said, coming forward to give me a hug also, wrapping his arms so tightly around me I could barely breathe.

We were soon all chatting loudly together as the family toured the condo. They commented on everything, loving all that they saw. When we stepped out onto the balcony, they raved over the beautiful scene in front of us.

"Would you look at that view!" Dad exclaimed as he leaned over the railing. "This is gorgeous!" He turned and pulled Mom into his arms.

"It really is pretty!" Mom agreed, leaning her head back against him.

"Shelly and I thought you two could take the master

bedroom," I said to my parents. "We'll move into Brad's room, and he can share with Vance."

"Nonsense!" Mom replied. "We booked the room right next door. The rest of the coven members have their own rooms all over the hotel. We figured your condo could be our home base, since it's the largest."

"All right," I said smiling.

"Pumpkin, these brownies are divine!" Dad said through a mouthful. "I've been starving for some good Christmas goodies!"

"Did you make all this stuff?" Grandma asked as she bit into one of her own.

"Yes, Shelly and I did. And it was old-fashioned style, you know ... no magic," I replied, with a grin, knowing it would please my mother.

"The boys didn't help out?" Grandma prodded.

"Of course we did! We were the official taste testers," Vance said with a little laugh.

"Ah! I see," she said, patting him on the shoulder. "So how's everything else going? Any news?"

"No, No!" my dad said, stepping between them and waving a finger at Grandma. "There'll be no talking about that tonight. Tonight we'll put aside our cares and celebrate the holiday."

Chapter 8

Christmas morning dawned clear and beautiful.

My family, Brad, Shelly, and the rest of the coven gathered together at the base of the tree to open the few presents we had for each other. The wrapping paper was soon piled up around us, as we laughed and smiled over each other's gifts.

Vance seemed to really enjoy the pullover sweater I bought for him, though I felt completely cheap when he surprised me with a diamond tennis bracelet.

"You really shouldn't have," I said to him during a private moment together.

"Why not?" he asked as he smiled softly at me. "I love you, and I enjoy showering you with beautiful things."

"Yes, but all I got you was a sweater," I complained, feeling badly.

"That was exactly what I needed," he said. "I love it! It's perfect!" He grinned brightly at me.

"Whatever," I mumbled, moving away from him.

"Hey," he said, reaching out, turning me back so he could look deep into my eyes. "I've never received a bad gift from you. I absolutely treasure everything you've ever given me, whether it's a physical gift or an emotional one." He lifted my hand and ran his finger over the diamond ring there.

"You agreeing to marry me was the one thing I really

wanted. Nothing I could buy for you will ever trump that," he added as he reached out to stroke a hand over my hair. "I love you, Portia."

My eyes watered slightly at his words, and I threw my arms around his neck, hugging him close to me.

"I love you too, Vance. Thanks for being so good to me," I replied right as my mom interrupted, calling out that it was time for the blessing on our Christmas breakfast.

We had a lovely meal, which Mom, Grandma, Shelly and I prepared for everyone. It was complete with eggs, ham, sausage, biscuits and gravy, and hash browns. We also had eggnog and orange juice to drink.

When the meal was over, everyone just spent the day hanging around visiting, watching movies, and eating way too much food.

"I feel like a stuffed turkey," Vance commented with a laugh, as we lounged together on the couch that afternoon. "See? Look how fat I am!" he added, patting his sculpted abdomen.

"Whatever," I said rolling my eyes. "I could scrub laundry on that washboard stomach of yours."

He leaned over to give me a quick peck on the cheek, flashing his baby blues at me in the process.

"So you still find me attractive even when I'm fat dogging it on the couch?" he asked, his eyes sparkling in amusement.

"I always find you attractive, no matter what you're doing." I smiled back at him, meaning every word of it.

"Good to know. And I wouldn't be too horribly opposed to watching you try to wash stuff on my abs," he added in a whisper, his expression clearly hinting he was flirting with me.

I blushed furiously at his remark, the image of me scrubbing wet material across his chiseled stomach burning into my mind, but I didn't get a chance to answer him as our conversation was interrupted.

"Portia, Vance?" my dad called to us from out on the patio where he was sitting with Mom. "Could the two of you come out here?"

I stood up, turning to pull Vance to his feet. The two of us walked hand in hand out onto the balcony.

"Close the door," Mom said gesturing to the sliding one we just walked through.

Vance turned and shut door before walking over to join me at the outdoor table.

"Have a seat, kids," Dad said, as he patted the chair next to him.

"What going on?" I asked, as I sat down.

"I thought maybe you could tell us," Dad replied, giving me a questioning look.

I was at a complete loss to what he was referring to.

"I asked her to marry me," Vance piped up.

Suddenly, I realized what was happening as I followed their gazes. I still had my engagement ring on and my parents had noticed the bejeweled finger.

"It's a little early for that, son, don't you think?" my dad asked, staring up at Vance, his expression unreadable.

"I had every intention of asking you before I gave it to her," Vance said politely. "I'm sorry that didn't go as I'd planned, but I want you to know this is not something I did lightly. I love Portia, and I know our love is the real deal. We've been through a lot together, and I wanted to give her something tangible that signifies my commitment to her."

"And what about her safety?" my mom interjected, frowning slightly. "I understand that even though you're no longer going through a demon conversion the desire is still there for you. Isn't that a threat to her?"

I could see he was struggling with his answer. "It could

be," Vance agreed, nodding. "Portia has been trying to help me see I'm still responsible for my own actions, though. She's really helped me to learn to exercise control over my cravings."

"So, can you say for a certainty there will no longer be any danger from you toward her?" my dad asked, looking at him with a hard expression.

I watched the emotions on Vance's face as they warred with each other before he replied. "No, sir. I can't," he replied truthfully.

"Well, you must understand our concern," my dad replied, leaning back in his chair and folding his arms across his chest. "I had once sworn to myself you would never lay eyes on her again after I had to sit there helplessly and watch you feed on her. I was very angry with you. I feel you broke my trust in every sense of the word that day."

I couldn't take anymore. "That was my choice," I spoke up loudly, defending him. "He had nothing to do with it."

"He could have killed you, Portia!" my mom complained, throwing her hands into the air. "In fact, he almost did."

"Exactly!" I said, standing up suddenly. "He almost did, but he didn't. He was able to stop himself."

"After which he basically begged you to surrender your virtue to him," my dad reminded me.

I walked over to the railing, looking out at the sea before me. I took a deep breath before I spoke my next words, knowing they would spark a discussion I didn't really want to have.

"If it makes you feel any better, I already offered it to him. He refused to take it."

"Uh, no!" my dad said, sitting up straighter in his chair. "That doesn't make me feel any better. Why would you do something like that?"

I turned around to face them all, my tears running down my face.

"I love him," I said, with all the emotion I could muster. "I'd do anything for him. Anything! I just don't want a life without him."

I looked straight at Vance, letting my words sink in. I needed him to understand the depth of my feelings.

"So you haven't been intimate together?" my mom asked, softly this time.

I shook my head. "No. It's not because we haven't wanted to, though. Vance feels that part of our relationship is best saved for marriage."

"I can live with that," my dad said, with an obvious sigh of relief.

He looked at Vance, who had quietly been observing our interactions.

"So what are your intentions exactly?" Dad asked him.

"Well, right now pretty much everything in my life is hinged on the fact that something needs to be done about my dad. If we can get it all worked out, I would like to ask your permission to marry Portia before her senior year of high school. I figured I could look for a job in Flagstaff and we could get a little place there. She could still drive to Sedona for school, while I start at Northern Arizona University," he explained.

"Before her senior year?" my mom asked with a little gasp. "And how do you know that you'll be able to provide for her adequately, or yourself for that matter? It's hard to work and go to school at the same time."

"I'm guessing you don't know about the money then either?" I asked, with a sardonic smile.

"What money?" Dad asked, looking confused.

"Vance happens to be a millionaire," I said, enjoying dropping the bomb on them.

"What?" they said in unison, looking at Vance.

He shrugged modestly. "I have a trust fund," he offered as a simple explanation.

"The trust fund Marsha told us about?" my dad questioned.

"That's the one," he replied, looking completely unaffected by the subject change.

"I had no idea it was anything like that!" Dad said in shock. "I thought maybe a few thousand ...." He trailed off.

"We didn't want to advertise it," Vance explained simply. "We didn't know if my dad would try to trace the money. Besides, we were both quiet, down to earth people who liked living things out in a small, comfortable way."

"Wow!" was all my dad said in response, his eyes wide as he shook his head slightly.

We sat together in silence, letting things sink in, before Dad finally spoke up again.

"Vance, you're already like a son to me. It's been hard to watch you go through the trials you've had lately. That being said, though, Portia is my flesh and blood. Our flesh and blood," he amended, reaching over to grasp my mom's hand. "We want the best for her. I know she wants you, and I know the two of you are linked in a special way that's been pretty much unheard of before now. I understand you're older too, and in a place where you have more interest with moving on with your life." He paused for a minute, as he looked Vance over again, as if considering his next words carefully. "I guess I'm saying if things work out okay then Portia's Mom and I will consider your request to marry her early. I'm not promising anything, but with the way you're together now, an engagement isn't going to hurt anything."

"Thank you, sir," Vance replied, unable to stop a smile from spreading across his face as his gaze moved from my dad to me.

"I do have a couple of stipulations, though," Dad added, causing Vance to redirect his attention back to him.

"What's that?" Vance asked, leaning forward to listen.

"I don't want to let her get married before her senior year, and I'd like her to be seventeen first. She'll have her birthday just a few weeks after school starts. And second, if I see you're going to be a threat to her in any way, I'll call this whole thing off. Binding spell or not, it's her safety first," Dad was clenching and unclenching his fist, and I wondered if he realized he was doing it.

"I understand," Vance replied, looking back over at me. "Her safety should always come first, Sean."

"Do you understand, Portia?" my mom asked.

I nodded.

"Very well, then," my dad said. "The two of you have our permission to officially announce your engagement if you'd like."

"Really?" I asked, a smile I couldn't possibly hold back breaking across my face.

"Really," Dad said.

I ran over and threw my arms around his neck, squeezing him in a giant bear hug.

"Thank you, Dad," I said before turning to hug my mom also.

"Welcome to the family, son," my dad said as he extended his hand out toward Vance.

"Thank you, sir," Vance said, shaking his hand vigorously, and I saw he was beaming also.

Dad nodded his head toward the glass door which was separating us from those who were inside.

"Might as well go and break the news to everyone else," he said as he stood up, offering Mom a hand.

The four of us walked inside together, and Mom went

over to the kitchen counter, picked up a glass and began tapping it with a spoon.

"Could I have everyone's attention?" she asked over the din.

Everyone stopped whatever they were doing and turned to look at her.

"Vance has something he wants to tell all of you," she said, and all eyes turned to look over at him.

He lifted my hand to his lips and kissed my ring finger in front of everyone before he spoke.

"I've asked Portia to marry me, and she has consented," he said with a smile, as he stared into my eyes, never looking away from me. "Yes, this is early, and we aren't really sure when a wedding might happen. But for now, at least, we're officially engaged."

Some people started clapping, and others let out a happy cheer. Soon we were surrounded by well-wishers giving us hugs and kisses.

It was a wonderful feeling, and I couldn't help letting out a girlish giggle in all the excitement.

"You're my fiancée," I whispered to him with a smile, as I squeezed his hand in delight.

He pulled me close to him then and kissed me proper, much to the joy of everyone else in the room.

I couldn't stop smiling later that evening, as we strolled along the beach hand in hand, Brad and Shelly walking beside us doing the same.

We decided to take a walk after Dad and Grandma asked us to leave for a few minutes so they could meet privately with the rest of the coven.

"This has been my favorite Christmas ever!" I said with a smile.

"Why is that?" Vance asked as he gave my hand a tender squeeze.

"Because I got you for Christmas," I replied, grinning from ear to ear, still unable to believe it was really true.

"Well, I hope I'm a gift you won't ever want to return," he said, jokingly.

"Not a chance!" I said and threw my arms around him and kissed him.

He responded by picking me up and twirling me around in a circle, without breaking the kiss.

"Get a room!" Brad complained with a laugh.

"No kidding!" Shelly laughed, too. "It's like being stuck in a romance novel or something."

"Sorry." I blushed, as Vance lowered me back down until my feet were touching the sand, even though I wasn't sorry at all.

Vance graciously changed the subject. "We've been out here for a while now. I'm sure we could head back to the condo, if you'd like," he said as he looked back down the beach in the direction we had come.

"What do you think they're talking about?" Shelly asked.

"I have no idea," I replied, shaking my head, thinking it had indeed been a curious thing for them to ask us to leave and to take Brad and Shelly with us.

Usually when the coven met together, everyone was involved, especially lately as things were almost always regarding Vance.

"Let's go find out then," Brad suggested, and he started moving in the direction of the hotel.

We walked back up the beach to the grounds of the resort, passed the sparkling swimming pools with Jacuzzis, and through the breezeway to the elevator.

The coven was still seated together talking when we re-entered the room.

"Come on in, kids!" My dad waved at us with a smile.

"We have some things to discuss with you."

The four of us went and sat down, cross-legged on the tile floor, next to the others who were gathered.

"We have a proposition for you," Grandma said, looking specifically at Shelly and Brad. "We've discussed this with everyone except for Vance and Portia, but they can feel free to give any comments they have on the matter also."

"All right," Brad said, looking a little bit apprehensive.

"We'd like to extend an official invitation for the two of you to join our coven," Grandma stated, looking closely at both of them for their reaction.

There was complete silence in the room for a moment.

"But we aren't witches … or warlocks," Shelly said, looking over at Brad.

I was very surprised by this request, but it also seemed to make perfect sense to me, and I wondered why I never thought of it before.

"You've been offering your services to help further the causes of this coven and the people involved in it," Grandma continued. "By inducting you as official members you'll be under the protection of the powers that are in this coven. If we're to be involved in some type of confrontation in the near future, this will greatly enhance your chances of survival.

"Plus, there are a lot of things we can teach you that would give you some magical benefits. For instance, making healing medicines or even using some minor spells. You'd be able to keep your magical talismans and learn how to use their powers to strengthen yourselves in other areas. Basically, the power of the coven would supply you with magic so to speak," she explained as she watched them both.

"You wouldn't ever surpass the level of an apprentice witch or warlock, however," Dad said, letting them know there would be limits to what they could actually do with their borrowed powers.

"What do you think about it?" Brad asked, turning to look to Vance for some advice.

"I think it's a smart idea. I feel foolish for not having thought of it myself," he replied.

"What do you think, Portia?" Shelly asked me.

"I agree with Vance," I said. "Something like this would've protected you from being susceptible to what you went through before, when Vance's mom placed the spell on you. Both of you are very close to the coven, and you know our secrets. Making you official members would not only protect each of you, but would protect the coven also."

We all sat in anticipation as Shelly and Brad thought things over carefully for a moment.

"I accept," Shelly said, giving Brad's hand a squeeze and looking at him with a questioning gaze.

"I'll do it, too," he replied.

"Wonderful!" my dad said. "This will actually give us the equivalent of having thirteen witches in the coven even though we'll actually be fourteen in number. It was a great misfortune for us to lose Marsha."

Everyone was silent for a moment as we recalled Marsha and her sweet disposition. I knew Vance would always love her and be grateful for the help she had rendered him.

"I propose we dedicate the rest of this evening to Marsha's memory and induct Brad and Shelly into the coven tonight," I suggested.

"That sounds like a perfect idea!" my dad said. "Do we have all the magical items we need here to do that, Mom?" he asked Grandma.

"Yes, we do. I brought everything I thought we might possibly need," she replied as she stood to leave the room, my dad following after her.

We soon stood in a circle in the center of the floor, all of us in our ceremonial robes, even Brad and Shelly, which proved Grandma and Dad had indeed planned ahead for this very thing.

The elements were called, and the circle was cast. Brad and Shelly were officially introduced to each member of the coven with a kiss and the Blessed Be incantation. Afterward they were invited to stand together in the spot that had once been Marsha's place in the order. Then they were given a candle, which they both held together. It was lit in her memory.

Vance spoke of Marsha and of the good she'd done in her life during the time he knew her. Afterward he thanked her, becoming a bit emotional in the process, and his voice cracked slightly over the memories of an individual who had been like a mother to him. When he was done speaking, he leaned over and blew out the candle to signify setting her spirit free.

Dad then began explaining about the earth and its creations, much as he had when I had been inducted into the coven. Tonight, however, he spoke at length about the birth of the Christ child and the blessings His life and death had brought to all of mankind. It was a beautiful Christmas sermon.

When Dad was done speaking, Grandma presented Brad and Shelly each with a beautiful round, smooth crystal, about the size of golf ball. She said these also held magic in them and she would show them how to use them properly. She explained that between the power of the amulets they were wearing and their crystals, they would probably be surprised by the things they would now be able to do.

She did caution them, however, that they needed to take great care with keeping the crystals safe, as they were something anyone could pick up and use. There was no fail-safe charm on them like with the talismans. Also, if they were to get damaged, it could affect the power in them.

We released the circle afterward, and Brad leaned over to whisper something in Grandma's ear. She smiled and whispered something back, making a slight gesture with her hand.

Brad stepped forward and gave his ring a slight twist before he raised his arm into the air and spoke a word I didn't recognize, swinging his hand and the crystal in a full swoop around his head.

Instantly large snowflakes began falling from above, over our heads and drifting down, dissipating before they hit the floor.

"Merry Christmas!" He smiled widely.

"Merry Christmas!" everyone replied, and we all took turns hugging one another.

Chapter 9

When we awakened the next morning, it was back to business as usual. The warm and fuzzy holiday memories in our heads were placed on the back burner as the coven met together to form a plan with one another.

The first thing on the agenda was a complete circle which was held over Vance. He was suffering from serious withdrawals this morning that had everyone very concerned about his wellbeing.

Grandma was working over him now as he lay on his bed curled up in a ball, dressed only in a pair of long gym shorts, while he fought the spasms wracking his body. His eyes seemed even more bloodshot than usual to me, as Grandma passed smoking herbs up and down him, while reciting an incantation.

When she was finished speaking, I quietly brought my concern up.

"He seems much worse to me while we're performing these rituals," I complained, feeling upset about his reaction.

"The two kinds of magic are warring against each other in his system," Grandma explained softly. "Try not to let it worry you. We need your positive energy right now to help him."

I wanted to beg her to stop, since it seemed he was far worse than he'd ever been before, but I also knew she wouldn't be doing anything intentionally to hurt him.

As it turned out, his withdrawal phase this morning lasted a much shorter amount of time, though it was so much more painful for him.

I hadn't been able to help myself, crying softly as I watched. He hadn't screamed out or even made a sound, but I could hear the torture as it ran through his head, and it had been excruciating.

When the worst of it passed, the coven released the circle and one by one the members slowly filtered out of the room. After they were all gone, I closed the door behind them and went to lie down next to him, wrapping my arms around him.

He was damp with perspiration, as if he had done a really hard work-out. He didn't speak to me for a while—he just lay there and rested, but his eyes never left mine.

Lifting my hand, I moved to brush some of the sweaty hair off his forehead, away from his face, letting my fingers trail slowly down over his sculpted features after I was finished.

"I'm okay," he said finally, and I heard the exhaustion in his voice.

"I want this to be over," I replied, snuggling up closer to him, nuzzling under his chin with my nose. He lifted it a little, and I placed a kiss against his neck. "I'm sorry, but I don't like these treatments."

"They're helping to some extent," he said, as he traced a finger slowly in a small circle on my back. "I go through it all a lot faster than usual."

"It breaks my heart to watch it."

"You don't have to stay if you don't want to. Just wait outside until it's finished."

"No. The coven's magic is weaker without me. Besides I want to be with you whenever you need me."

"Thanks," he said with a small smile, before reaching up

to run a hand against my arm that was draped over him. "I appreciate it."

He rolled away from me, over onto his back, turning his head so he could look at me. I propped up on my elbow, so I could lean over him, and gave him a tiny peck on the lips. He smiled softly back at me, as he ran his hand over my hair.

"I should probably go get in the shower now," he said, looking a little regretfully at me. "I don't want to keep everyone waiting on me."

"All right," I replied, taking my cue for dismissal, rolling off the bed to walk toward the door. "Call me if you need me."

"I always need you," he answered with a slight laugh as he sat up on the edge of the bed.

"You know what I mean," I said, smiling at him as I slipped out the door, not missing the playful wink he sent in my direction.

Breakfast was in full swing by the time Vance got out of the shower. I told him to sit, while I served him a heaping plate of pancakes and sausage.

"I'm fine now, you know that right?" he asked, as I sat his plate in front of him. "I can dish my own food. I'm not an invalid yet."

"I like serving you." I laughed, before leaning over to give him a kiss. "Besides, I'm going to be your wife someday. I figured I should practice up on waiting on you—after all, it will be my job." I turned to step away from the table to go back toward the kitchen.

His arm snaked out quickly and caught me by the wrist, pulling me back toward him.

I looked at him with a puzzled expression as he pulled me down to where my head was next to his.

"I want you to understand something," he began, in a low voice meant only for my ears. "You will never be my servant. We are partners, equal to one another in this relationship. I'll never do anything to dominate you."

I smiled at his deadly serious comment. "I know that, silly. But I like doing things for you, and nothing you say will ever make me change the way I feel about that, so get over it." I jabbed him in the ribs with one of my free fingers.

He let go of my wrist, and I saw some deeper emotion flicker through his gaze.

"I love you," he said, as he continued to watch me closely.

"I know," I replied, flashing my eyes at him and giving a Cheshire cat grin, before turning to walk away, though I could still feel his stare burning a hole in my back behind me.

When breakfast was over, we all met to begin discussions on what to do with things surrounding Vance's father. My dad turned the floor over to Vance to explain what was going on to everyone.

"We haven't actually made any contact with him," Vance began, as he ran a hand through his hair. "I'm just assuming that he's here because of what we've found out."

He went on to tell everyone about Juan and what he had told us in his store. He also told them we had found the warehouse on the shipping address and how it was heavily guarded with a lot of activity going on around it.

"We need to send out a scouting party to go and case out the warehouse," Dad said as he looked around the room. "Do we have any volunteers for that job?"

Of course, Vance shot his hand into the air immediately.

"No," Dad said, shaking his head. "Too dangerous. They've been looking for you specifically. I'll not send you right into their lair. We need someone else to go check stuff out."

Sharon and her brother, Fred, both volunteered at this

point.

"They wouldn't have any reason to know who we are," Sharon spoke up. "And both of us have Hispanic heritage which would make it easier for us to blend into the local environment."

"That's a good point," Dad said in agreement. "Now we need someone to go talk to the shop keeper on Benito Juarez again. I want to see if he'd be willing to let us use his place as a home base of sorts, while we're trying to keep tabs on the comings and goings at the warehouse property."

"I can speak Spanish, and I already know Juan. Vance and I could go," Brad offered.

"I don't think I'm the best choice of person to approach Juan," Vance spoke up as he shook his head slightly at Brad. "I had a little flash of blood thirst the last time I was there," he explained to everyone else. "I don't think Juan trusts me. Plus, if he were to find out I was actually the son of the 'demon warlock' he fears so much, I don't think he'd be too inclined to help out."

"I agree with you," Grandma added. "I think it would be wise for someone other than the kids to go. If anyone were watching Juan's place, they'd recognize right away the kids had already been there. I think I should go. I have my own shop and I can make it look like something to do with business."

"But what if the coven was watching you when Krista came before?" I asked. "They might know who you are."

"I'll go," Babs piped up. "I work in the store. I can make it look like a legitimate business interest also."

"I don't want anyone going out alone, though," Dad said. "You'll need to pick someone to go with you."

Alice, the Pilates instructor from the Fountains at Fontane, volunteered to go with Babs.

"Great." Dad smiled as he rubbed his hands together.

"Okay, the rest of us will take turns driving in different vehicles around the property to avoid detection. Rule number one is to not approach Damien Cummings if you find him. If you do happen to see him, then report back to the rest of the group, please. If we need to, we can set up a tail to follow him and see where he goes. All of you have been provided with cell phones with good service here in Mexico. Don't hesitate to use them." He paused a second before he continued on. "Rule number two is to try and find out what's being shipped in those crates being moved around. Knowledge is power in this case. We don't want any surprises."

When everyone was fully briefed on what they needed to do, Dad started sending people out the door.

"So what can we do?" Vance asked, as we approached him when all the other members of the coven had gone.

"Man the phone," Dad said, handing his cell to Vance.

"You're kidding, right?" Vance slowly reached for the phone, eyeing it a bit distastefully.

"Nope," my dad replied and crossed his arms over his chest. I could see he knew he was in for an argument. "I'm trying to keep you safe, and for right now that means completely out of the line of fire. In fact, I'd go so far as saying you and Portia shouldn't even leave the hotel. That way you'll have less of a risk that someone who might know you will see you and report to your father."

"So, I basically get to sit here and do nothing?" Vance turned to walk back over to the couch, plopping down on it in frustration.

"Pretty much. Sorry, son. I know you want to be out in the thick of things, but I just can't, in good conscience, allow it. "

"So what do you want to do all day?" Vance asked, giving up much easier than I thought he would have. He looked at me with a dejected sigh. "I wasn't counting on being placed on house arrest."

"Well, we could help Mom cook more food for everyone," I suggested as I sat next to him, placing my hand on his knee.

"We need more groceries, though," my mom piped up from the kitchen as she was rummaging through the cupboards.

"Why don't you take Brad and Shelly with you to the store then?" Dad proposed.

"Do you mind coming with me?" Mom asked, turning to look toward them.

"Not at all," Shelly replied, moving to walk toward the bedroom. "Let me get my purse."

"This is just great," Vance mumbled underneath his breath. "I'm not even worthy to buy groceries."

I just laughed as I scooted closer to him so I could wrap my arms around his shoulders, giving him a little squeeze.

"You *are* worthy," I whispered, nuzzling against his ear. "They're just worried about you. Besides, what is your favorite thing to do?"

He smiled then as he nudged my face back with his. "Why, to cuddle up with you, of course," he answered with a wink.

"Well, unless we get a phone call, we get to sit here and do just that," I reminded him.

"You always know how to cheer me up." He smiled, with a devious grin, and he adjusted his position so he could pull me into his arms and onto his lap.

He began to kiss me passionately, just as my Dad walked back into the room from the patio.

"Hey! No hanky panky!" Dad said sternly to us.

Vance and I both busted up laughing.

"Come on," I said, sliding off his lap and pulling him to

his feet. "I think there's still a cake mix in the cupboard. We'll make it while everyone else is gone."

We walked over to the kitchen together where I began pulling out ingredients, setting them on the counter next to a mixing bowl and cake pan.

"How about you mix up the cake, while I stand here and do this," Vance said as he wrapped his arms around my waist and kissed my neck, which sent delightful little shivers dancing up my skin.

I just laughed as I started to blend up the ingredients, while he used levitation magic to measure everything out so it was ready for me whenever I needed it, dumping the contents in the bowl whenever I asked for them.

"This is kind of fun," he said with a grin, as he continued to lean his head over my shoulder, resting his chin there.

"I thought so, too," I replied, turning my face to rub my cheek against his in return.

We poured the batter into the pan and placed it into the oven, setting the timer. Then we cleaned up the kitchen and loaded the things we had used into the dishwasher.

"Now what?" Vance asked, when we were finished, looking around with a bored expression already.

"Let's go sit on the balcony and watch the surf," I suggested, tugging on his hand to pull him in the direction of the door.

"I don't know if that's a good idea," my dad said, peering up from some documents he was looking over, at the dining room table. "Vance's father could have spies anywhere."

"Dad," I said, with mounting frustration, "don't you think if Damien had any idea that Vance was here, he'd have been swarming all over this place by now?"

"You can never be too careful," Dad replied with a shrug, looking like he wasn't too willing to give in on the issue.

"Dad," I groaned, dragging his name out like a disgruntled child would, "we've been here for a lot longer than anyone else and haven't seen anything suspicious. We've eaten at restaurants, shopped and walked on the beach. That would've been more than ample opportunity for someone to attack us, or even kidnap us, if they were really following us around."

My dad dropped the papers he was holding back onto the table, leaning back to cross his arms across his chest.

"I suppose you're right," he finally said with a sigh. "It's just we're going to start stepping up our game now and it'll draw attention if anyone is trying to look for things out of the ordinary."

"Tell you what," I replied, trying the negotiating tactic, as I could feel Vance becoming tenser beside me. "If you let us sit out on the balcony, we'll sit up next to the wall. That way we'll be able to watch the ocean, but no one from the grounds or the neighboring condos will be able to see us. They'd have to be on a boat out in the middle of the water with binoculars to be able to spy on us."

"That could easily happen," Dad said, pursing his lips together. "There are a lot of fishing boats that cross by on their way out in the mornings. He could be watching us from anywhere."

"Dad!"

"Okay. Okay," he replied, raising his hands in surrender. "Maybe I'm over reacting. You may sit on the porch next to the wall. Just please try to stay out of sight, for my sake."

"Thank you!" I said, fighting the urge to roll my eyes. Vance and I walked over to the large glass door and opened it.

We stepped out and pulled a couple of the chairs up against the wall.

"Sorry about my dad," I apologized as Vance reached over to hold my hand, his fingers toying with the diamond solitaire that graced my finger.

"Don't worry about it. I know he means well." He continued to rub his finger over my ring. "Do you like it?" he asked, changing the subject, looking from it to me. "You never really said."

"I like it a lot," I replied and smiled. "It's very beautiful. I think you chose well."

"I wasn't sure where your tastes ran when it came to engagement rings." He chuckled, and his eyes sparkled like the water of the ocean. "It was kind of a blind shot in the dark. I finally just ended up choosing the one I could imagine seeing on your finger."

"Well, that was a good way to do it then, because I think it's perfect."

"Not as perfect as you."

"Now you're just being cheesy." I laughed, but leaned over to give him a kiss anyway.

"Hey. Whatever works, right?" He smiled. "You can't blame a guy for spreading a little cheese now and then."

"I can when he's as smart and talented as you are," I teased him as I lifted my hand to give him a little pinch on the shoulder.

"Now who's laying it on too thick?" he asked, reaching to poke me in the ribs with a tickle.

We didn't continue our little confrontation because my dad's phone suddenly began to buzz in Vance's pocket.

"Phone!" we said in unison, and we both jumped up and hurried back into the apartment.

Dad looked up as we came into the room, Vance holding the phone out in front of him, as he quickly moved to give it to him. He took it from him and answered it.

"This is Sean. Talk to me."

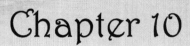

Chapter 10

We waited with baited breath as Dad listened intently to the person on the other end. After a second, his body totally relaxed, and he inhaled deeply, before letting out a sigh of relief.

"Good grief, Stacey. Are you trying to give me a heart attack?" he asked, looking over at the two of us with a shake of his head. "Your mom wants to know if you bought any baking soda the other day."

"I did," I replied, going over to the freezer and pulling out the box, shaking it a little, while looking inside. "It is about half empty."

Dad relayed the message to Mom, while Vance and I sauntered back out onto the balcony together.

"I hate sitting here, doing nothing," he complained, sitting down on the lounge chair.

"I know," I said, as I sat next to him, reaching over to pat his hand. "But Dad must figure it's pretty important for you to be here. He stayed here to protect you himself."

"Is that what he's doing?" Vance rolled his eyes and flopped his head back against the seat. "Marvelous."

"Don't be so hard on him. If he didn't really care about you, he wouldn't be here. Welcome to the close family life you've always been longing for."

He just answered me with some sort of grunt, before he moved his hand to lace his fingers with mine.

We didn't talk much as we sat together, allowing the soothing sounds of the ocean to wash back and forth over our senses.

I found myself slowly being lulled to sleep as I lay with my eyes closed and my head leaned back into the comfortably padded lounge chair. I didn't realize I'd actually fallen asleep though until I felt Vance shaking me gently.

"Portia," his sultry voice called out to me, and I lifted my eyelids to look at him. "Hey, baby." He smiled. "You've been sleeping for about an hour now. Some of the coven members have come back. I thought you might want to hear what they have to say."

"Oh … okay," I replied, taking the hand he extended to me, letting him pull me up.

We walked back inside, anxious to hear what the others learned while they'd been out on their expeditions.

Sharon and Fred were inside talking to my dad.

"We were actually able to talk to the security guard at the facility today," Sharon was saying, as we came through the sliding door. "We noticed there was a sign advertising one of the warehouse units available for lease. We went up to the gate pretending to be people who were interested in putting a business in there. The guard gave us a card to the listing agent.

"We also asked him about security on the place," she continued. "He told us they keep a guard posted at the gate all day and there are three security cameras, one for each of the other walls around the property. He then informed us there's a group which rents one of the larger units at the facility and they conduct their business there mostly at night. They post their own security guards there in the evenings. He said the name of the business was called Cummings Enterprises. He gave us a card for them also, in case we were interested in contacting them and asking how they like the facility."

Fred pulled a card from his wallet and handed it over to my dad for review.

"So now we have an address and a phone number," Dad smiled, as he looked over the card, before glancing up to give Fred and Sharon a nod. "Great work, you two. I'm really proud of you."

Vance walked over to my dad and asked if he could please have a look at the card, holding his hand out expectantly.

"He's really here then," he said somberly, running his thumb over the card absently for a moment, before snapping back to reality. "This is a home address," he pointed out, as he leaned over toward me to show me the writing. "We passed the turn to Las Conchas when we were downtown. I believe it's a resort housing area."

"Well, it's evident he isn't trying to hide if that's true," I replied, as I looked between my dad and Vance. "That goes right along with what Juan told us. He isn't afraid of anything or anyone getting in his way."

"Did you perhaps find out any clue to what Damien is shipping there?" Dad asked Sharon and Fred.

"No," Fred answered, with a shake of his head. "We didn't even ask after the guard mentioned all the business dealings were kept confidential. We felt he might get suspicious about it."

"No worries," Dad said as he flipped his cell phone open. "We'll find out somehow."

"Hi, Mom," he said when Grandma answered her phone. "You can send the other drivers back now, but I need you to go check out a different location." He gave her the address. "It's located in the Las Conchas housing area. I just want you to find out where the property is, though.

Please don't slow down or try to observe anything other than the obvious. After you find the place, go ahead and come on back to the hotel."

We waited around for about thirty minutes after Dad talked with Grandma, before everyone made it back to the condo and came to report their findings to the rest of us.

"So I found the address without any problem," Grandma said, looking around at each of us. "It's easily the largest beachside home in the vicinity, though I didn't notice any activity whatsoever on the property as I passed."

"How about you two?" Dad asked turning to look at Babs and Alice. "Did you have any success?"

"We were able to speak with Juan," Babs said. "He seemed to be willing enough to help out however he could, but he's a little nervous about everything, especially since Damien threatened him and his family if he tried to get other people involved in this situation."

"That's understandable," my dad replied, as he thought about it for second. "If he wishes, we can conduct our business there during the evening hours, after the shop is closed. He wouldn't even need to be there at all, if it was to be his preference and, of course, if he feels he can trust the place to us."

"That might help," Babs said, nodding. "We'll talk to him again and see what his feelings are about it."

"Good," Dad replied. "Now we just need to decide what is the best way to do some surveillance on this property located out in Las Conchas. If it's indeed Damien's personal residence, you can be sure it'll have powerful protection charms all over it. We need to find the weakest spot and attack things from that vantage point."

"That would be from the ocean," Vance spoke up. "All of those homes are loaded with glass windows that face out from every room to maximize the view. It would be easy to sit out on the water with binoculars or even a telescope. We'd be able to see virtually everything happening in the house, without ever setting foot on the property. That would eliminate the worry about activating magical charms or wards he may have placed around the area."

"That's true," Dad replied, pondering on what Vance had suggested. "This is a very good idea. We'd need to come up with a boat of some sort we could use, though."

"No problem," Vance said with a slight shrug. "I've seen a lot of those fishermen stay out on the water well after dark. I think we should offer to pay one of them to use their boat for the whole day. It wouldn't seem suspicious to anyone who was watching to see a regular local craft out on the water. In fact, keep the crew on and let them fish. Tell them we'll pay them all double their draw for the day."

"That could cost a pretty penny, though," Dad reminded him.

"I'm not worried about the money." Vance said, dismissing the comment with a shake of his head. "I do have one stipulation, though."

"What?" Dad asked, looking at him in question.

"If I'm paying for it, then I'm on the boat, and Portia comes with me. She's seen images of my dad through our mental link. We're the only two here who can positively identify him besides you. I'll not leave her behind." He stared at my dad seriously, driving his point home, and I knew he wasn't going to budge or negotiate on the subject. He was tired of sitting on the sidelines.

Dad mulled things over for a minute before he spoke, and I could tell that he wasn't too thrilled with the suggestion, but he knew Vance's idea was sound in its logic.

"Fine," he finally agreed. "We should be far enough away to keep you safe from being seen by anyone."

"It's too late for us to get on the boat today, though.

We'll have to shoot for tomorrow," Vance said, and I could see he was feeling frustrated by having to wait even longer to get going on this plan.

Bruce, who owned the restaurant in Sedona, volunteered to go down to the docks and wait for the fishing boats to come in, to see if he could make the arrangement we needed to acquire.

"I can inquire about fresh shrimp for the restaurant while I'm down there looking around for a suitable boat. It'll be a good cover," he said.

Hal also volunteered to go to the marina with him, too.

"Awesome," Dad said, and I could tell he was enjoying the thrill of the hunt we were finding ourselves drawn into. "Now we need to figure out some surveillance plans on this warehouse for this evening."

Everyone was soon surrounding my dad as he knelt down on the large tile floor, where he spread out documents detailing his previous searches for Vance's father, along with the schematics for all the warehouses Damien had previously used in other locations.

While I was surprised by all the detail these documents contained, I was most caught off guard when he rolled out an entire blueprint of the warehouse here in Rocky Point, along with all the surrounding property and businesses, clear up to Juan's store on Benito Juarez.

"Dad?" I asked him, in front of everybody, as he was busy circling areas of the blueprints in red marker. "Where did you get all this stuff, and what is it exactly that you do? And I don't want any more of this encyclopedia salesman that you've been feeding me my whole life."

A slight chuckle made its way through the rest of the group as Dad looked up at me with a grin.

"Pumpkin," he replied, "it may not be in your best interest to know that I may, or may not, be an agent of the

United States federal government."

"What? Are you like a … a spy or something?"

"No. Nothing that glorious." He bent back over the map of the building. "All you need to know is_I have my resources, but I'm not going to go into any more detail than that."

I threw my hands up in the air and turned to walk away as I began to mutter quietly to myself.

"Pumpkin, I'm an encyclopedia salesman," I mimicked him. "But really I'm a warlock. Oh, and did I mention I'm a federal agent also?" I paused. "Is there anything else that I need to know about you?" I added loudly, calling to him over my shoulder, as I cast a glare back at him.

His only response was laughter.

"I'm such an idiot!" I said to myself.

"You really are," Vance added with a grin, coming up behind me.

"What's that supposed to mean?" I asked, looking at him in surprise over his agreement with my self-assessment.

"Encyclopedia 'salesman'?" he said with a smile. "Ever heard of the modern convenience called the Internet? Who in their right mind would purchase a set of encyclopedias when all the information they need is right at their fingertips with a touch of a button?"

I'd been played, and I knew it. "You've known all along, haven't you?" I asked, staring at him with an incredulous look on my face.

"Well, he was the reason Marsha and I came specifically to this coven," he offered as an explanation.

"Why didn't you tell me?" I felt like a complete idiot for not even knowing my own father.

He shrugged nonchalantly. "I figured if Sean wanted you to know what was going on, he'd tell you," he said as he watched me.

I felt betrayed.

"Don't take it personally," Vance said, coming closer to rub his hand down my arm. "It was a means to protect you and your family from anyone who might want to harm you."

"Yeah, well I feel like Lois Lane must have when she took off Clark Kent's glasses and found out he was Superman."

Vance just laughed at my comment and reached out to pull me closer.

"Come on, silly girl. Let's go see what your dad is planning," he replied, after placing a chaste kiss against my forehead, leading me back over to the group even though I was still scowling at him.

Dad began by pointing out the locations of the security cameras on each of the walls. Each of them had a small point where they didn't quite cover the area over to where the next camera picked up.

"Even though these are weak points, we can count on them being reinforced," Dad explained. "I'm positive Damien has looked for these kinds of flaws himself and has placed magical charms all over the area."

"What about this building?" Vance said, leaning over and pointing out a two-story building on the left of the compound.

"That was what I was thinking," Dad replied, nodding his head. "We won't be able to breach the perimeter of the warehouse, but we can observe it from the roof of this building. Now Damien may have anticipated this also, so we'll need to proceed with caution and check it for any type of alert system."

"How will you know if they're there?" I asked, curious.

"Magic has a strong energy field," Grandma explained to me. "It looks different than regular energy, and there are ways to see it with certain spells. I imagine Damien may even be using the same sort of thing to search out some of the powers of his victims."

"Makes sense," I agreed, pondering this new information. "There's so much I don't know," I added with a sigh, speaking directly into Vance's head.

"You're doing fine," Vance said, back into my mind, and he gave my hand a little squeeze. "Be patient. Things will come to you in time."

I turned my attention back to Dad and what he was saying.

"I think we should move a surveillance team into the room at Juan's place. We can send another team to the roof of the building next to the warehouse to check things out. If they can get on the roof without being detected, we'll have them set up a camera. We'll rig things up so we can send the feedback to Juan's store.

"I want Vance, Portia, and myself stationed at the store," he continued. "Once the camera is in place, I want everyone out of there to avoid any detection. The three of us will monitor things and call in any additional support if it is needed."

Dad looked up at each of the people surrounding him. "Any questions?" he asked.

Everyone shook their heads.

"All right, then I want my mom to lead the group that's going to attempt the roof. She'll check for any magical barriers. If all is clear, then Brad and Shelly can go to the top to place the camera. Once we verify the feed is coming through okay, I want all of you to leave the area as quickly as possible," he said, looking seriously at each one of them.

"Understood," Brad said, as Shelly nodded her head, and I could see what looked like anticipation on their faces at the idea of their role in this.

"And my job will be to have delicious food ready for all

of you people," my mom piped up with a laugh, breaking the serious mood.

Dad stood and went over to give her a hug. "Which, of course, will be our favorite part," he said with a smile. "I appreciate everything you do for us, Stacey," he added quietly.

"Like I've always said, I leave the magic to the experts." She smiled brightly. "Besides, I like cooking for everyone."

"Speaking of food, let's all pitch in and get some lunch together," I said. "I think we've had a pretty productive morning."

"Sounds good," Dad agreed turning to Mom. "What can we help you with, honey?"

"Well, we're in Mexico." She smiled. "I got stuff for burritos, enchilada style. The tortillas were made fresh this morning. They're still warm."

"Delicious!" Dad said, rubbing his hands together. "Let's get to it. I'm starving after all this planning."

I was soon grating some cheese, while Vance stood at my side shredding lettuce. Brad and Shelly were across the counter from us, dicing tomatoes and onions, and Grandma was getting some serving dishes out of the cupboard.

Mom mixed up the meat to go into the tortillas, while Dad stirred the enchilada sauce in a saucepan.

Soon we were ready to serve the main dishes, along with a large pile of chips and salsa. After a quick blessing on the food, everyone formed a line down the edge of the counter buffet style and started dishing up their plates.

"Oh! I'm getting a call," Babs said as her phone started loudly vibrating in her pocket.

She reached her hand into her clothing and pulled it out, answering it quickly. We could all hear someone speaking loudly and excitedly on the other end. Babs listened intently on this end, occasionally speaking a couple of words in Spanish during the conversation.

"Okay. Thank you," she finally said, and hung up, turning to the rest of us. "That was Juan. He says he just saw a truck which hauls for Cummings Enterprises pass by outside his store. It turned at the corner and is headed down the street toward the warehouse. He believes Damien is receiving a new shipment."

The Demon Kiss

Chapter 11

"Dang it!" my dad said, pounding his fist down on the counter. "We need the camera up there on that building now!"

"It's too risky to do it in the daylight, son," Grandma said, shaking her head to discourage him. "We would be like sitting ducks."

"I know, I know," he replied, before beginning to tap his fingers against his head repeatedly. "Think, Sean! Think!" he said, to himself.

"I know how we can get in," Vance suddenly piped up, looking at Dad seriously. "But you aren't going to like it."

"Tell me," my dad demanded. "We can't afford to waste any more time with this."

"Send Stacey," he replied, motioning over toward my mom. "She isn't magical, so she won't set off any type of detection. She can call the realtor and tell her she's interested in seeing the property, but it has to be this afternoon. She could also talk to some of the people from Cummings."

A look of horror passed over my dad's face. "Absolutely not!" he responded firmly, shaking his head.

"I told you that you wouldn't like it," Vance said.

"I think it's a great idea!" my mom popped up, walking into the middle of us. "Let's do it!"

"No, Stacey! It's too dangerous!" my dad said, putting a

hand onto her shoulder and turning her back to face him.

"Dangerous to you maybe," my mom replied, completely unfazed by his concern over the situation. "But not to me. I'm no one as far as Damien Cummings is concerned. He would rather swat at a fly than look at me. I'd be able to move in right under the radar."

"It actually makes sense, Sean," Grandma spoke up, seeing the possibilities in using Mom for this task.

"I don't like it," Dad replied, frowning around at the rest of us. "Not one little bit!"

"Look, Sean, we'll send everyone else to take turns driving up and down the road outside the property. The regular security guards are on during this time of day. Cummings Enterprises isn't going to try anything with the whole place watching them. They're trying to keep up appearances, not blow their cover," Vance said matter-of-factly.

Dad paced the floor letting Vance's words sink in.

"Make the call," he said finally, handing the realtor's business card to my mom, before turning to face Vance. "But if anything happens to her, I'll hold you personally responsible for it."

"As well you should," Vance agreed. "But I think we have her covered. I wouldn't have suggested it otherwise."

"Hola?" Mom's voice broke into the conversation, and we all turned to watch her talk to an unseen person on the phone. "Se habla English? Yes, my name is Maria Sanchez, and I'm looking to possibly rent a warehouse unit that is located off Freemont Boulevard. Are you the listing agent for that property?"

She paused for a moment to allow the person on the other end of the line to respond.

"Well, here's my problem. I'm only in town on business for the afternoon before I go back to the States. I wouldn't be able to come back and see the property for several months. Is there any chance you could squeeze me in this afternoon before I have to leave? I'd really like to be able to tell my boss I found a place for him here in the area."

She waited again before she started speaking.

"In an hour? Perfect! Thanks so much! I'll meet you at the gate," she said before hanging up the phone and turning to my dad. "I need to go get changed, and you'll need to come up with a convincing story for me to tell."

She gave him a peck on the cheek before she sauntered out of the condo to head next door to the one she, Dad, and Grandma were staying in.

"Story, people! Now!" Dad said snapping his fingers consecutively at the rest of us who were left standing there.

"Her boss is a supplier for all the tourist trap shops around here. He needs to move from his current location because the building is located on the wharf and has some mold damage which needs serious repairs. Her boss has sent her here to appraise the damage, make sure everything is legit and that the guy running the warehouse here isn't just trying to take him for a ride," Vance offered up.

"Did you just come up with that off the top of your head?" I asked looking at him in wonder.

"Yep." He smiled. "You might as well know I happen to be a great liar." He shrugged at my look. "It happens after spending years on the run."

"I think I'm going to have to watch you a little more carefully," I said, with a worried gaze.

He just grinned at me. "You don't have anything to worry about," he replied softly. "I always do my best to be honest with you."

"So let's think of a company name, and I'll get a business card printed up for Stacey real quick," Dad said.

Everyone began to throw in their suggestions. We

ended up choosing one of Hal's ideas.

The fake company would be called International Tourist Treasures, and Hal even volunteered to be Mom's boss, putting his phone number on the card just in case anyone decided to check out her references.

Dad printed out about five of the business cards in the end to make it seem more believable.

"What do you think about this?" he asked, when he was finished, handing a card over to me.

I took the card and it read:

International Tourist Treasures
Hal Breck and Associates
Maria Sanchez, Administrative Assistant
1-800-555-5353

It also had a small decorative set of maracas in the lower right corner.

"It looks really good," I replied, handing the small paper back to him. "Not overly flashy but very business-like."

"Good," he said, turning to look as Mom re-entered the room. "Wow," he added after he saw her.

Mom had her dark hair all piled in a chic looking knot on the top of her head. She was wearing a very smartly cut pin-striped suit in a dark gray, with nylons that were just a shade lighter, along with pair of comfortable but sassy gray heels with a pretty silver buckle.

"You brought that outfit with you?" Dad said eyeing her up and down. "What could you have possibly felt you might have needed it for?"

"A woman always comes prepared for any situation which might arise," she said with a smile as she did a quick pirouette for him.

"Well, that explains the four suitcases you had to bring," he replied, a little under his breath.

"Hey! Be nice!" she responded, with a playful slap to

his shoulder.

"I was being nice. I didn't add the rolling tote and three purses you insisted on packing also."

"You can never have enough purses," Mom said as she looked at his hand. "Are those the business cards you were making?" She reached out so Dad could place them in her palm.

"Yes," he replied as she checked them out. "Vance, I was wondering if she could borrow your car. It probably says 'money' a little better than anyone else's. No offense to the rest of you," he added with a quick glance around the room.

"No problem," Vance replied, reaching into his pocket to pull out the keys and toss them to Dad.

"All right," Dad said with a sigh, and I could feel the tension running through him. "Is everybody set?"

Everyone nodded their heads and began heading to their respective vehicles.

Dad turned toward Vance and me, as we started walking toward the door, opening his mouth to speak.

"Don't even say it, Sean. I already know the drill," Vance said interrupting him with a sigh. "Portia and I are to stay here and man the phones."

"Good boy," Dad replied, patting him on the shoulder before turning to run out the door after the others.

"I'm really starting to dislike your Dad," Vance said facetiously, as he turned and wandered back down the hall into the living room to sit on the couch.

He picked up the remote and turned on the television.

"Well, there's one good thing about all this," I said as I sat down and sidled up against him.

"What's that?" he asked, without looking at me

"They left us all alone."

He did look up from the TV in interest then.

"They did, didn't they?" he said with a small smile as he reached his arms around my waist and pulled me onto his lap. "It seems like a long while since I had a good kiss from my girl, too many prying eyes."

He tilted my face up next to his and kissed me passionately. After a moment he pulled away from me when the phone suddenly started vibrating in his pocket. He shifted a little so he could dig the phone out.

"Hello?" he said with a sigh at the interruption.

"No hanky panky!" I heard my dad's voice come loudly over the receiver, followed by what sounded like laughter.

"Dad!" I yelled, as Vance snapped the phone shut and threw his hands up in the air.

"I can't catch a break today," he said, in frustration, as he slouched back against the sectional.

"Don't even worry about it. Just kiss me," I replied, placing his arms back around my waist. "Now where were we?"

I leaned my head in, and he met me halfway as we resumed what we had been doing before the annoying phone call.

"How are you doing?" I asked, as we pulled apart.

"I'm okay," he said, and I believed him as his eyes were still his normal startling color of blue.

He kissed me again, this time much more heatedly than he had the first time.

I reveled in the feel of him.

He had one of his hands tangled in my hair, his other around my back pushing me closer to him, while his mouth ravaged mine.

Shifting, he moved sideways so he could lay me over onto the sectional without breaking our kiss. My arms wrapped around him trustingly as he followed after me.

His lips moved expertly over mine, and I could feel the

intensity level of our exchange start to rise. It was always like we couldn't get enough of each other. I opened my eyes to stare straight into the red demon eyes that looked back at me this time, but I didn't stop.

I let him leave my mouth to trail his kisses down to my throat, and he licked the now fully healed, light scar on my neck where he had bitten me. I sighed slightly at his touch, and I ignored the warnings that ran through my head when I felt his teeth grazing there, moaning softly as he placed a small nip.

And then he was gone, leaving me to go stand at the window, looking out at the deep blue sea.

"I love you," I said, sitting up slowly, after a disappointed moment and running my fingers through my disheveled hair.

"I love you, too." He turned his bloodshot eyes toward me, but didn't move, keeping his distance from me.

"So, I have a very personal question I want to ask you."

"Shoot," he said, turning to lean his back against the glass so he could look directly at me.

"How will this bloodlust thing affect you when we do finally decide to … um," I trailed off, searching for the right words to use, "you know … consummate our relationship?" I fumbled nervously with the bottom of my shirt, and when he didn't answer immediately, I continued. "I mean is there some part of you that's always going to be holding back from me? Will you be afraid you might hurt me? Because when we get to that spot in our relationship, I want to know I can be with all of you, not just bits and pieces."

His eyes never left me as he thought about my question. "Portia, I honestly don't know the answer to that without having experienced it. I would like to think I could give you every part of me and not be swayed to harm you in any way, but I really just don't know."

"Well, then how is it now?" I asked, continuing to push this line of conversation. "Do you always want to bite me when you kiss me?"

He sighed heavily, running a nervous hand through his hair. "Almost every single second of it," he answered me honestly.

"Oh." I said, feeling bit dejected about that.

"But you have to understand I felt that way to some extent even before I experienced all this demon conversion stuff," he added.

What he said was true. I remembered back to the night in my bedroom when he had trailed love bites down my neck for the first time. I'd seen the red marks he left on my skin in the mirror. His dad had drunk blood from him prior to that, but Vance had never been given any blood in exchange.

"It is like the lust and the bloodlust are all tangled into one thing now. One thing always seems to activate the other," he said a little frustrated. "I wish I could explain it better to you."

"I think I understand. At least I'm trying to." I bit my lip for a moment before I continued. "So you're saying that even after marriage, being together physically could be a hard thing for us."

He just looked at me for several long moments, and I knew his answer before he spoke it.

"Yes," he said finally.

"So what do we do about it?" I asked, feeling completely helpless, wishing there was something proactive I could do.

"I don't know," he replied, pushing away from the glass to walk toward me. "I guess we'll just carefully cross that bridge when we come to it."

At that moment, I actually wished Damien Cummings

was standing in front of me so I could lash out and destroy him, the same way he was destroying my life—Vance's life— our life together. I shook with anger inside.

"It'll all work out somehow," Vance said sitting down next to me, but not touching me. "Don't worry about it."

"I do worry. There are so many things we don't know. Do demons ever father children? I mean I assume they can. Could the problems from this condition pass on to one of them? I don't know enough about this, and everything I want for us could be hanging in the balance," I said, feeling very exasperated.

"Portia, you don't have to marry me," he said softly, and I could hear the hesitation in his voice as he struggled to say these words. "If this is going to be too difficult for you, then we'll just be together, but not together. Do you know what I mean?"

"Yes, I do. And frankly that isn't an option for me. We just have to find some way to help make you better. That's the only choice there is."

I felt the relief at my answer flood through him. He stood and pulled me up after him before bending to place an arm under my knee, swinging me up into his arms so he was holding me.

He left the living room, carrying me into the master bedroom, laying me gently on the down comforter. He went over to the large window and closed the wooden blinds to darken the room before coming back over to climb up onto the bed so he could lie next to me.

"You've been tired today, and I've missed sleeping with you," he said, gently changing the subject. "Let's take advantage of the quiet time and take a little nap together while everyone is gone. Shall we?"

I nodded as he moved up against my back, wrapping one arm under my neck and the other across my waist. I closed my eyes as I listened to the comfortable sound of his breathing mixed with the sounds of the waves as they crashed against the shore outside.

"Mmm," I whispered, softly. "I could lay here like this for the rest of my life and I would still die happy."

"I know what you mean," he said, lifting a hand to stroke the side of my face and down my hair.

"That feels good," I replied with a sigh, relaxing completely against him.

"So, I have a personal question for you now," he said softly, his breath whispering across my ear.

"Okay."

"If you could have any one wish granted to you right now, what would it be?" he asked me, and I was surprised.

"That's easy. I'd wish for you to be completely cured of the things you've had to go through lately."

"You'd waste your wish on me?" he asked, seeming truly astonished by my answer.

I rolled over in his arms so I could face him. "I'm not wasting anything. I want you to be well more than anything in the world. I'd even sacrifice my own life if it would accomplish that for you."

"Don't even talk like that!" he said harshly, his eyes flashing at me. "I'm not worth your sacrifice. Besides, what good would it do to be cured if I had to live my life without you? I'd be miserable."

"I know exactly how you feel. I remember when I thought you'd die and I'd have to live my life without you. It was the most excruciating pain I'd ever felt. It encompassed my whole being. And you hated me because I wouldn't feed you. I could feel your anger boiling over towards me."

"That wasn't really me, baby," he said softer now, his gaze relaxing. "I would've never treated you in such a way if I'd truly been myself. That was the talk of uncontrolled demon emotions. Please forgive me for hurting you that way."

"No. You were right. I fed you and ultimately that was what ended up saving your life," I reminded him.

"No. It was the binding spell and your healer's magic that did it. Had you fed me any sooner, while I was stronger, I would've killed you. There's no doubt in my mind," he stated as he looked at me. "I'm sorry, but it's the truth."

"Let's not talk about it any longer," I said placing a finger over his lips. "It's done now. We got our miracle. You're still alive and you haven't been converted into a demon. We can work with that."

"I agree," he said, leaning in to kiss me, placing his hand against my cheek.

This kiss was very sweet, almost chaste at first, but suddenly I felt an emotional barrier break and a sob catch in my throat.

"What's the matter, baby?" he crooned softly against my ear, as he rubbed his cheek up against mine.

"We have just been through so much," I choked out, feeling my carefully controlled emotions suddenly spinning out of control. "I can't believe you're really here with me sometimes. It's like I'm dreaming and I'm afraid every time I go to sleep I'll wake up and find you're going to be gone again. I'm so happy when I'm with you, yet at the same time I see this dark looming cloud which is threatening our future."

"I'm really here, Portia, and I'm not going to leave you," he said, as he pulled me closer, kissing me hard and aggressively as if trying to drive his point home.

He rolled me over onto my back as he leaned over the top of me. The kissing intensified so greatly at this point that I felt as if he were bruising my tender lips beneath his own.

He broke away from me suddenly, looking deep into my eyes, and I could see several emotions pass through them. "Touch me, Portia. I'm real and I belong completely to you," he said, breathing into my ear as he reached down to lift one of my hands, placing it on his chest, near his heart. I let my fingers run over the chiseled muscles I could feel beneath, marveling over his physique.

"What are you doing?" I asked, in confusion at his actions, not understanding what he was asking me to do.

"I was wrong to leave you before," he said, trying to explain to me. "I'm sorry. I just want you to know I am real and I'm here with you right now. I'll do everything in my power to always be with you. Please, please, forgive me for hurting you."

He lifted my hand then and turned it so he could place a kiss in the center of my palm. When he opened his eyes, I could see the dreaded red streaks flaring to an all-new level in his irises as he struggled for some semblance of control once again.

"Get some rest," he said as he climbed off the bed, laying my hand gently back at my waist. "I'll be in the other room if you need me."

Chapter 12

I woke up less than an hour later when I heard all the voices of the coven members entering the condo in high chatter.

"Shhhh!" I heard Vance hiss quickly, from the other room. "Portia's sleeping."

"Sorry!" I heard someone whisper apologetically, as I was climbing down off the bed.

"It's all right. I'm awake," I said as I walked out of the bedroom door, running my hands over my hair trying to smooth it. "How did things go?" I asked, as I looked around at their bright faces.

"Have I ever told you how awesome your mother is?" my dad said, smiling as he grabbed her around the waist from behind, leaning over her shoulder to kiss her on the cheek. "She walked in there like a pro, fooling everyone involved. She even snowed me, and I knew who she was."

"He's blowing it all out of proportion," Mom laughed as she waved him off. "I just met the realtor lady, walked in to look around, taking a quick minute to speak to a couple of the guys who were unloading the truck from Cummings Enterprises, and asked them how they liked the facilities. Piece of cake really."

"And she learned the truck was delivering the same long narrow crates we found at the other warehouses," Dad added, giving a squeeze to her shoulders.

"I only asked them if they found easy access to the loading dock," she replied, shaking her head at Dad. "It just so happened the truck was open while I was talking to them."

"Did the men seem suspicious at all?" Vance piped up, looking a little worried about it.

"Not that I could tell," Mom answered, looking at him. "They were very kind to me actually."

"That's because they thought she was hot," Dad said, with a knowing grin. "They were totally checking her out." A stormy look suddenly passed over his face. "Dang it! I should have stormed in and punched them both!"

"Easy, Dad!" I laughed, as I patted him on the shoulder. "Try to step it down a notch."

"Tell them what else you did," Dad smiled, speaking to Mom again, giving her a little nudge of encouragement.

"Well, I happened to be able to place a microphone on the premises," she replied with a nonchalant shrug.

"A microphone! She did it all on her own!" Dad exclaimed, sounding totally amazed. "I didn't even know she'd taken one out of my briefcase. She's a natural at this stuff!"

Vance leaned forward, placing his elbows on his knees.

"So we'll have audio with our video tonight?" he asked, lifting an eyebrow in interest.

"Yes, we will," Dad replied, nodding excitedly, as he continued to proudly pat my mom on the shoulder.

"That's great!" Vance said, a slight smile moving across his face. "Good job, Stacey."

"Thanks." She smiled and looked around at everybody. "Well, I guess I need to go change so I can get dinner for this brood started. We need to get everyone fed before you all have to take off again."

"You want me start cooking anything for you?" I called

after her, as she walked off down the hall, toward the door. "I bought stuff we can grill tonight," she called over her shoulder. "You can start the coals in the barbeque grill out on the patio if you'd like."

I did as she asked, and after several minutes the coals were ready for cooking, though Dad insisted on being the grill master, since it was a "man's job" as he put it. I didn't argue with him, but I realized I'd never understand the whole male testosterone fascination with cooking outdoors.

Vance, Shelly, Brad, and I helped Mom out in the kitchen. We all did a little magical slicing and dicing, since there was so much more food to prepare this time around.

As soon as Dad had the meat all cooked and ready, dinner was served. Steaks, hamburgers, and pork chops graced the table, along with mashed potatoes, gravy, corn on the cob, and green salad, followed by a gelatin dessert.

"This looks delicious!" Hal exclaimed, as he reached over to grab up a plate and start the buffet line.

When everyone had their food dished up, we had a blessing on the meal and over the evening's activities. Then we began eating.

"So, each of you are clear with your assignments for tonight?" Dad asked, as he looked carefully around the room.

Everyone nodded their heads, between mouthfuls of food.

"Good. I think Hal and Bruce should go down to the marina as soon as they're done with dinner to start trying to catch the fishing boats as they come back in," Dad suggested. "Mom, you, Brad and Shelly should head out as soon as it's dark to get the camera set up. Vance, Portia and I will leave right after dinner also to get things going at Juan's place."

The sun sank speedily after that, so it seemed, and soon

it was time for all of us to get to our jobs we had been assigned.

"Let's take our car since Stacey drove yours earlier today," Dad said to Vance, as we headed out of the elevator and into the parking lot. "Just to be safe, in case anyone would remember seeing it from this afternoon."

We walked over to the dark-tinted Toyota Camry and climbed inside together, though we were silent for most of the drive.

There was a lot of traffic out for the evening. We weaved our way through it, across town, over to Benito Juarez. Dad pulled around when we arrived so we were behind the shop in a little alleyway.

"I think we shouldn't have the car out in the open, since it should be well past closing time by now," he said, though neither Vance nor I had questioned his motives.

Juan was waiting for us at the back door. As we exited the vehicle, he eyed Vance carefully, the distrust still plainly visible in his eyes.

Vance greeted him kindly and pretended he didn't notice the nervous stares coming his way as he helped Dad unload some surveillance equipment from the trunk. They carried the items into the store.

Juan stood nearby the whole time, but stayed out of our way, choosing to observe us instead. We soon had the monitor and recording devices all set up on a small table ready to go.

"Should be anytime now," Dad said looking at his watch. "My mom should be checking the building perimeter for any magical barriers as we speak."

We each pulled up a folding chair and sat down to wait. It seemed like the time was dragging slowly, and I watched as Vance rubbed his hands slowly together, trying to calm his own anticipation.

Soon the point where we should've received a signal had come and gone. Dad stood up and started pacing the floor nervously.

"What is going on out there?" he asked in frustration, to no one in particular as he kept checking and rechecking his watch.

He had ordered that no one use their cell phones during this time, so as not to draw attention to the trio while they were setting things up.

Suddenly, a flicker crossed the television, followed quickly by a clear, black and white picture.

"There we go!" Dad said in relief as he clapped his hands together. He sat down and adjusted a few things until we had some audio also, although it sounded a little bit scratchy.

His cell phone rang, causing us all to jump as the unexpected sound pierced the silence.

"All clear," Grandma's voice came out from the speaker. "Sorry for the delay. There was a man out walking his dog by the building, and the dog chose that place to sniff around for a little potty stop."

"No problem," Dad said, smiling. "I'm glad it all worked out okay. Everything looks good from this end, so you three go ahead and return to the resort for now."

He hung up after he said goodbye, and we all moved our chairs closer to watch the streaming feed.

The delivery truck from earlier in the day was still there, parked up against the bay. Though we couldn't see into the back of it, it appeared to have been completely unloaded as several of the crates were stacked upon each other against one of the walls inside the roll-up door in the storage area.

"I wish the truck would move," Dad complained, as we watched the small screen. "I can't see into the warehouse or if anything is going on inside it."

After several minutes of nothing, we finally saw some movement. We watched with piqued interest as a worker came out onto the dock and lit up a cigarette while checking his watch.

"He's waiting for someone, it looks like," I said, after he continued staring off into the distance and repeatedly looking at the time.

The nervous man paced back and forth for a while, until we noticed that he straightened up suddenly and quit moving completely after flicking his cigarette to the ground beneath him, crushing it out with his foot.

A long black sedan pulled into the picture, the sound of the tires crunching on gravel as it moved. The car pulled up next to the truck at the dock, and the man jumped down to open the back passenger door.

A tall man exited the vehicle. He was dressed to the nines in a dark suit, his semi-dark hair cut close to his head. He turned a bit, looking around while he adjusted his sleeve and cuff links.

"That's him," Vance said, leaning back into his chair a little, a strange emotion flitting briefly over his face.

I could see Vance must've gotten some of his looks from his dad. I might have called Damien handsome, except that his face was so hard looking that it seemed more like I was looking at the devil himself. There was no friendliness there. He exuded danger in his very persona.

"Why was the truck so early today, Marco?" Damien's smooth cultured voice echoed out into the lot. "And why is it still here so late?"

"I'm sorry, sir. I didn't mean to get here so early. I must've miscalculated due to the change in time. Peter's asleep in the truck cab. He had a long night last night after we picked up the shipment."

"Did he indeed?" Damien quirked an irritated eyebrow

at Marco, as he walked up the steps of the platform and inside the warehouse.

He passed out of view behind the truck, Marco following, and we could no longer see anything useful.

"I knew that truck was going to be a problem," Dad grumbled, but he stopped as the speaking resumed.

"Open this one," Damien's voice came over the scratchy speaker.

"Right away, boss," Marco said.

We could hear some scraping sounds, like metal rubbing against wood, and we assumed one of the crates was being pried open with a crowbar.

"Ah! Very good! Where is this one from?" Damien asked about something we couldn't see.

"India," came the reply.

"Yes. I can see that now. I should've known. Very nice indeed and quite refined looking."

"Maybe he's still importing artifacts," I said softly, wondering what else he could possibly be speaking about.

Damien began talking again. "Let me see the invoice," he demanded.

There was silence for a few moments before he spoke again.

"Bring these four to the house. The rest you may divide amongst yourselves," he said.

"Will do, boss. Thanks!" Marco said, and we could hear him scuttling around, making loud sounds.

Damien exited the building and walked toward the waiting car. The driver suddenly hopped out and opened the rear passenger door. He held it while Damien climbed back into the vehicle, closed it, and then returned to the front before slowly pulling away from the lot, out of the range of the camera.

"Well, we know for certain he's here now," Dad said, as

he looked at Vance. "I don't think we've learned anything else, though. We still have no idea what he's shipping in the crates."

"What would he be taking to his house and dividing the rest among his staff?" I asked, completely perplexed at the conversation we'd just heard.

"We need to get hold of Hal and Bruce and see if they were able to charter a boat for tomorrow. We have to start surveillance on that place," Vance said to Dad. "That's probably the only way we're going to be able to find out what's being delivered there."

Dad flipped out his cell and dialed up Bruce, talking for a few minutes before hanging up.

"He got a boat called the Deep Fisher. It frequents the waters in that area regularly. He'll have a light crew on so there'll be plenty of room for the three of us to go with them. They leave at first light."

"We'll be ready," Vance said, reaching for my hand.

We continued watching the monitor until we saw Marco reappear and shut the door. He hopped into the truck and drove out of the picture.

"Let's call it a night," Dad said, reaching over to turn off the equipment. "I doubt they'll be back again this evening. We'll set people up in shifts around the clock in the morning if we need to."

My dad thanked Juan in broken Spanish and informed him someone would be probably returning in the morning.

Juan shook hands with him and followed us as we left the shop, locking the door behind us.

We went back to the hotel, where we met everyone in our condo and told them what we learned this evening.

Dad set up a schedule of assignments for Juan's shop to begin first thing in the morning. Then the group broke up and headed off to their rooms.

"So how was your evening?" I asked Shelly, after everyone had left and we were straightening up the condo.

"It was awesome!" she replied, smiling broadly. "Brad and I had a great time with your grandma when we went to set up the camera. We were all dressed head to toe in black. It was like we were spies or something."

"Well, you kind of were," I replied, grinning at her enthusiasm.

"Your grandma showed us how to use our crystals to reveal any hidden alarms or charms that aren't visible to the naked eye. We could easily see the fields surrounding the building next door, but there was nothing on the building we put the camera on. It was so cool," she added, her eyes flashing brightly.

"I'm glad everything went all right for you. We were beginning to worry about you when the signal was late."

"Stupid guy and his dog held us up," Brad said over a mouthful of leftover mashed potatoes and gravy. "We could've been in and out of there in the amount of time we had to wait for him."

"We'd better call it a night, baby," Vance interrupted, looking at me. "We have an early morning ahead of us."

"Oh!" I said, thinking of something else I wanted to ask him about. "Are you going to be okay to go? What about your withdrawal?"

"I'll wake up early," he said with a shrug. "Hopefully that will help."

"I hope so, too," I replied feeling worried about him and wishing there was some way I could help him.

He reached a hand down, pulling me up off the couch and started walking me toward my room.

I pulled back on his hand to stop him from going any farther, and he turned to look at me with a puzzled expression.

"What is it?" he asked, stepping closer to me.

"I want to spend the night with you tonight," I said, searching his eyes for some clue he wanted to be with me, too.

"You know that isn't the best thing for us anymore," he said softly, and I saw regret flash over his face briefly.

"I know," I agreed, knowing he was trying to protect me. "It's just you found your dad again tonight and I can feel the conflicting emotions running through you. I don't want you to be alone. That's all."

He sat there staring at me, weighing the situation in his head, before turning and walking toward his room, pulling me behind him.

"Goodnight," I said to Shelly as I passed her.

"Goodnight to you," she said giving me a knowing smile, along with a wink in my direction.

Vance flipped the light on in his room without touching the switch as we walked through the doorway. He let go of my hand, and I crawled up onto his king-sized bed, while he went over to the dresser and got out some sweatpants.

I lay my head down on one of the pillows, watching as he pulled his shirt off, and I was glad he didn't look over at me because I couldn't take my eyes off his fabulous physique. When he reached for the button on his pants, however, I demurely closed my eyes. I felt him sit on the end of the bed to remove his socks and shoes, before he stood up again.

"Here," his voice said to me, and I felt something soft hit my face. "Get comfortable. I'll be back in a minute."

I opened my eyes to find one of his t-shirts lying there. He wanted me to sleep comfortably. It melted my heart.

I stood up and quickly removed my own clothing and pulled the soft shirt over my head. It hung to mid-thigh on me. I looked in the mirror, rubbing my hands down over the fabric. I liked wearing his clothes.

Suddenly, I realized that seeing me dressed like this might be a huge turn on for him, so I quickly folded my clothes, placing them neatly on the dresser, and climbed back into the big comfy bed.

I flopped back onto the fluffy pillow and pulled the comforter up to my chin, just as the door to the room reopened.

"All comfy?" he asked casually, softly closing the door behind him.

"Yes," I replied, as I snuggled down farther into the pillow, suddenly feeling very relaxed.

"Good," he said, as he flipped the light off with a snap of his fingers, enveloping the room in darkness.

He walked over to his side, but he didn't get in. Even though it was dark, I could feel his stare as he looked at me.

"Do you promise to be good tonight, Portia?" he asked me from the edge of the bed.

"Of course I do," I replied, knowing I wouldn't move an inch all night long if he'd let me stay with him.

I was very surprised at his next move, when he lifted the covers and crawled in next to me, scooting over to be clear up against me, with nothing in between us. This was something he rarely, if ever, did ... and certainly not given the circumstances surrounding us lately.

"I know. I'm tempting fate," he said with a sigh, as he wrapped his arms around me. "I hope you'll forgive me, but I've missed you, too. So, I'm going to do my best to think chaste thoughts and not about how sexy you might look in my shirt right now. Tonight we sleep."

"I understand," I said, moving my arm to rest against his, patting it slightly. "Goodnight, love."

"Goodnight," he replied softly as he cradled me in his arms.

I closed my eyes, taking a deep breath and tried to relax. After a moment, I realized I could hear music coming from somewhere. It took me a minute to place the source.

"Are you singing the Star Spangled Banner in your head?" I asked, unable to suppress a little giggle.

"Yes," he replied, gruffly. "Now go to sleep before I have to move on to church hymns."

"All right," I said smiling, as I closed my eyes again, letting my body rest against his loving arms.

It was touching that he was trying to be so conscious of himself around me. I was happy he let me come in here with him. I was just sorry I was the reason he often had such a difficult time.

My breathing became slower and deeper, and I found myself snuggling closer to Vance, albeit somewhat subconsciously. I hadn't realized how physically draining all this emotional turmoil had been weighing on me lately—it just felt so good to be lying in his arms.

The last conscious thought I had actually came from him, something about a red glare and bombs bursting in air. He was repeating the song, I realized. I slowly smiled once more and let sleep claim me as the sound of his beautiful baritone voice danced and swirled in my head.

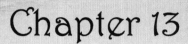

Chapter 13

It was before dawn when I was awakened very abruptly— due to the fact Vance had nudged me hard in my ribs with his elbow.

"Portia, I need you to leave now," he said, his voice sounding like he was speaking through gritted teeth.

My eyes opened instantly. I could see his eyes were glowing brightly. He was shaking violently against me, and I could see the cords in his neck straining as he fought for control.

My heart went out to him immediately, and I just wanted to gather him to me so I could help him through this, but I resisted the urge, knowing it would only make things worse for him.

"Portia ... please go—now," he pleaded with me.

"I love you," I said, throwing the covers back. "I'll get you some help."

He didn't answer, and I quietly slipped out of the room, shutting the door behind me.

I hurried into the living room, finding Dad and Grandma sitting in there on the sectional visiting together quietly and looking over some papers together. They both looked up at me as I approached.

"Is it time?" my dad asked, his gaze washing over me with a disapproving glance as he took in my t-shirted appearance.

"Yes. He's shaking pretty badly this morning. He had to wake me up and ask me to leave the room," I replied, concerned about him. I lifted my hands to comb my fingers through my wayward hair, trying to straighten it a little so I wouldn't look quite so bedraggled.

"Go get yourself ready, so you can leave when it's time," Grandma said, nodding toward my room. "I'll take care of him."

"Don't you need everyone from the coven to come?" I asked her, wanting to help Vance somehow.

"No. I want to try something different with him today, and if he asked you to leave then I don't want to make it harder for him by having you in there with us."

I watched the two of them gather up several magical items they had and head into the bedroom.

I sighed, feeling a bit dejected, and turned to go into my room, trying to be quiet so I wouldn't wake Shelly. I only made it two steps into the room before I heard her speak.

"How's Vance this morning?" her sleepy voice said, full of concern.

"Sorry to wake you," I apologized, looking over at her. "He's bad, not doing well at all."

"So what happened between the two of you last night?" she asked, as she sat up a little.

"What do you mean?"

"Did you sleep together?" she asked me bluntly.

"Yes," I replied, suddenly knowing right where she was heading. "Emphasis on the sleep."

"So the two of you have never …?" She let her sentence trail off as she watched me curiously.

"No. Not that it's any of your business," I said with a laugh as I bent over to pull some clothing out of the bureau drawer.

"How come?" she asked, continuing to press the issue,

moving to sit up completely in the bed so she could look at me better.

"Really?" I replied, as I turned to face her again with a bit of an incredulous look. "Not feeling any boundaries here with this line of discussion this morning, are you?"

"Sorry," she replied, though she didn't even try to look apologetic. "I don't mean to be nosy. It's just that Brad and I decided to wait a long time ago. From my experience of listening to others at school, most kids don't do that. We're different. I wanted to know why you were waiting. I mean, you're engaged and everything, so why not take it to the next level?"

"Well, part of the reason is Vance wants to wait until we're married, and the other reason is his current condition. He's afraid he might want to hurt or even kill me if we try it. This whole demon bloodlust thing is pretty mixed up with his hormones right now," I explained, finding myself interested in the fact she and Brad had chosen to wait also.

"Oh," was all she said for a moment while she considered what I said. "So if that were different, would you try it?"

I was surprised at her comment, and I had to stop to really evaluate my morals in that moment. I knew I wanted to be with Vance in every way possible and physically being with him was one of the top items on the list, I had to admit. Then I thought about all the things that I had been taught over the years of my life and really looked deep into myself.

What did I believe?

Shelly sat patiently in the bed, waiting for an answer, while I struggled to find out what the truth was in my heart.

"No. I wouldn't," I said, after several moments, a little shocked at my own answer. "I guess being able to be with him in that way would be something so special to me I wouldn't want to mar it in any way. I want it to be perfect, at the right time and place. Waiting for marriage is the right thing to do, I think." I sighed, before I continued, amazed with my own self-revelation.

"I remember when my mom would take me to church when I was younger," I spoke, letting the images of the past wash over me. "The minister would talk about the scriptures, doctrine, and the laws of God. He said the act of physical intimacy was a beautiful thing, but it's considered an abomination if you aren't married to the person you're with. I don't think I ever really understood what he was talking about at the time. Whether or not the perspective of the church is the truth ... well, I don't know if I've really ever thought about it for myself. But Vance likes to talk about our relationship in the terms of an eternal perspective, so I guess if we want to be together for eternity, we probably shouldn't do anything God might frown on."

"Makes sense," Shelly said, with a slight shrug, after listening intently to me.

"You aren't getting off that easy. This street goes both ways." I laughed at her. "Why did you and Brad decide not to?"

"Well, it was mostly because we both just wanted to make sure our feelings for each other were real before we took it to the next level," she answered. "Neither of us wanted some casual fling we would just walk away from someday. Don't get me wrong. It isn't like the attraction isn't there or anything. It's there, and sometimes it's hard. I don't know. I just don't want it to happen because we lost control or something. I want it to be planned and special when it happens."

"I know what you mean," I replied, as I left her sitting there, so I could make my way into the other room. "I'm going to get cleaned up now," I called out to her. "I don't want to keep anyone waiting on me this morning."

Once I was in the bathroom, I turned the shower on so the water could heat up while I undressed. I climbed in when I was done and closed the shower curtain, letting the hot water stream over my skin for several minutes.

My mind continued to wander over the things I discussed with Shelly while I moved about automatically, getting ready for the day.

I got dressed in a form-fitted, long-sleeved, black turtleneck and blue jeans with a black stripe running down the seams.

After I was done dressing, I decided to wear my hair up in a French twist, secured with a claw clip, since I thought it could be breezy out on the water while we were in the boat. I carefully applied my makeup when I was finished with my hair, so I wouldn't be terrible to look at. After all, I was going to be with Vance all day. I wanted to look good for him.

I left the bathroom to find Shelly sleeping soundly once again on the bed. I quietly sat down on the overstuffed chaise lounge chair beside the bed as I pulled on my slim, black sneakers. Then I quietly left the room, closing the door gently behind me.

No one was in the living room, so I went straight to Vance's room.

"How's he doing?" I asked quietly as I entered cautiously, knowing Vance hadn't wanted me in there.

"He's having a hard time," Grandma said, stepping away from him. "This is the strongest one he's had yet. We can't stop the shaking." She shook her head in discouragement. "I'm beginning to think he's getting worse instead of better."

I moved the rest of the way inside, shutting the door before going over to his side and sitting on the edge of the bed.

"You shouldn't be here, Portia," he said, with a slight

stutter to his speech, and I felt like my heart was breaking into a million pieces for him.

I could see he was in agony as the spasms wracked his body unmercifully, calling out for him to do something against his nature to appease them.

"May I try something?" I asked him quietly as I observed. "I'll need to touch you, though."

He looked at me for a moment, his eyes flaming brighter before he nodded.

I reached over and gently placed my hands on either side of his head. I closed my eyes and thought of healing him like I had before, when he had been going through the conversion. I concentrated every effort of my being into my hands before I finally felt a warmth move through them.

When I opened my eyes, I saw a gentle white light passing from me and into him. I could actually see the light as it penetrated his skin, passing down through his veins and moving over his entire body. After a minute, his tremors began to ease. When he stopped convulsing completely and the red had disappeared from his eyes, I removed my hands.

"Thank you," he said the relief apparent in his voice and in the relaxed position of his body.

"It occurred to me we'd never tried to heal you again after the conversion was stopped. We just assumed I'd already done everything there was to do. I doubt this will stop the withdrawal, but apparently it can stop an attack once one has started," I said as I looked between the three of them.

He lifted one of my hands to his lips and kissed it. "You truly are an angel," he said softly, his eyes full of a deep emotion as he looked at me.

I laughed with a snort. "Not even close!" I said, as I bent over to kiss his forehead lightly, feeling like his tortured morning must have addled his brain a little.

"I'm not joking, Portia," he said, seriously. "You have no idea what this means to me."

"Vance, you'd do the same for me if our situation were reversed," I said squeezing his hand. "Now I don't mean to rush you, but you'd better get ready or we're going to miss our boat."

He nodded, sitting up easily.

Dad, Grandma, and I, left the room to give him some privacy.

"I don't know why I didn't think of that," Grandma said as she shook her head. "I guess I'm just still getting used to the fact your powers are so much stronger than most of ours. We need to start utilizing them more."

"I'm willing to try whatever you want," I said, with a shrug. "I just don't know what to do most of the time."

"Maybe when all this is over and we have a little more time, we can play around a bit," she said.

"We should run back through our genealogy and see if any of our ancestors experienced anything like this before," my dad suggested. "I mean, I assumed Vance's powers were so strong because he was the product of two magical parents. But Portia only has one. It doesn't make any sense unless there's some genetic thing we're unaware of."

"That's actually a really good idea, Sean," Grandma replied with a nod. "I'll look through our pedigree sometime when I have the chance and see if anything pops out at me."

Vance came out of his room a short while later, fully dressed and ready to go, looking like complete perfection as usual. One would never guess at the suffering he'd been through this morning.

He walked straight up to me, pulled me into his arms and kissed me hotly, not caring Dad and Grandma were watching both of us.

"I have no idea what I'd do without you," he said

seriously when he was done.

"Let's not find out, okay?" I replied with a smile, placing my hand lightly against his face. He leaned in to kiss me again, and I responded by wrapping my arms tightly around his neck.

"I hate to break up the love fest, but we need to get moving," my dad reminded us, turning to walk over to Brad's bedroom door, knocking. "You ready, Brad?" he called to him through the door.

We stopped kissing, although it was reluctantly, and turned to follow him into the hallway.

"Brad's coming?" I asked, just as the bedroom door opened and Brad stepped out, running a comb through his blond locks.

"Yeah, I figured we might need to use him as an interpreter," Dad said, as he clapped Brad on the shoulder with a grin.

"Thanks for everything this morning, Milly," Vance called back over his shoulder to Grandma as we walked down the hall toward the doorway.

"No problem. I didn't really do anything to help, though." She smiled before calling out after us, "Oh! Wait, Sean! Don't forget your cooler."

I turned to see her grab a very large, very heavy looking cooler off the counter and waddle after us.

"Oh thanks, Mom," my dad said, quickly hurrying back to take it from her. "Your mom is afraid we're going to starve today," he added to me with a grin, nodding toward the object in his hands.

"I don't know how that would be possible. This thing looks like it's laden with enough food to feed an army," I laughed.

We went out to Vance's car and loaded up the cooler, along with Dad's duffle bag, which contained who knew what in it, into the trunk. Then we got into the car and headed off to the marina.

We found the boat called the Deep Fisher easily, even though the sun was barely beginning to peek over the horizon. We were soon welcomed onboard by the skipper whose name was Enrico. He politely introduced us to the three other men on the boat named Miguel, Mio, and Pablo. Enrico told them we would be doing some observing of a possible wanted fugitive who was hiding in the area and that everything we said or did was confidential.

The men nodded in understanding as they helped to haul the cooler full of food and Dad's bag of equipment onboard.

Brad asked them to please place the items in an area where we would be out of their way, letting them know that we would work around them as needed throughout the day.

They ended up placing our belongings in the forward cabin, which had a table with two benches that sat beneath the large windows and offered a full view of three sides of the craft.

"This is perfect!" Dad said to Enrico, while Enrico started the engines up, and we began puttering out to sea.

We had been moving for several minutes when Mio appeared in the doorway, smiling broadly.

"Come!" he said with excited eyes as he motioned with his hand for us to follow after him.

We moved to the stern of the boat, peering out over the edge as Mio pointed down into the water.

Suddenly a dolphin jumped from the water into the spray the engine from the boat was making, followed by another one.

"Dolphins!" I said happily, brushing at the minute droplets of water that sprinkled up onto my face.

Vance stepped forward, kneeling down to reach one of

his hands outside the watercraft. He emitted a low series of whistles, and to my surprise one of the dolphins jumped up to touch his outstretched hand, nudging it higher into the air.

"How did you do that?" I asked in amazement as I watched, feeling a little like a giddy schoolgirl as I stared at the display.

"Come here!" he shouted to me with a smile over the loud noise of the engine and churning water.

I knelt down next to him, and he motioned for me to reach my hand out like he was doing.

He began the low set whistles again and this time both dolphins jumped out of the water, at the same time, to hit our hands with their bottled noses.

"How are you getting them to do this?" I asked again, laughing at the interaction I was getting to experience with these beautiful creatures of the wild.

"I just said hello." He smiled as he winked at me.

"Whatever! How do you say hello to a dolphin?" I asked, leaning over to elbow him slightly in the ribs.

"Like this!" he shouted and whistled again.

The dolphins jumped into the air once again.

"Dad! Brad! You've got to try this!" I hollered to them over my shoulder.

They quickly traded places with us, stretching out their hands, as they had seen us do. Vance whistled into the air once more, and the dolphins jumped to greet my dad and Brad.

"This is so cool!" Brad called out, above the engine noise.

Soon we had Mio, Miguel, and Pablo also leaning over the edge, as Vance worked his magic with the playful sea creatures.

Miguel shouted something over to Brad in Spanish.

"He wants to know how you're making the dolphins dance," Brad translated for him, relaying the message to Vance.

Vance shrugged with a smile. "I'm not doing anything. They're just friendly, I guess," he said with a grin, but I knew better.

He might be trying to be modest, but he was definitely using his powers to communicate with them.

The dolphins followed us until we reached the coordinates Dad wanted, and Enrico had called out to him, letting him know we had arrived. After the boat came to a complete stop, the mammals disappeared under the surface of the water, not to be seen again.

I sighed in disappointment when they left, having enjoyed the unexpected treat of interacting with them. Our little group left the stern and went back into the forward cabin.

"I wanted to start farther out this morning, and then we'll work our way in closer to the house as we crisscross the area to avoid suspicion. The only time we'll stay in one spot is if the crew starts making a good haul in that area," Dad explained to the rest of us, as he started digging through his giant duffle bag.

We watched the men working, while Dad was setting up a telescope so we could see from the far distance. The crew soon had large fishing nets unraveled on both sides of the boat and hanging from two big pulley systems with mechanical arms, which they used to drop the nets into the water.

"Okay," Dad said finally, straightening back up from leaning over the sensitive piece of equipment. "It's all set up. I want each of you to look through it and make sure you can see everything well enough. I figured we would each take turns using the glass to break things up."

Vance moved forward to lean in first, looking things over carefully as he moved the scope around slightly to check the area out.

"Looks good to me," he said, before stepping back so Brad could check it and give his opinion.

He agreed, and I went to look after he was done.

"No signs of life yet," I said, as I stared into the big empty windows of the gigantic beachside house. "Whoever is in there must still be sleeping or they're gone," I added as I stepped away.

"I'll take first shift," Dad said, trading places with me in the confined space. "Why don't the three of you dig into some of the food Stacey sent along? She'll be mad at me if I bring that stuff back," he added with a laugh. "I hope you're hungry. I don't want to have her lecturing me about how you all aren't eating enough. Eat a lot!"

We soon found being on stake-out was extremely boring. We finished with breakfast, cleaned up and began to intermittently wander around the tiny cabin restlessly. Thankfully, Dad packed a deck of cards and we were able to play some games together to help pass the time.

After about an hour of watching the beach house without seeing anything, Dad stepped down and Vance moved to take his place.

Dad opened the cooler to pull out some of the sausage patties and biscuits Mom had packed. I dealt him in to the new hand Brad and I were playing as he settled onto the small bench at the table with us.

"See anything at all?" I asked him as he took a big bite of his biscuit while checking out his cards in his other hand.

He shook his head. "Not a soul," he answered after he finished chewing and swallowing. "I did get a pretty good idea of the surrounding area, though, in case we were to ever need to try and approach the place. I also noticed the house right next to him is available for rent, so we could even go in there if we needed to."

"You want to be his neighbor?" I asked, in surprise, peering over the cards in my hand to look at him.

"Not at all," he replied, shaking his head. "I prefer to stay as far away from the guy as possible personally, but it's an option if we were to need to move in closer for some reason."

"What time is it?" Vance spoke up, from where he continued to look through the telescope.

"It's about seven," I answered, looking down at my watch. "Why? Did you see something?"

"He's up. Log it," he replied back, not looking up, and I could hear how tense his voice sounded.

"What do you see?" Dad asked, dropping his biscuit back down to the tabletop. He quickly reached into his bag, digging out another slim case that contained a smaller telescope.

He quickly assembled it and placed it in the window next to where Vance was leaning.

"Nothing really," Vance replied, continuing to watch, moving the scope slightly to adjust the angle. "He's walked up to the large window in the living room. It's almost like he's looking out right at me. He's wearing a pair of leopard print silk boxers and a matching robe," he added with a snort.

Dad was already peering into his glass. "I got him," he said, adjusting the telescope a little, trying to sharpen the image.

"I want to see this guy," Brad said, and Vance stepped to the side so Brad could take a look.

"So that's your dad, huh?" He watched him for a moment before he moved away.

"Unfortunately," Vance said stepping back up to the

scope to continue watching the scene before him intently.

"He looks like he's drinking a cup of coffee or something," Brad said nonchalantly.

"It isn't coffee," Vance replied somberly.

"How can you tell what he's drinking from this distance?" Brad asked.

"From the look on his face," Vance said stepping back from the glass, flashing his red eyes at Brad, and I knew he was craving blood after what he had seen.

"Oh," Brad replied, and he took an involuntary step away from Vance, clearing his throat nervously as he glanced away.

Vance turned away from the scope and walked across the cabin. "I shouldn't have come," he said, closing his eyes as he leaned his forehead against the opposite window. "I'm going to blow our cover," he added motioning with his hand toward the guys working outside.

I stood up and went to him. "Are you okay?" I asked, a little afraid to touch him for fear it would make things worse.

"I'll be fine," he replied, turning his head slightly so he could look at me. "I just need to get a little control over myself."

"Can I try to help you again?"

He watched me for a moment before he nodded, and I noticed Brad stepping between me and the doorway to block us from the view of the men working outside.

I reached up and placed my hands near his temples, and let a little of the soft white light flow from my fingers into him. The magic came much easier this time, and I watched as his eyes began to change colors until they were once again the ocean blue I loved so much.

"Thanks," he whispered, leaning in to kiss me on the cheek. "You have no idea what a gift you are in my life."

"Any time," I replied, wrapping my arms around him, feeling his arms going around me also. "I like being able to help you."

"Damien's leaving the window. I think there's someone at the door," my dad said, interrupting our moment together. "I can't quite see into the house that far, but I can see a light coming in from the other side of the hallway now, like he opened a door somewhere."

Vance let go of me and hurried back to the other telescope. "It looks like the delivery guy from last night at the warehouse. What was his name? Marco?" he said after gazing intently for a few moments.

"I think you're right," Dad agreed.

"Wait. There's someone else there, too. I can see a third shadow moving against the wall," Vance added. "Do you see it, Sean?"

"I do," Dad replied, as he continued peering intently into the distance. "It's another man."

"I think it might be the other delivery guy Marco was talking about last night. He has something on a dolly," Vance said.

"You see it?" Dad said suddenly very excited.

"Yeah," Vance replied, acknowledging whatever Dad was seeing. "They're bringing in last night's shipment."

The Demon Kiss

Chapter 14

The sun moved higher into the sky as noon approached. We had all taken turns monitoring what was going on at Damien's house.

Four of the long narrow crates which Mom had described to us from her visit to the warehouse had been brought inside, but they remained sitting where they had been placed ever since. There hadn't been any noticeable movement in the house for over two hours now. It was as if everyone disappeared.

Brad was taking a turn at one of the scopes while I was setting out lunch items for everyone. We offered to share our food with the fishing crew outside, but they politely declined, motioning to their own lunches that they brought with them.

We ate together at the table in reflective silence, waiting for something, anything, to happen.

After lunch, Pablo set lines up on a few big fishing poles and let those of us who weren't at the telescope try our hand at some deep-sea fishing. It was loads of fun, and we reeled in several flounder, red snapper, and grouper.

The fishing helped immensely. It allowed us to pass the time after we had to quit looking at the house completely that afternoon. The sun had begun to drop in the sky, and it reflected badly against the large glass windows to the point where we couldn't see anything of the house except for its blinding glare.

We also used this time to relocate the boat again, but also slightly off to the side to try and avoid being too obvious to anyone who might be watching our actions.

The fishermen cast their nets into the water once more as the sun settled down behind the horizon. It was at this point we started to notice the lights beginning to click on in the house.

"All right," Dad said settling in behind his scope again. "This is what we've been waiting for."

Off in the distance, I became faintly aware of the sound of an engine moving closer toward our position.

"There's a boat coming in around us from the port side," Vance said suddenly, removing the telescope from the window and placing it down on the table completely out of sight.

Dad quickly did the same, and we all sank down in our seats, trying to avoid any detection. Even though it was nearly dark, the lights from the deck where Enrico and his crew were working reflected through the cabin behind us.

The motorboat zoomed on past and continued heading in toward the shore, slowing until it actually slid softly aground on the beach.

Dad and Vance lifted the scopes to begin watching again while I went over and closed the cabin door so there would be nothing to illuminate our silhouettes in the large window.

"Apparently my father has company," Vance said as three figures emerged from the boat and went up the beach toward the dwelling.

"Damien is meeting them out on the patio," Dad added. "He's waving them inside."

They didn't say anything else for a few moments and I began to feel impatient. "What's happening?" I asked.

"They all walked inside and are standing around the

crates now," Vance replied, continuing with the play-by-play commentary for me. "They're talking among themselves and gesturing over the boxes."

"Here comes someone with a pry bar," my dad added. "I hope we can see whatever is inside those things."

I started fishing through Dad's giant duffle bag, looking for the two pairs of binoculars I'd seen in there earlier, not knowing if they would help from this distance or not.

"Here!" I said, handing the extra set to Brad. I leaned over the back of Vance to look out the window.

I finally found the target and adjusted the focus until I could plainly see the four individuals standing in the living room.

Two of the men were lifting the lid off one of the crates, and everyone in the room leaned forward, peering in.

"Can you see what's inside?" Dad asked Vance, sounding very frustrated.

"No. We're not at the right angle."

One of the men reached into his pocket and pulled out a pair of rubber gloves, placing them on his hands before reaching inside the box.

"What's he doing?" I asked, curious about what they could possibly need latex gloves for.

"I can't tell," Vance answered me.

The woman who was kneeling on the floor suddenly sat up. She had an I.V. bag, like those used in hospitals, which she was holding in her hand. She lifted a syringe and poked it into the port on the bag, injecting the contents inside.

"Is that what I think it is?" Brad asked, sounding puzzled as we watched the scene unfolding in front of us.

"If you think it's an I.V. bag, then yes," Dad replied.

"They're a medical team!" I said as the pieces suddenly clicked into place. "There's something alive in the box!"

As if in answer to my comment, the two men reached

into the crate and lifted out what appeared to be an unconscious woman, moving her to lay on one of the couches.

"What the heck?" Dad said to no one in particular, as we watched in confusion, unable to figure out what was happening.

"I think he might be importing witches and warlocks from all over the world so he can feed on them," Vance said, and I felt the wave of nausea he experienced at that thought.

"Why?" Dad asked. "It doesn't make any sense. Can't he just search for any witch or warlock to feed on? Why go to all the pain and expense to ship them in?"

I pondered on his comment for a moment, thinking things weren't adding up properly.

"What if he isn't feeding on all of them?" I replied, an idea suddenly popping into my head that could possibly explain what was happening.

"What do you mean?" Dad asked.

"Maybe he's performing a demon kiss. Don't you get it? He's probably searching out the most powerful people of the magical community and having them shipped here so he can steal all their powers. I mean, I'm sure he's probably feeding on some of them to help build his strength, but he saves the best, the power he desires the most, for the kiss."

They were all quiet for a minute while they pondered this.

"She makes sense," Vance said finally, agreeing with me. "It would be harder to find someone more powerful with each kiss he performs, which would be what he craves. If he's sending scouts out to look for those kinds of people, then drugging them and shipping them here ... it really does make sense."

"But why does he need the medical people?" Dad

asked. "He could just kill them easily right now by drinking all their blood. Why treat them?"

"I remember watching an interview with a serial killer on television once," Brad said. "All he could talk about was how superior he was to his victims. He wanted to show them how devious he could be. That was how he got his thrill."

"Maybe Damien wants them awake so they know what's happening to them," he suggested. "He wants to show his power for an audience. That's what Juan kept saying. The demon warlock kept talking about how powerful he was and how no one could touch him."

"Yeah, well, I'd like to get a hold of him and touch him right about now," Vance mumbled angrily.

"We need to get those people out of there!" I said, feeling a bit frantic over their situation, knowing their lives were in jeopardy.

"It's too late for these people," Dad replied, giving a slight shake of his head. "We can't just try to storm in there without a plan. We'd just end up being his next victims."

"So we're just going to sit here and watch?" I said horrified, a sick churning feeling beginning to start in the pit of my stomach.

Vance moved away from the glass and turned around to look at me, a concerned expression on his face.

"You don't have to watch, Portia," he said, running a hand down my arm, trying to soothe my temperament. "But we do need to find out what's going on here, not to mention seeing exactly how this kiss thing works. If this gets to be too much for you, then just turn away, okay?"

I nodded, and he gave me a gentle squeeze before turning back around. I lifted the binoculars to my face again, focusing in on the scene playing out in front of us.

We continued to watch as the three remaining crates

were also opened and soon the medical people had their contents set up with an I.V. also.

It wasn't long before we noticed the woman on the couch was beginning to thrash violently, almost like she was having a seizure of some sort.

Damien calmly went over to her and placed a hand on her head, eerily the same way Vance would do to mine when I couldn't sleep. He bent over her, muttering something and the woman calmed almost instantly.

"I wish we had a microphone," Dad complained, to no one in particular.

After a little while, we noticed Damien did the same thing to the other three individuals still lying in their boxes.

When this was done, he waved at the two medical men standing by, and they came and lifted one individual out of the crate, carrying his limp form over to a solid looking high-backed chair.

The man was placed on the seat, and the woman who was with them came with a set of manacles and began securing his arms to the chair.

"All right. This is starting to feel a little too familiar to me," I said, remembering when I found Vance being held prisoner in almost the exact same setup as this.

The medical woman placed a second set of irons around the man's legs, after which Damien came over to touch each of these. A magical force field surrounded them instantly in a glowing fashion.

This same pattern was followed with the next two victims, who were also men of different ethnical origins. Then the woman was lifted to a waiting chair, but was left unrestrained.

The medical crew then went over to the wall, and I watched in surprise as they moved something. I realized then, it was actually the wall which was in motion. It began to turn slowly around, until the opposite side was facing outward into the room to reveal a new set of curious items. The wall had some type of pulley system on it with several brackets.

One of the men pulled a belt down from the pulley system and wrapped it around the unconscious woman's waist. Then as the man and woman on each side of her steadied her, the third man pulled on the system, hoisting the woman up off the chair, until she was touching the wall. They slid her body down gently until her feet were near the floor, snapping her arms and legs into the waiting brackets.

Damien began to walk around the room, snapping his fingers in front of each of the individuals who were restrained in front of him. They came instantly awake as if they had never been drugged.

I watched as they slowly became aware of the predicament they were in. I couldn't hear their screams as they realized where they were, but I could plainly see them.

My stomach began to churn even more violently, but I couldn't look away. It was like a bad horror movie where you knew someone was going to be slaughtered, but you still had to watch through your fingers. My mind kept telling me to lower the glasses and look away, but the message never reached my hands, which were frozen in place, as if they had turned to stone.

Damien walked over to the first man in the chair and calmly took out his athame. He lifted it and sliced hard into his victim's restrained arm. Blood sprayed everywhere, violently pumping from the deep arterial wound.

I felt Vance physically flinch beside me at the sight, but I couldn't even speak to ask him if he was okay.

Damien placed a silver chalice beneath the wound and magically guided the blood into it. When the cup was full he waved his hand over the wound and closed it.

I could see the man in the chair was gasping in agony. The two male victims sitting next to him were watching in wide-eyed terror, and the woman hanging on the wall was sobbing.

Damien casually swirled the blood in the chalice, then sniffed it as if he were sampling a fine wine. He lifted the drink to his lips and took a large swallow, right before he spit it out again and tossed the goblet onto the floor. He clearly didn't care for the taste.

He motioned for the medical crew, and I watched in horror as they transformed into their demon forms, like Krista had done once before in front of me. The small fleshy horns protruded from their head, the brows furrowed, and their teeth lengthened into rows of uneven fangs.

They pounced on the man while he screamed—ripping chunks of flesh from him as they bit into his skin to feed on him, blood spraying in every direction.

Vance was at my side instantly, ripping the binoculars from my grasp, his eyes flaming red.

"Don't look, Portia!" he said, as he buried my face against his shoulder. "They're going to kill this one."

I let him hide my face there, not wanting to see what was happening to the poor warlock who sat in that chair. I could feel Vance shaking, though, as he fought for control over his own desires.

All I could think of was that Vance had once been subjected to something very similar to this, only he had been allowed to survive. I started weeping into his shirt as he ran his fingers up and down over my back trying to sooth me.

"It's okay, baby. It's okay," he repeated, his clenched teeth belying the calmness he was trying to exude over me.

I turned to look toward the cabin door, worried about whether or not any of the fishermen were hearing us, but it sounded as if they were still busy hauling nets in with loud whirring machines.

"He's gone," I heard Dad say in a low voice, and I knew he meant the man was now dead.

"What's happening?" Vance asked, as he continued to cradle me protectively.

"Your dad is testing out his next victim," Brad replied, pausing for a moment. "I guess he likes this one," he added, disgust dripping from his voice. "He's going back for seconds."

"Will he let this one live?" I asked against Vance's shirt as I held onto him as if I were drowning.

"It depends on how many cups he has," Vance answered honestly. "His chalice is big. It looks to be about the size of a pint. If he stops after eight, then they probably plan on changing him. If he drinks more than that, he'll probably just let him die."

My dad and Brad continued to watch while Vance held me tightly in his arms, his chin resting on the top of my head.

"He stopped at ten," Dad finally said, after a long silence. "But he's letting the others take the rest."

"This is so sick," Brad said sourly, continuing to watch the scene unfold in front of him.

"He's starting on the final man now," Dad added.

"He isn't going to keep any of them, is he?" I asked, feeling my heart break painfully for the victims involved with this monster.

Vance shook his head. "I don't think so," he whispered as he hugged me closer.

"He just passed him off to the others," Brad said several minutes later. "I think he's going for her now."

"We have to watch," I said, pushing Vance away and reaching for the binoculars on the table again. "We have to learn what it is."

"Portia, I'll do it. You don't have to," he said, concerned, placing a hand of restraint against my arm.

"No!" I replied, harshly. "I involved in this, too! I need to know what we're going up against."

He looked at me for a moment before he released my hand, and I brought the binoculars back up to my face, finding the target once again, as Vance returned to the spyglass he'd been using prior.

Thankfully the bodies that had been in the chairs were no longer visible. I didn't dwell on what that fact might mean, and I followed as Damien began to stalk his new prey.

I watched as the woman on the wall began screaming, tears rolling down her face. I could see she was trying to throw a magical force field around herself for protection, but it wasn't working.

"That's why he has the I.V.," Dad said, in sudden understanding. "He's drugging them so they don't have proper control over their powers. He's running interference."

Damien walked up close to the woman, reaching through her flimsy barrier of protection, and grabbed her jaw so she faced him head on. He placed his other hand on the back of her head. I could see her trying to say something as he leaned in close, and it almost looked like he was going to kiss her. He stopped when he was about two inches away from her mouth, suddenly dropping his jaw open and inhaled as if taking a very deep breath.

The women's body went completely stiff and she began jerking in spasms. I could actually see the essence of her powers, in the form of light, very similar to the glow I witnessed from my own healing powers.

I watched as the light flowed rapidly up though her veins, into her neck and then out of her mouth, passing out of her body and into his. It was all over in about thirty seconds, and she slumped heavily against the wall.

Damien dropped his hands from her body then. He began to shake as the new powers ran through his body, lighting his veins as it moved through him, until it filled his entire being. He held his hands out away from him, and I saw what looked like sparks shooting out from the ends of his fingers. It appeared as if he was in pain as he convulsed with the power. Finally, after several long moments, his body began to assimilate the new powers and the lights running through him began to slowly fade away.

"That was some trip," Brad said quietly, mostly to himself. "I think I'm going to vomit."

The medical staff hurried to the wall and removed the woman from it. She was carried brusquely out the door, down to the beach and unceremoniously tossed, rather roughly, into the waiting motorboat.

We heard the engine sputter to life in the distance and begin to head back out to sea.

"Portia! Hand me the night vision goggles in my bag, quick!" my dad called out to me.

I dropped my binoculars onto the table and hurriedly rummaged through the duffle bag until I found them.

"Here!"

He had them on in a flash, looking about, scanning the waters for the small motorboat.

"There!" he said pointing across the bow as he located them.

We moved our line of sight, following the point of his finger, but couldn't see anything out in the dark night, though we did hear the engine slow slightly.

"They dumped her into the water!" he exclaimed suddenly.

"Dad!" I shouted in dismay. "We have to go get her!

She's too weak and she'll drown!"

"It'll take too long to get this thing started!" he replied, shaking his head as he looked over at the controls. "If we fire it up right now, it'll alert them also," he added as he looked out over the water.

Vance was instantly out the door of the cabin, and suddenly I heard a splash.

"He's swimming to her!" I said as I ran out the door, trying to see him in the dark but to no avail.

"They're leaving now, in a hurry," Dad said as he continued to watch out the window.

"Enrico!" I shouted from the door, trying to get his attention, just as Brad appeared at my side.

"Tell them to drop the nets!" I begged Brad, gesturing toward the working men. "It'll take too long to pull them in!"

Brad ran forward toward the fishermen gesturing wildly with his hands, speaking rapidly in their native tongue.

Enrico balked and was shaking his head violently, arguing back in Spanish, clearly not wishing to drop his load.

"Tell him we'll buy him all new nets if he'll drop them now!" I shouted, before turning back to my dad. "Can you see them? Is Vance okay?" I hollered at him, feeling my nerves rise to an all-new extreme.

"He's moving quickly through the water. I think she's face down in it! He isn't near enough yet, though!" he called back to me.

I turned to look at Brad, who was still arguing with Enrico and the other crewmembers.

"Screw this!" I said under my breath and I strode out onto the deck.

I centered all my emotions, feeling the urgency and the energy racing through my veins. I lifted my hands out, raising them in a slow motion high into the air.

A hard wind suddenly raced through the atmosphere, whipping my hair free from the claw that held it, thrashing it wildly around my face.

The nets began lifting up out of the water, following the motion of my hands, until they were swinging in the pulleys full of fish. I moved my arms in toward my body and the large metal robotic arms swung the nets into the boat.

The fisherman were screaming and hovering into a corner now as they pointed first at the nets and then over at me, terror written plainly on their faces.

"Get this thing moving!" I yelled to my dad and I heard the engine fire up at that exact moment.

The boat started forward slowly as Dad turned it slightly to adjust the course, heading in the direction where we needed to go.

Brad was frantically trying to calm the screaming men behind me and keep them from jumping overboard.

I rushed around to the port side and leaned over the edge, looking out into the darkness as we picked up speed, looking for any sign of Vance, or the woman, out in the wave-rippled water.

"Over there!" I yelled to my dad, pointing as I spotted him, his red eyes glowing in the distant darkness.

He was treading water in the spot where he flipped the woman over, and he was holding her head up trying to keep the waves from washing over her face.

Dad maneuvered the boat up alongside him, and Brad and I reached down into the water to grab the woman.

We hauled her up onto the boat as the fishermen looked on in amazement, being silent for the first time. Their moment of silence lasted until Vance climbed back into the boat. They got one look at his red eyes and started screaming again.

This time Enrico jumped overboard.

"Oh, good grief!" Vance said, throwing his hands into the air, before diving back into the water after him.

Chapter 15

We went to work quickly on the woman, laying her flat on her back on the deck, while Dad checked her.

"She has a pulse, but she isn't breathing!" he said, and he slightly tilted her head back and began to blow into her mouth.

Brad and I watched him work quickly with her. After a few breaths, the woman started coughing violently, and water began gurgling out of her mouth.

We rolled her to the side so the liquid could drain from her without choking her again. She took several gasps of breath.

"Brad, ask one of the guys if they have any oxygen onboard," I said, knowing she needed extra help.

He relayed the message to the three remaining fishermen onboard who looked at him with wide eyes like he was crazy. I didn't think they could even comprehend a thing that he was saying to them.

"I think they're in shock," he replied with a shake of his head. "They aren't answering me. I'll go look for some in the cabin."

We heard a squeal from the men and looked up to see Vance dripping wet, dragging an equally soaked Enrico back onboard the vessel.

Vance sat Enrico down with the other men and touched each of them, effectively freezing their bodies with a spell to keep them from moving. He sloshed his way back across the deck and knelt at my side.

"How is she?" he asked, panting slightly.

"She isn't conscious yet," I said. "She had a lot of water in her lungs."

"Heal her," he stated, looking at me.

"What?" I asked in shock, his words not really registering.

"Heal her," he replied again, wiping his dripping hair away from his face. "I don't want to try it while I'm having these demonic reactions. I don't know if they'd affect my magic."

I nodded in understanding before turning back to the woman. I reached out and placed my hands gently on both sides of her head, letting my energy flow from me into her. The soft white light moved quickly throughout her body as it searched out the areas in need of attention. When the transfer was finished, I removed my hands and sat back.

A few seconds later she slowly opened her eyes and looked around, flinching visibly when she saw Vance leaning over her.

"You're all right now," I said, nodding my head toward him. "He saved you from drowning."

"What happened?" she asked with a cough, and I could hear the accent of her native Indian tongue coming through.

"You were the victim of dark magic tonight, and you've lost all your powers through something called a demon kiss. Your body was discarded into the ocean afterwards," I explained.

"Where am I?" She looked around.

"You're in Mexico, on a fishing boat in the Sea of Cortez," I replied as she looked at me.

She glanced back warily at Vance again. "He isn't a demon?" she asked, with trepidation creeping into her voice, her nervousness apparent.

"No," I said shaking my head. "Someone tried to change him, though, and he still suffers from reactions to the near conversion." I wanted to help her to be able to relax around him and not fear him.

She looked him over for a moment as if trying to decide whether or not to believe what I was saying.

"Thank you then," she finally replied, her gaze holding his own. "And I'm sorry for your suffering."

"I'm fine," he said with a soft smile. "I just want to make sure you're all right."

"Would you object to coming back to shore with us and telling our coven what has happened to you?" my dad asked gently. "We're trying to stop the person who did this to you."

"No. Not at all," she said. We helped her to her feet and guided her into the cabin out of the night air.

Brad wrapped a blanket he found around her, and we helped her to sit down on the bench at the table.

"What are we going to do about this other mess we've made tonight?" Dad said as we looked out at the magically restrained fishermen.

"I have no idea," I said, biting at my bottom lip. "I didn't really have time to plan correctly before I cooked up that little show of power I made out there. I'm sorry about that."

"Don't worry about it, Pumpkin," my dad replied. "We'll think of something to tell them."

"I suggest we try honesty first and see if that works," Vance said. "If it doesn't, then we'll try Plan B."

"It can't hurt, I guess," I replied, figuring since I was the one who caused the commotion then I should be the one to explain things to them.

I left my dad with the woman and walked back out onto the deck to stand in front of the crew.

The four of them stared up at me with wide eyes, and I turned to look back at Vance who was leaning casually in the doorway with his arms folded across his chest, watching me closely.

"All right," I said, taking a deep breath. "First of all, I want to apologize for scaring you nearly to death. That was truly never my intention."

Brad stepped up next to me and began translating my words into Spanish for them.

"We never meant to expose you to any of this," I began again, when he paused, waiting for me to continue. "I need to tell you some things that will be difficult to believe. Do you understand me so far?"

Their eyes switched from me back to Brad as he translated, then back to me when he was done.

"Do they understand what I'm saying?" I asked him, unable to tell.

"I'm not even sure if they know who they are right now," Brad said, a slight grin creeping onto his face as he fought back a chuckle. He was trying to remain solemn over the situation and failing miserably at it.

I turned back to face Vance.

"Now what?" I asked, lifting my hands uselessly before dropping them. "I don't think anything I'm saying is computing."

He moved away from the door and walked up next to me, before reaching out and touching each one of them on the forehead once again, this time effectively putting them to sleep.

"We need to construct a believable scenario— something they can wake up to and think they'd just experienced a horrible dream."

"Like what?" I asked, not even knowing what kind of believable scenario we could build out of this mess.

"Well," he said, thoughtfully, "I think we should call your grandma and have her meet us at the marina first of all. She can take our new lady friend back to the condo with her and get her taken care of."

"Yeah, then what do we do?" I asked, curious about where he was heading with all this.

He looked over my head at the metal mechanical arms holding the bulging fishing nets on the boat.

"Then we should go back to the original coordinates we were at when we were watching the house. We'll drop one of the nets back into the water, and we'll construct an 'accident' with the other. I think we could make it look like one of the arms broke and let the net fall on these four knocking them out. When they wake up, hopefully they'll just think it's all a crazy dream they had when they were unconscious."

"But both nets were still in the water when this happened. And what about when they start telling each other about the nightmare they've just had?" I asked, feeling doubtful about whether or not this would work.

"I find the human mind tends to want to accept the most plausible reason it can find for something." he replied. "I'm sorry, but it's what I've got. Take it or leave it."

"I'll take it." I said, stepping up to him and placing my hands on his temples. "But we have to get rid of these red eyes for it to work."

We told our idea to Dad, and he agreed this was probably the best course of action. He called Grandma, and soon we were on our way back toward the tiny marina.

Thankfully, all the other boats that were normally stationed here were either docked and sitting empty or hadn't come in yet.

Grandma and Shelly were waiting for us at the pier. They took the woman, whose name was Sarit, with them, and Dad turned the boat around to head out to sea once again.

When we finally reached our original coordinates, Dad shut the engine down, and we went to work turning on the same lights, setting out our food, cards, and telescopes the way they had been.

We dropped one of the large fishing nets back into the water and made the metal bend and give way in one of the joints of the arm on the other to look as though it had strained from serious metal fatigue.

We moved the men into position, pulling their bodies around and scattering them about on the deck, strategically placing fish net over them. We took extra care to make sure Enrico and Vance were both completely dry also.

"You guys ready?" Vance called to us as we took our places inside the cabin, pretending to be watching the house.

"Yes!" I called back, and he waved his hand over the men before running back in to lean over in front of me.

"Ahhh!" I heard one of the men scream loudly. He grabbed at the fishnet over his body, struggling to remove it.

The others' voices soon joined his as they tried to push up out of the nets, calling out for help.

"Oh my gosh!" I yelled, running from the cabin. "What happened? Dad, Vance, Brad, come quick!"

The three of them dashed out of the cabin, pausing for a second to look at the scene ahead of them before rushing to help, trying to gather the heavy net and pull the men from beneath it.

When we freed the men from their restraints, they huddled together looking confused at us, as Brad excitedly pointed up to the broken beam in Spanish.

The crew looked up in awe and dismay.

"No! No!" Enrico shouted when he saw the damage,

grabbing his hair in his hands and talking rapidly in Spanish.

"Ask him what happened?" Vance said, prompting Brad.

Brad relayed the question, but the men just looked dazed and confused, shaking their heads as they talked rapidly to each other, and I was afraid they might be sharing their stories about us and what they'd seen earlier.

Dad stepped up and asked Brad to translate for him. "Tell them we'll pay for the damage to their boat since it happened while they were trying to help us out," he prompted.

Brad relayed the message, and Enrico grabbed Dad's hand, shaking it vigorously out of gratitude.

"Gracias! Gracias!" he said over and over again, bowing his head down to each of us, happy to know he hadn't just lost his way to make his living.

"No problem!" Dad said with a smile as he shook Enrico's hand back. "Tell them we're done with our investigation and ready to leave whenever he desires."

The men worked to quickly pull the other full net up and onto the boat. Enrico made his way to the controls, and we headed back to the marina once again.

The rest of us packed up our belongings in the cabin and went back out onto the deck to help the fishermen load their catch down into the cargo storage hold beneath the floor.

When we pulled up to the dock, Dad pulled a very large roll of American one hundred dollar bills out of his duffle bag and handed it to Enrico.

"Gracias!" Enrico called out again, as he profusely shook Dad's hand over and over.

I thought it was funny how they just assumed the money came from Dad. I knew it was from Vance's bank account, but Vance didn't seem to be bothered one bit by the whole exchange, not even blinking an eye.

We climbed off the boat, and Miguel handed our stuff over to us. We left the smiling men waving at us as we walked away.

We quickly threw our stuff in the trunk and climbed into the car, and we drove off, leaving the smiling men behind us none the worse for wear.

"Do you think they bought it?" I asked with a laugh, now that we were finally out of earshot.

"I think so," Vance replied with a smile. "They were awfully friendly there towards the end when they saw all that money."

"I hated breaking their boat," I said, truly feeling bad it had come to that and hoping it wouldn't take long for them to get it repaired.

"Well, we couldn't let Sarit drown, and we couldn't leave them there freaking out like they were," Brad said.

"What's done is done," my dad added. "Thankfully it seems to have all worked out. This has definitely been one crazy night."

"I'm afraid it's only going to get worse from here," Vance added, growing serious once again.

"I'm afraid you're right," Dad said echoing his concern.

The whole coven was waiting for us when we entered the condo, sitting around Sarit, who was eating a fresh bowl of hot soup on the couch.

I was happy to see she was dry, dressed in someone's borrowed clothing, and covered in a warm blanket.

"So we've all heard Sarit's side of the story," Grandma said, looking us all over. "How about yours? It sounds as if you've had a dreadful experience this evening."

Dad began to fill everyone in on the things we had seen and experienced, though he edited the gory details extremely out of deference toward Sarit and all she had been through.

Vance leaned in toward me while Dad was speaking, looking very tired and worn out.

"I'm going to go get in the shower," he said softly. "I positively reek of fishy saltwater."

"Okay," I said, as he leaned over to give me a peck on the cheek, before he walked off.

Everyone was listening with rapt attention to Dad as he explained the events we had witnessed. I stood up not wanting to hear any more about it and walked into my own bedroom, thinking a shower sounded just like the thing I needed to do, too.

I got a tank top along with some shorts, and headed into the bathroom. I let the shower water rush over me as I tried desperately to not think about the images that were trying to invade my mind.

The door to the bathroom opened quietly a few moments later.

"It's just me," Shelly said softly, as she entered.

"Hey, Shelly," I said, continuing to shampoo my hair.

"Was it awful?" she asked bluntly.

"It was worse than awful," I replied honestly as I massaged the sudsy bubbles into my scalp. "Can we not talk about it right now, though? I'm really tired, and I'd just rather forget about the whole thing for a little while."

"I understand," she said, and I thought I heard regret lacing through her voice. "I'm glad you're all safely back here, though."

"Me, too," I replied, meaning it.

"Are you going to sleep in Vance's room tonight again?" she asked, changing the subject.

"Most definitely," I answered. "I don't want him to be alone after everything that's happened tonight."

I knew the real reason was I didn't want to be away from *him* after all I had witnessed either.

"Well, sleep good then. I'll talk to you in the morning." Her voice sounded a little bit sad.

"Night, Shell," I called out as she left the room, feeling bad for letting her down when she was trying to talk to me about things, but I couldn't relive it yet.

I climbed out of the shower and got ready for bed. I pulled my damp towel-dried hair into sections before I braided it into one long single braid down my back.

Afterward I brushed my teeth and returned to the living room.

Everyone had already left our condo, and I was thankful since I didn't want to face any questions from the others right now. I assumed proper sleeping arrangements had been made for Sarit, since she was no longer here, so I made my way to Vance's room.

I knocked lightly on the door.

"It's open, Portia. Come in."

I walked in to see him lying in the bed with the covers up to his waist. His chest was bare, and his head was resting on his arms which were on the pillow.

"Come get comfy," he said reaching over to throw the covers back on the other side of the bed.

I crawled in and scooted over, laying my head against his bare shoulder.

He wrapped his arm around my back, and I just lay there in the dim lamplight, reaching out to draw lazy circles with my finger on his chest.

We didn't say anything, each of us lost in our own thoughts, though I purposely steered mine away from any events of this evening.

"Are you doing okay?" he finally asked, breaking the long silence between us.

I nodded, continuing my absent tracing of his sculpted muscles, trying hard to concentrate only on the beauty of his physique.

He toyed absently with my braided hair, seemingly as content as I was to avoid the issues at hand.

"You ready to go to sleep?" he asked a few minutes later. He reached down and picked my hand up off his chest, kissing each one of my fingertips.

I nodded again. "I have just one request."

"What's that?" he replied, looking down at me questioningly.

"Can we please sleep with the light on tonight?" I felt dumb to ask such a childish thing.

"Yes, baby," he said, understanding me immediately, pulling me into the comfort of his arms. He enveloped me completely within the safety of his warm embrace. "Yes, we can."

The Demon Kiss

Chapter 16

"*No! Stop!*" I screamed into the air as I was running, my lungs aching from breathing heavily in the darkness.

I couldn't get away. The fog swirled around me. I looked over my shoulder as Damien Cummings stepped out of the mist and into my view.

"Hello, Portia," he said, an evil smile stretching across his face as he stalked toward me.

"*Nooo!*" I screamed, turning to run again.

"Portia!" Vance's voice called out in the gloominess that surrounded me. "Portia! Wake up!"

I could feel him shaking my body as I slowly came to. I opened my eyes, trying to focus.

I looked around to see that I was still in his bedroom, the dim lamplight casting an angelic-looking halo around Vance's form as he held me, cradling me in his arms, a worried look on his face.

Grabbing him, I clung desperately as I started sobbing.

"It's all right now," he whispered into my hair as he placed tiny kisses against my forehead. "It was just a nightmare. You're safe right here with me. I won't let him hurt you."

He continued to hold me as I cried, and I could see my tears dripping against his bare skin.

He didn't rush me, letting me step firmly back into reality, before he leaned back against his pillows so he could take a good look at me.

"I'm sorry," I said, looking at him through my red swollen eyes, reaching out with one of my hands to wipe my tears off his damp chest.

"Don't apologize. You have nothing to be sorry for. I'm the one who should be asking for your forgiveness."

"For what?" I said, completely confused.

"For dragging you and your family into all this mess," he replied with a frustrated glance.

"It isn't your fault." I sighed as I looked at him. "You had no idea what was happening either."

"Maybe not, but it's my flesh and blood which seem to be causing all the psychotic problems in your life lately," he reminded me, looking truly sorry about it.

"If that's what I have to deal with to be with you, then so be it," I replied, laying my head back against him and wrapping my arm around his waist to give a little squeeze.

He didn't say anything. His fingers ran over the rubber tie that held my braid. After a few seconds, I felt him pull the band off and he began to run his hands through my still partially damp hair until it laid spread out across his body.

"You're so beautiful," he said softly, his hand continuing to stroke over the strands in a manner I found very relaxing. "Sometimes I still can't believe you want me as much as I want you."

"Well, believe it, because it's true," I responded, lightly rubbing his exposed bicep which rippled handsomely with every little movement he made, sending happy little shivers of attraction down my spine.

"What am I going to do about all this, Portia?" he asked in muted exasperation. "I have no idea how to stop him, but I can't let this continue on either."

"Don't worry about it right now," I replied, trying to think of a way to calm him as he was calming me. "We'll talk things over in the morning with everyone else and see if we can come up with something."

"I do worry about it. We can't have a real future until I figure out a way to fix this. I've been awake all night trying to outline some sort of plan. I'm at a complete loss."

"You've been awake all night?" I asked, lifting my head to look at him, worried he wasn't getting any rest.

He nodded. "I was watching you sleep," he said with a half-smile. "You make such sweet little faces when you're dreaming."

"And when I'm having nightmares?" I asked sarcastically.

"You start screaming," he said looking at me with concern. "I find it interesting that my father has been the horrible thing in the fog you've been running from all along," he added, as he brushed some of my hair back behind my ear.

I shrugged and placed my head back down on his chest, not really wanting to think about it anymore.

"Well, I don't blame you. I'm thinking he's a pretty scary monster right now myself."

When I didn't say anything, he nudged me with his arm.

"Hey," he said.

I looked up.

"Come here," he added with a little jerk of his chin.

I moved the rest of the way up his chest, until my face was directly above his.

He reached up and placed both of his hands on each side of my head, pulling me in so he could kiss me on the lips.

"I love you," he said, pulling back, his gaze flickering over the features of my face.

"I love you, too," I replied, knowing I'd never get tired of hearing him say those words.

"Portia, I won't let him hurt you—you know that, right?" he said as he searched my eyes, and I could see the love and concern written plainly there.

I nodded again, laying my head back on his chest, letting him hold me until I fell into a deep sleep once again.

When I finally woke up in the morning, he was still sleeping. I was lying on my side in the crook of his shoulder, facing toward him. His arm was wrapped loosely around me, his hand lightly resting on my shoulder.

I didn't move a muscle, reluctant to wake him. I also didn't want to do anything that might start his withdrawal process.

Listening, I could hear the rest of the family and coven out in the common area of the condo. I sounded like they were making breakfast while talking with one another, sporadic laughter filling the air. I knew I should get up and help out, but it was so nice right here in this moment.

My gaze wandered over the sleeping face I loved so much. He was relaxed and peaceful right now, giving his look a tender quality I hadn't seen in many days gone by.

I loved his thick dark lashes that lay gently against his cheeks. I loved looking at him period, never tiring of seeing him at any time, in any situation. He was a master at stealing my breath away, and I wondered if he were aware of that fact at all.

My line of sight continued down to his perfectly shaped nose and over the luscious full lips I delighted in kissing so much and having them kiss me so passionately in return.

I traveled lower, over his strong chin with its ever-so-slight cleft in the middle, and down his neck where I could see his pulse beating steadily.

Continuing my perusal, my eyes traveled down to where my hand rested lightly on his smooth, tanned chest, in between his perfectly toned and shaped pectoral muscles. The blankets were scrunched up at his waist, covering most of the six pack abs I already knew were underneath, so I let my vision trail a path down where his hips were hidden beneath the linens, and over the outlines of his long, strong, legs down to where his feet rested, with one foot kicked out from underneath the quilt.

He was such a perfect creature. He was all male, and sinew—muscle, magic, looks and power wrapped into one incredibly amazing package.

I closed my eyes and wondered what it was about me that had possibly attracted him.

"Apparently you've never noticed me looking at you like that before," his voice whispered into my head.

My eyes popped open to look at him.

His eyes were open slightly, and he was looking over at me with a soft smile spreading across his lips.

"Good morning," he said out loud in a quiet voice.

"How long have you been awake?" I asked, looking into the red eyes that watched me intently.

"Long enough to enjoy the thoughts in that pretty little head of yours," he replied, and I noticed the first pangs of his morning withdrawal as it shot through his body, causing him to clench involuntarily.

I reached up to place my hands at his temples.

He closed his eyes, and I let the magic flow from my fingers into him, past the redness in his eyes and throughout his body to stop any more discomfort before it started again.

"Thanks," he said, opening his eyes when I was finished, revealing the startling blue color I loved about them.

"You're welcome," I said, leaning forward to kiss him lightly.

"Sounds like everyone is here already this morning," he

commented, glancing over to the door. "I guess we should get out of bed and go out there."

"I don't want to," I said leaning in to kiss him again, purposely trying to distract him. "I want to stay in here with you all day and pretend the whole world out there doesn't exist."

"That would be nice, wouldn't it?" he replied, looking at my face while running his hand over the top of my head, across the length of my hair and down my back.

We just stared at each other, communicating a whole host of thoughts and feelings without words.

He ran the back of his hand down the side of my cheek, before turning it over to cup my face.

I leaned into his palm, rubbing against it, enjoying the feel of his sweet caress against my skin.

"So beautiful," he whispered, watching me.

He moved his hand down farther, placing it on mine where it rested against his chest, and began toying absently over the large rock that rested there on my small finger.

"Are you happy, Portia?" he asked me suddenly, looking up from the ring and into my face. "I mean, in spite of everything that's going on?"

"I'm very happy, Vance. You don't need to worry about that. You make life feel wonderful," I replied with a sincere smile.

I could see the doubt creep into his mind, threatening to shatter this moment as thoughts from yesterday began to return.

"It's just that I …." He stopped, as I quickly placed my lips over his mouth.

"Shhhh," I whispered against them. "Not right now."

He understood, wrapping his arms around me and kissing me thoroughly. I could feel his teeth as he softly nipped against my lower lip, before coaxing my mouth open with the tip of his tongue.

He rolled me onto my back, leaning over me as he continued his exploration of my mouth.

I closed my eyes and just enjoyed the feel of him, letting my tongue tangle with his, as we tasted each other.

He didn't move away from my mouth this time like he usually did, and I could tell he was keeping a rein on things, trying to not be too aggressive.

He pulled away from me, but he didn't let go of me, and to my surprise his eyes didn't have one hint of red in them.

"I love you," he said softly as he stared at me. "I know I say it all the time. It's probably just gibberish to you by now."

I shook my head as he spoke. "Coming from your mouth, they're my three favorite words in the whole world," I replied honestly.

He kissed me again, this time much more intensely, and I reached up to pull him closer, tangling my fingers through his thick hair.

Someone knocked on the bedroom door, but we didn't stop kissing, choosing to ignore them instead.

After a few seconds the knock came again, a little harder.

"You guys going to sleep in there all day?" my dad's voice called through the barrier.

Vance pulled away from me slightly with an extremely exasperated look on his face.

"You ready to get up now?" he whispered to me in a low voice.

I shook my head.

"Me either," he said with a grin. He lowered his head and continued on with his worship of my mouth.

I heard Dad give a huff and walk away from the door.

I started giggling. "We're so bad," I said against his

mouth.

"Yes, but I'm don't care because this feels so good," he replied, with a smile.

He kissed me for quite a while, and I began to notice I was starting to get a little whisker burn from the overnight stubble he had growing on his chin. I didn't mind, but he finally pulled away with a sigh and flopped over onto his back.

"I can't think of one morning in my life where waking up was as fun as this morning has been," he said, with a satisfied smile.

"It has been nice, hasn't it?" I agreed, rolling over to place my arms over his chest and leaning my chin on the back of my hands.

He watched me for a few moments, with a slight grin turning up the corner of one side of his mouth, popping one of those beloved dimples to the surface.

"I love your hair when it spills across everything like this," he said toying with a few strands.

"You mean when it looks like I just stepped out of a tornado?" I said with a laugh feeling a touch self-conscious about how I must truly look at the moment.

"I was thinking more along the lines of bedroom hair, but a tornado works, too," he replied with a widening smile.

"Why do you like it so much?" I asked, truly curious, since he was always playing with it.

"Partially because you look so dang hot," he replied honestly. "And it goes well with the swollen lips and the whisker burn, too," he added with a lusty look at me that made my pulse leap up in tempo.

"Is it that obvious that we've been making out?" I asked, lifting a hand to run over my face.

"Well, let me put it this way. When you walk into that room full of people a few minutes from now, they'll all know that you've been thoroughly kissed this morning." He laughed, not seeming a bit sorry about it.

"You're enjoying this way too much." I said, playfully taking a slap at his shoulder.

"Hey. You can't blame a guy for wanting to put his mark on his woman," he replied as he grabbed at my wrist, effectively stopping the blow from landing on its intended target.

"Is that what you're doing?" I lifted an eyebrow. "Putting your mark on me?"

"In any way, shape, or form I can," he replied seriously as he watched me. "Do you know how absolutely fetching you are this morning?" he added tenderly.

"No," I replied, wondering all of a sudden if he might be legally blind. "But I'm willing to lay here for the rest of the day and let you tell me all about it."

"I wish I could. But we have people waiting on us," he said, glancing toward the door.

"Do we have to get up now?" I asked with a dejected sigh, really wanting to just lay here like this for the rest of the day.

"We have to go out there and face reality sometime," he said seriously, dashing my hopes of keeping him here in bed with me.

"I don't like reality anymore," I said with a pout. "Let's just live in here for forever."

"I wish we could, baby." He gave me a light kiss on the lips, before he rolled over, pulling me up and out of the bed after him. "Come on. I've been blessed with a bout of amazing restraint this morning. Let's not try to push our luck any farther."

"All right," I grumbled, knowing it was the right thing to do and not wanting to tempt him beyond what he could stand.

He hugged me one more time, before placing a chaste kiss on my forehead.

"Let's get some breakfast," he said. He grabbed my hand, leading us both out the door in our completely disheveled state.

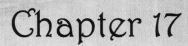

Chapter 17

I stepped gingerly out of the bedroom, knowing we were going to get many shocked stares looking like we did.

It didn't seem to bother Vance one bit. He strode straight into the dining room, not caring he was only wearing a baggy pair of sweat pants, and sporting his sleep tousled bed head.

It also didn't seem to bother him that he was towing me behind him feeling half-dressed in my white tank top and plaid boxer shorts. My hair was twisting out in every direction possible, and I knew my lips were obviously swollen from our previous kissing session.

"Morning, everyone!" Vance said cheerfully as if nothing were amiss, pulling me over to where the food was spread out on the buffet.

The chatter in the room went to complete silence as people looked up at us, taking in our appearance.

I couldn't even make eye contact with anyone, afraid of what the stares were saying. I let my thick hair fall forward around the sides of my face, trying to hide the humiliation that might be showing there.

But Vance was in a mood this morning, and he was intent on flaunting it for all who were present.

"See anything you want to eat for breakfast, baby?" he said with a smile as he pulled me close up to him, pushing my hair back from my face with one hand as he molded me against his body with the other. He proceeded to french kiss me in front of everyone.

He threaded his fingers into my hair, basically keeping my face pushed against his, so I couldn't pull away at all. Not that I really wanted to. I had to admit he was the best kisser in the world, and after a moment I forgot where I was. My arms moved involuntarily as they threaded their way around his neck, bringing him even closer to me.

I felt my face flush with color when he let me go, and I remembered where we were.

He, however, was grinning from ear to ear at the response he'd gotten from me, and I could tell he was feeling totally pleased with himself.

"Breakfast?" he asked again, lifting one of his eyebrows in question as he looked at me.

"Uh … the french kiss … um, I mean, the french toast looks good," I stammered, as I looked over at the buffet.

"French toast it is!" he said, still grinning triumphantly, while proceeding to place some on a plate for me and drowning it with maple syrup.

He took the plate over to the table and sat it down, pulled a chair out, and guided me into it like I was the Queen of England or something.

He bent over to peck my lips again once he had me settled into my place.

"Mmm," he said as he winked seductively. "You're sweeter than syrup this morning, Portia."

I couldn't hold it in any longer, and I burst out laughing—partially because he was funny, but mostly from the nervous reaction he was causing in me.

"What *are* you doing?" I asked quietly, my eyes widening in confusion as I looked up at him.

"I want everyone to know exactly how happy I am this morning," he replied with a smile.

"Well, I think you're scaring them." I whispered as I finally braved looking around at everyone else and finding them all watching our little display with extremely avid interest.

He turned, seeing them watching him with quizzical glances, looking like they thought he had gone completely off his rocker. I realized most of the people present had probably never witnessed this side of Vance, or anything even remotely close to it before. He always played the role of the aloof, tortured individual before this point as far as any of them had ever been concerned.

"Now I know you all have seen two people who are crazy in love before. Shut your traps and move along." He gestured, shooing them away with the back of his hands as if he were addressing a group of unruly children instead of some very educated, powerful, adults.

No one moved, and they continued to stare at him. It was quiet only for a moment though, and then Brad spoke up, breaking the tension.

"We can't move yet," he replied sarcastically. "We all need a cold shower after your little display."

Everyone started laughing at his comment.

"I just have one thing to say to everyone in this room," Vance replied, grinning over at Brad before turning somewhat serious. "You never know what life is going to throw at you, so grab the one thing that makes you happier than anything else and run with it."

"Amen," someone toward the back of the room replied.

The conversation went back to normal at this point, and Vance went over to the buffet and dished himself a plate also, coming to sit next to me when he was done.

He reached out and held one of my hands during the entire time we were eating, his thumb rubbing lazy circles against the back of my hand.

"So how did you sleep last night?" my dad asked, as he casually walked up to join us, pulling out a chair next to Vance and sitting down.

Vance looked over at him quizzically, his eyes narrowing slightly, before he spoke up.

"Well, let's see," he began, leaning back into his chair and releasing my hand so he could cross his arms over his chest. "Portia had nightmares. I spent most of the night watching her sleep, while trying to solve the puzzle to all of my life's problems, before I finally gave up and fell asleep myself," Vance replied. "Then I woke up to this beautiful angel in my bed, who magically took away the pain of withdrawal which has made me miserable every single morning lately, so I grabbed her and made out with her for close to an hour, loving every second I was able to forget about the world around me, while I did my best to thank her properly."

I coughed and almost choked on my food, turning to look at Vance incredulously, while Dad sat there looking stunned next to me.

"Did that answer the question you were really asking?" Vance asked, with a quirked eyebrow, as he reached for his orange juice and took a large swallow before placing the glass back down with a loud clank.

Dad just sat there for a moment, as if he were searching for his voice, before he answered.

"I believe it did," he said, with a slightly confused smile, though he nodded his head.

"Sean. You can trust me," Vance said seriously, not caring who could hear him. "I give you my word."

Dad just got up and walked past us, though he patted Vance on the shoulder as he moved by him.

"Hey," I whispered my eyes wide in disbelief as I kneed him under the table. "Do you think you could dial it down a notch this morning?"

"Why?" he asked, as he looked over at me, leaning forward to pick up his fork to stab it into his last piece of sausage.

"Because I can't tell if you're happy or angry," I replied, wondering what in the heck was going on in that handsome head of his.

He stopped and dropped his fork to his plate as he leaned back into the chair once again.

"I'm a little of both, actually," he replied, the frustration becoming apparent on his face.

"What do you mean?" I questioned him, not quite following his mood swings this morning.

"I mean I have everything I want right here at my fingertips." He reached out to rub his fingers over my hand before he continued. "And everything out there is threatening to take it all away from me."

"Not everything," I reminded him. "Just one thing."

"I'd fight to the death for you before I let that happen," he said leaning in close to me.

"Then we don't have anything to worry about, do we? Because I'd do the same for you," I replied with a smile, and he leaned in the rest of the way to kiss me again.

I let him kiss me for as long as he wanted to this time, knowing things were rough for him right now.

"I love you, Portia," he said when he pulled back. "Thank you for everything you do for me."

"You don't have to thank me for anything. It's my pleasure." I smiled. "Are you done with your plate?" I asked, changing the subject.

He nodded, and I picked it up with mine to carry to the sink.

"Morning, Mom," I said, as I entered the adjoining kitchen area. "Breakfast was delicious. Sorry I wasn't up to help you."

"That's okay. I figured you needed your rest this morning after last night. Besides, Shelly, Milly, and Sarit helped me get things ready for everybody."

"So how's Sarit?" I asked, looking across the room to where she was seated in the middle of a group of coven members.

"She's doing all right, considering everything she's been through," Mom said, casting a sympathetic look her direction. "I'm sure her friends and family are crazy with worry over her right now."

"We need to get her home," I replied, nodding my head in agreement with her. "I'm sure Vance would purchase an airline ticket back to India for her."

"Actually, he gave your dad the money for it last night while you were still in the shower."

"Oh," I said feeling a little surprised at that bit of information. "He didn't tell me."

"Yeah. He wanted to make sure we got her a first class ticket. He said it was an abomination she had to come here in a box—the least he could do was send her back home in comfort."

"I think he feels responsible for his father's actions. Though I don't know why he does," I said looking over at him.

He was sitting at the table, his eyes following my every move. I was sure he was listening to everything we were saying.

"He shouldn't feel that way at all," my mom said, unaware he was eavesdropping on our conversation. "He's nothing like that monster."

"I know," I said, continuing to make eye contact with him, hoping he was getting the message. "I just don't think he does."

He stood up and came into the kitchen.

"I'm going to go get cleaned up for the day," he said, before giving me a peck on the cheek.

"Okay," I answered, smiling at him, before he turned to walk away from me. "See you in a bit."

Dad called the group to attention a few minutes later. He told everyone that Sarit was going home today and she wanted to say a few words.

Sarit stood up in front of everyone and thanked them for the hospitality they had shown her. She said while she was already missing her magic greatly, she was very thankful to still have her life and was anxious to get back to her family.

Everyone gathered around her after she was finished speaking, giving her hugs and well wishes. When they were done, Sarit singled me out in particular.

"Thank you, Portia, for your help," she said as she grasped my hand warmly in between both of hers. She looked around the room, searching for something. "I do not see Vance anywhere, but please tell him I greatly appreciate him and the services he has rendered to me. Without him I surely would have died." Her eyes misted over a little at this point. "I truly hope everything works out for him and the two of you will find the happiness together you seek." She smiled.

I removed my hand from hers and hugged her. "Thank you, Sarit. I'll tell him. I wish we could've met in a different place and time, under better circumstances."

"I do, too," she replied, as she stepped away from me. "If you ever find yourselves in India ...."

"We'll be sure to look you up." I smiled at her.

"That would be wonderful," she agreed as she walked slowly away. "Then my family could meet you, too."

Dad left with her, taking her to the small local airport

that would transfer her to a larger plane in Mexico City.

Once they were out the door, I closed it behind them, turning to go into my room to get showered and cleaned up. Shelly followed right after me.

"So, that was some show the two of you put on this morning," she said, with a short laugh.

"It was, wasn't it? I don't know what was up with him!" I laughed lightly. "He was talking all about making his mark on me and things like that. One minute he was deliriously happy, and the next he was upset."

"I think you make him feel so happy that he gets desperately afraid of losing you," Shelly replied, offering up an explanation for his strange behavior.

I shrugged my shoulders, thinking she could possibly be right. "I don't know what he's afraid of losing me to. I don't plan on going anywhere without him ever again."

"I think the two of you are acting out because you're avoiding the real issue," she said, solemnly, watching me closely.

"What do you mean?" I asked, confused over what issue she could possibly be talking about.

"I saw the terror on all of your faces when you came to drop Sarit off at the dock. Whatever the four of you witnessed out there scared the heck out of all of you," she stated flatly.

I felt myself take in a sharp breath. "You're right. I am avoiding the subject." I walked into the bathroom, closing the door abruptly behind me.

I felt bad for cutting her off, but I didn't want those images flashing through my head right now.

"She's right," Vance said in my head, and I realized he had been eavesdropping again. "We are avoiding it. It actually has a name. It's called Post Traumatic Stress Disorder."

"So that's the reason our emotions are all over the place?" I sighed, listening to him even though part of me didn't want to.

"Yes. It's the natural way the body reacts to something it has a hard time dealing with," he explained.

"So how do we make it better?" I asked, not really wanting to talk to him about this at all right now.

"By doing the one thing we don't want to," he said, as if he were reading my thoughts. "We're all going to have to sit down and talk about it."

"You go ahead and do that. Let me know how it goes," I mentally replied to him, while turning the shower on and climbing in.

I realized then I was showering in complete darkness. I hadn't even wanted to turn the light on. I just wanted to hide in a safe, dark, place.

Changing my mind, I decided at that point to settle down into the tub instead, letting it fill high with the water as hot as I could stand it, before turning on the Jacuzzi jets. I closed my eyes and let my body relax under the heat.

I didn't know I'd fallen asleep until I heard the door to the bathroom open and close as someone entered the room.

"Are you all right?" I heard Vance's voice in the darkness.

"Mmm. Yes. I guess I fell asleep," I replied a groggily. "I'll be out in a little bit."

"Do you want to talk to me about it?" he asked from the other side of the shower curtain.

"Not now," I said, knowing he was trying to help. "If I start crying, you'll be tempted to reach in here and hold me. It wouldn't be good."

"I understand," he answered quietly, and I heard him open the door to the bathroom again. "I'll wait for you in the living room."

"Okay." I didn't hurry to get out, taking my precious time so I could delay the inevitable as long as possible. I just tried to relax as well I could in the water. After a while I sat up and took my time shampooing and conditioning my hair, then shaving my legs. When I couldn't think of another feasible reason to stay in the soothing bath any longer, I finally got out.

I went into the closet and got dressed in a sweet little blue and green plaid top, with a scooped neck that went up into a high collar around the back, and belted with a thin strip of material at the waist. I slid on a pair of boot cut blue jeans and stepped into a cute pair of moccasin-looking clogged heels.

I took the time to dry my hair with the blow dryer and pulled it into a chic looking ponytail, with my long bangs across my forehead and tucked back behind one ear. Then I carefully applied my makeup, so it was in complete perfection, dark eyes, soft pink lips, and a little bronzer to give my pale skin a sun-kissed glow.

Digging through my bag, I found my favorite body spray scent, caramel green apple. I applied a little of it behind my ears and on my wrists before spraying a couple of pumps into the air and walking through it.

Afterward, I went to my jewelry bag and pulled out my large silver hoop earrings and placed them through the single holes in my earlobes.

Then I surveyed myself in the mirror. I looked good, but I knew I'd spent way too much time getting myself ready in an effort to avoid everything else.

Time to face the piper, I thought.

I took a deep sigh and walked out of the bathroom, through the bedroom, and into the living room.

Vance wasn't in there, so I swung around to look

outside and found he was standing on the balcony, staring out into the ocean.

I quietly stepped out the patio door, closing it softly behind me and walked up behind him. I intended to sneak up on him so I could place my arms around his waist to hug him, but he turned to face me as I approached, leaning back against the rail.

"Wow!" he said, as his eyes ran up and down the length of me, a smile of appreciation gracing his face.

"Wow, yourself!" I said back to him with a smile, as I checked him out in return, thinking how delicious he looked just standing casually there with his arms across his chest.

He was wearing the long-sleeved, dark gray, pullover sweater I gave him for Christmas, over a pair of dark indigo-colored low tide Levi's, with a pair of Kickers sneak high shoes.

His hair was textured into that perfectly messy look I loved so much, and I could smell the cool scent of his aftershave wafting through the air as the breeze blew it toward me.

He reached a hand out, and I accepted it. I let him pull me up against him so our faces were mere millimeters apart, and our bodies in full contact with each other.

"You smell good enough to eat." He smiled with his sexy grin that he saved exclusively for when he was alone with me, and he nudged my nose slightly with the tip of his.

"Thank you. So do you." I chuckled, loving the feel of being next to him. "I have to warn you, though," I said, suddenly serious. "I'm overripe."

I held up my pruned looking fingers which had been in the water far too long, showing him their wrinkled appearance.

He just laughed and slipped his fingers through mine so they were intertwined together.

"I thought you had drowned in there," he smiled gently with a concerned look.

"Sorry," I apologized, feeling bad now for keeping him waiting. "I got a little too relaxed."

"Looks like your dad is back," he said, as his gaze moved away from my face to glance over my shoulder though the glass into the living room. "Shall we go in and have a chat? I think we have some planning to do."

"Lead the way," I said, though I wasn't at all eager to get into the Damien Cummings issues surrounding us.

We went back into the condo, where the coven was gathering together to talk things over. Vance led me over to the wall and leaned on it, pulling me so my back lay against him.

We had been standing there for a few minutes, waiting for things to get started when I noticed our reflections in the large mirror decorating the opposite wall.

Vance had apparently noticed the mirror also since he was already looking at me through the glass. I never realized what a handsome couple we made together before now. There was something about us that just fit. It was like we were two separate parts of something that made a whole picture.

I looked at him in question as these thoughts ran through my mind.

He nodded slightly in acknowledgment. "I see it, too," his voice whispered into my mind.

I couldn't look away from the image in front of me. There was just something there, something different about each of us that made us the same. I couldn't explain it, except to say he was my other half, the thing that completed me, and I him.

We just stood there staring at each other until he leaned his head forward and kissed me softly on my neck.

I liked watching him do that in the mirror, and I leaned my head slightly to the left to see if he would do it again.

He laughed quietly, a quick grin spreading across his face, but he still leaned in and obliged me once more.

"Temptress," he accused, and I gladly accepted the title.

Dad began speaking, and I reluctantly turned my attention away from the mirror and the special moment the two of us experienced.

"We need to have a discussion and make some decisions," he said, looking around at each of us seriously.

Grandma stepped forward. "As you know, things are much worse than we expected them to be. We're all kind of at a loss about how to deal with this problem. We've never had to be involved with anything like this before, so any suggestions you may have would be greatly appreciated."

"I think we need more help," Babs said, looking around with a concerned expression. "This guy has proven he's completely evil and has no concern over who he destroys."

"We need to get out of here before we all end up being his lunch, too," Hal said, shaking his head. "I mean, don't get me wrong, I'm all for confronting the guy, but it would be better on our own turf and under our own conditions."

We listened quietly as the conversation bounced back and forth, realizing everyone here was seemingly scared to take Damien on. Not that I blamed them for feeling this way. He terrified me, too.

Finally, Dad turned toward Vance and me. "The two of you have been awfully quiet over there. Do you have anything you want to add?"

I shook my head, not even wanting to be here for this discussion, but Vance spoke up quickly.

"I think we need to bring him to us," he said matter-of-factly.

"What do you mean exactly?" Dad asked, clearly

wanting a better explanation from him.

"I mean I think we should set up a trap for him."

"What kind of trap are you suggesting?" Grandma asked, leaning forward in interest.

Vance shrugged his shoulders, as if setting a trap for his father should be no big deal.

"I say we let him think he's found his next victim. You know, get him really excited," he said.

I turned to look at him with wide eyes, knowing the answer to my question before I even asked it.

"And who, pray tell, will be the bait?"

Chapter 18

"I will be, of course," he replied nonchalantly, looking back at me and holding my gaze stare for stare.

"Absolutely not!" I replied, folding my arms over my chest, knowing this was an issue I wasn't going to budge on.

"Why not?" he asked, quirking an eyebrow, actually having the gall to try and look surprised at my reaction to his suggestion.

"Well, let's see," I began, feeling the heat from my frustration creeping into my cheeks. "You've been running from him your whole life. You lost your mom because of him, and Marsha, not to mention the fact this coven has spent the last two years of their lives trying to keep you hidden from him. Now you want to just waltz in for a family reunion? No! It's too dangerous. I don't want him to hurt you."

I stared, waiting for him to say something, but he just stared back at me. After a moment passed, I turned to face the rest of the group.

"I'll be the bait," I offered, stepping forward, knowing the coven needed another option or they might actually consider what he was suggesting.

"What?" he said loudly, grabbing me by the arm and turning me back to face him. "No! Absolutely not!"

"Well, now you know how I feel!" I shouted back, my eyes flashing in anger as I returned his angry look.

"Kids! Kids!" Dad spoke above us. "Relax! Let's calm down and talk about this together."

Vance and I both stood there glaring at each other, neither one wanting to be the one who gave in.

"I think Portia would be a good person to use in the trap," Dad said, surprising everyone in the room.

"What?" Vance and I both said in unison, as we turned to look at him.

Dad sighed as he shook his head slightly in frustration. "I'm saying I think your idea to reel him into a trap is a good one, Vance, and I think Portia should be the bait."

"Not a chance!" Vance argued, stepping protectively in front of me as he glared angrily at my father.

"Listen to me, Vance," Dad said, holding his hands up in front of himself, trying to calm him down. "I have no intention of putting my daughter in any real danger. We'll just use her to draw him out so we can get him alone somewhere, into a position where we can contain him."

"Contain him? How? And if you manage to succeed, then what?" Vance asked, not letting his guard down for one second.

"I don't know! That's why we're having this little get together," Dad replied in irritation as he waved his hand around at the rest of the group.

"I'd rather you use me as the bait," Vance said in a steely determined voice, not willing to let it go.

"Think about it, Vance," Grandma said suddenly, standing up and coming over to put an arm around his shoulders. "We've been protecting you all this time, and your dad knows it. He sent your mom to get you. You killed her, and disappeared. If all of a sudden you show up right in front of him, in a different country no less, don't you think it would make him a little suspicious?"

The muscles in Vance's jaw were working back and forth

the entire time she was speaking to him, as he clenched his teeth together.

"All right! I see your point," Vance said, folding one arm across his chest and resting his opposite elbow on it so he could reach up to pinch near the bridge of his nose before rubbing there as if he were starting to get a headache. He sat there with his eyes closed for several moments before he spoke again, looking directly at my dad.

"So if I agree to this, and I mean *if,* what do you have in mind?"

"We would need to get him someplace where we'd be able to use our magic without alerting a bunch of people to the fact there are real witches and warlocks out there. And we'd definitely need all of our powers to contain him," Dad said.

"And then what?" Vance asked, becoming quickly agitated again. "We keep him as our pet demon? Come on, people! Think!" He looked around at all of us. "This is a powerful warlock we're talking about. We have no idea how this demon kiss thing is affecting his powers! Does he retain all the power he steals? Does it wear off eventually? If he is retaining everything he steals, then it's going to be a twenty-four-hour job for this coven to contain him, if they even can contain him! And what about when he goes into withdrawal? Are we all just going to sit there and watch him shrivel up and die? He needs to be destroyed … immediately."

Everyone sat there quietly, not knowing what to say to help make the situation better.

"You're right. We aren't prepared," Dad said, standing up to pace the floor. "We need to keep up the surveillance for a while longer, learn his habits and his patterns before we try to make any kind of move."

"Thank you!" Vance said with a wave of his arm,

sounding relieved at the turn of events, before turning around to face me. "You," he said pointing directly at me. "Follow me." He strode past me and down the hall to his room.

I turned to look at Dad, suddenly wishing he needed me to continue on with the conversation.

"Go," he said, waving his hand in dismissal.

I sighed and turned to follow down the hall after Vance. He was standing at the door holding it open for me. I walked through, and he closed it behind me.

"What the heck was all that? Offering yourself up as bait! What are you thinking?" he asked, walking up to stand toe to toe with me, glaring down.

"I'm thinking I've nearly lost you twice because of this man. First, when your mom took you, and second, when you left me to chase him. I won't let it happen again," I said stubbornly lifting my chin, returning his glare.

"So you're just going to sacrifice yourself to the cause?" he asked angrily, pursing his lips together in a flat line.

I knew he was really mad since I could see flaming red lines beginning to shoot through his eyes.

"If it's what it takes to keep you safe," I answered softly, not looking away.

"Portia," he said, shaking his head as he lowered his voice a little, "you're a walking ball of contradictions. You keep talking about how you don't want to lose me. What exactly do you think will happen if he gets his hands on you?"

I turned away from him and walked over toward the dresser reaching out to run my finger absently along the edge of the fine wood.

"If I were captured I know all of you would come after me," I said, afraid to look at him for fear of how he would react to my reasoning. "Hopefully, he'd consider my powers worthy enough to perform a kiss on rather than kill me or change me. You guys could catch him, destroy him, and I'd still get to have you. I'd just be completely human," I stated, biting my bottom lip in trepidation as I waited for him to respond.

"So let me get this straight," he said, coming up behind me, and I could feel his warm breath blowing against my neck, he was so close. "You're willing to risk being captured, losing your powers, or being killed, on the off chance it might do something to protect me?"

"That about sums it up," I said quietly, too nervous to turn around and confront him directly at the moment.

"Aarrrgh!" he grunted loudly.

I heard him walk away from me, so I turned and was just in time to see him running his hands over his face in an extremely irritated gesture.

He went across the room and leaned up against the opposite wall, staring over at me.

I leaned against the dresser, returning his look.

"Heck, Portia. I don't know whether to kiss you or strangle you right now. I just don't get how you think!" he complained loudly.

"What's not to get?" I stepped angrily toward him, shouting because he wasn't listening. "I love you! I don't want to see you get hurt! I can't lose you! How do you not understand that?"

"Exactly!" he hollered back. "But you're willing to sacrifice yourself and put *me* through the very same horror!"

I suddenly realized what he was saying. The two of us were fighting over the same thing.

"So it's okay for you to do it to me, but not the other way around?" I asked, hurt by his double standard.

He rubbed a hand over his face in frustration once

again. "Yes. No. I don't know." He looked at me seriously. "It's my job to keep you safe, not the other way around."

"Maybe you haven't heard about this woman's rights movement we have in society today. It isn't your job to do anything!" I said loudly to him. "When people love each other, they should both be looking out for each other. I'm a big girl! I can sure as heck take care of myself!"

He pushed away from the wall and walked over next to me, and I could see a dangerous glint in his eye.

"You listen to me and you'd better listen carefully," he said deadly serious. "It will always be my *job* to take care of you! Maybe that's a poor choice of words on my part, but you need to get this through that thick skull of yours! I love you, and there's nothing, *nothing*, more important to me than you or your safety. I'll do *anything* required of me to accomplish that goal! Do you understand? Because I'm not going to keep fighting with you about this!"

"So this subject is closed then? The mighty Vance has spoken. I have to do whatever you think is best, regardless of what I think?" I threw back at him.

"Sounds good to me," he said, crossing his arms over his chest, refusing to budge on the issue.

I glared up into his red eyes. "You're being a selfish pig!" I shouted at him, resorting to name calling since that was the only weapon I had left.

"Better than being as stubborn as a mule!" he shot back angrily.

"Well, forgive me for caring!" I yelled, shoving passed him to go out the door, slamming it behind me as hard as I could.

Twelve faces stared in shock at me from the other room, and it was clear they had heard pretty much every word we said to each other.

"I'll be on the beach!" I said way too loudly to them,

before striding down the hall and out the front door.

I ran down the stairwell instead of waiting for the elevator, and I kept running, through the breezeway, past the pool, and down the concrete steps toward the ocean.

When I reached the sand, I sat down on the steps and removed my shoes, before walking out onto the clean, beautiful beach.

A vendor selling straw bags immediately approached me, trying to sell his wares to a new potential client.

"No, thank you." I said passing him quickly, not wanting to talk with anyone let alone haggle over the price of something. I continued down to the water's edge, walking to a spot where no one else was around.

I sat down, pulling my legs up to my chest and wrapped my arms around them. The tears came of their own accord. I couldn't stop them, so I let them flow down my cheeks freely as I watched the waves rolling in to crash upon the shore.

This was our first big fight, at least the first that had occurred when he wasn't going through a demon conversion.

I didn't know how I could make him understand my fear of losing him. It was all-consuming to me these days. When he left me, it had broken my heart, not to mention that I feared for his life. Now, after seeing his dad in action, these feelings had only intensified. I wished I could make him understand how desperate I felt about the situation.

I didn't look at him when he came and sat next to me in the sand a few moments later.

He didn't say anything, and neither did I.

Eventually, he started digging for broken shells, accumulating quite a pile before he began throwing the hard objects out into the water.

I watched as he would get them to skip across the

surface, amazed he could do it over the moving surf, but I still didn't speak, and neither did he.

When he finally got tired of throwing things, he lay back onto the sand, placing his hands behind his head and closing his eyes. He was still for so long, I started to wonder if maybe he had actually fallen asleep next to me.

I didn't move, though, instead choosing to continue staring out at the water in front of me.

The sun continued its trek across the sky, until it was beginning its late afternoon dip.

We still hadn't said a word to each other. The tide started to drift out, and he got up to walk out in front of me, exploring over the wet sand the water had left behind, kicking things here and there with his bare feet.

I watched him walk over to where some rough corral was exposed, leaving some little pools of water captured in its borders.

He sat on his haunches and looked into the water, checking for any hidden treasures that might have been left behind in the tiny pools. I saw him smile suddenly, and he pushed up the sleeves of his shirt, reaching into one of the holes to pull something out.

He trotted back over to me and plopped back down into the sand by my side. He gently placed a big beautiful white shell next to me.

I paused for a moment before I picked it up and examined it. Whatever had lived in it wasn't there anymore. It was cracked open enough to show it was empty inside.

"Clam shell?" I asked, curiously as I ran a finger over the hard ridges in its design.

He nodded.

"It's very pretty. Thank you," I said, turning it over in my hand, continuing to look at.

"No problem," he said.

We looked at each other for a few moments, several emotions mirroring on each other's faces.

"Aren't you going to say anything?" I sighed, feeling exhausted over the whole ordeal.

"Nope," he said, shaking his head. "I figured when you were ready to start talking to me again, then you would."

"So you'd rather just sit here in silence and let me pout?" I asked, wondering if I'd ever truly understand how the male brain worked.

"Are we talking now?" he asked, watching me intently.

I thought for a moment before I answered him. "Yes. I believe we are."

"All right, then understand this please, Portia," he began. "I'd rather sit right here next to you and have you never speak to me again, then to have you walk out on me like you did earlier. That was a horrible thing to experience, and I don't want to ever feel that way again."

I swallowed hard as the tears threatened to make their way to the surface once more.

"We've never fought like this before," I said softly.

He scooted up next to me, placing his arm around me and pulling me up against him.

"Don't cry, please," he whispered into my hair near my ear as he nuzzled against me. "Please forgive me for being so awful."

"I was the awful one." I sniffed, wiping away a traitorous tear with the back of my hand.

"Okay," he said with a little grin. "We were both awful. How about we just call a truce?"

I nodded. "I want to do that, but I still feel the same way about everything."

"So do I," he replied. "We're arguing for the same thing, though, just from each other's different perspective on the issue."

"I know. I just don't know how to make you understand."

He laughed then. "And I feel exactly the same way."

"So we just agree to disagree?" I asked, wondering how that made things any better.

He nodded. "On this subject, yes, I think it would be for the best."

"And what happens when the coven picks one of us to be the lure?"

"We'll cross that bridge when, and if, we come to it," he stated very matter-of-factly.

"And what about the fighting? I don't like it," I said. I leaned my head against his shoulder.

"Me, either," he replied, giving me a little squeeze. "I hate it. But I do think it's stemming from things we've gone through lately and things we haven't addressed."

"So now we can't handle stress?" I asked, feeling like I was failing miserably at the tests and trials of my life lately.

"Portia, what we've been experiencing does not fall into the simple bounds of stress. We sat and watched as three innocent people were eaten alive, ripped to shreds before our very eyes," he reminded me.

"Don't talk about it!" I said sharply as the images flashed before me, and the awful churning in my stomach returned instantly.

"We have to," he said, taking my chin in his hand and turning me to face him.

I tried averting my eyes.

"Portia, look at me," he said softly, his face filled with love and concern for my wellbeing. "We need to acknowledge the truth. What we saw was awful and evil. But that isn't what's really bothering you."

I did look at him, wondering where he was heading with this conversation, but he stopped speaking as he stared at me.

He stood up and offered his hand out to me.

I took it, letting him pull me to my feet, and followed him as he led me back up the beach.

"Where are we going?" I asked, wondering why we were leaving when we'd just started communicating.

"To finish this discussion in a more private place," he said, rubbing his thumb over my hand as we walked together.

We entered the condo quietly, and he led me into his bedroom where he shut and locked the door behind us.

I went over and sat on the end of the bed, looking up at him as he moved to stand in front of me.

"You're frightened because he's my father," he said, jumping right back into the conversation without any preamble to give me warning where this conversation was headed.

I shook my head and looked away. "No," I said, unable to meet his gaze since he was hitting far too close to the truth for me to feel comfortable.

"Yes," he said, kneeling down in front of me, forcing me to look at him. "It's all right, Portia. I'm not going to turn into him."

"How can you know that for sure? It's been his intention for you since you were young. He's been chasing after you your whole life, not to mention he almost succeeded with his plans once."

"But he didn't, thanks to you and your magic." he replied, reaching out to take both of my hands in his.

"Yes. And you just keep running back to him now, don't you?" I said with a hint of accusation in my voice.

"Is that what you think?" He looked up at me, searching my eyes. "That I want to go to him?"

"It's all you talk about," I said, my emotions beginning

to surface once again. "It's always about leaving me to protect me, and going to find him. I can't take it anymore."

"But I'm doing it because I love you and I want a life with you," he sighed in exasperation.

"I know, but it still seems to bring the same result," I said, really trying to explain to him, to help him understand what I was really feeling. "You're gone, and we're not together. Whether it's because you've been taken against your will, or because you've chosen to face it head on, it always results in you leaving me, and it hurts."

"Oh, baby, that's not my intention," he said softly. "Not ever. It hurts for me too when we're apart, remember?"

"Yeah, but that never seems to stop you," I replied, honestly, wanting to let him know just how much it wounded me.

"Well, consider it stopped as of right now then. I promise not to ever leave you behind again," he stated, a light beginning to shine in his eyes. "All right? We'll fight this thing together or not at all."

"Really?" I asked, afraid to believe in what he was telling me. "No more of this super protector thing?"

"Who am I kidding?" he laughed. "You're the one who's done the majority of the saving in this relationship. Maybe my ego is bruised and that's why I'm acting this way."

"Whatever," I said, with a small smile, loving that his sense of humor was surfacing.

"Are we good?"

"We're good," I said, returning his smile.

"Come here." He stood up and pulled me tightly into his strong embrace.

I wrapped my arms around his neck, laying my head against his shoulder, my eyes watching his pulse beat strongly in his neck.

He clasped his hands together around my back,

squeezing me hard in a giant bear hug.

"I love you so much, Portia," he said softly against my ear. "I wish I knew how to show it to you so you could really understand."

"Just having you here with me shows me enough," I said, tipping my head back to look up at him.

He bent over and kissed me.

The Demon Kiss

Chapter 19

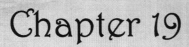

It was evening when we finally finished up dinner with everyone and gathered to discuss things once more.

"So, let's try this again," Dad said, giving a warning glance over toward Vance and me.

"Wait," Vance said abruptly, and all eyes turned to look at him. "I have something I need to say to everyone."

"Go ahead," Dad replied.

"Well, first I'd like to apologize on behalf of Portia and myself for our behavior earlier. We've been under a lot of strain lately, as you all know, and we'd reached a breaking point. I know this doesn't excuse the way we acted, but we're both truly sorry for any discomfort we may've caused any of you during our little tirade."

Everyone nodded in understanding as Vance looked around at each one of them before he continued.

"The second thing I need to tell all of you is, regardless of however we decide to handle this thing, neither Portia, or myself, is to be used as the person who will draw my dad out into the open."

Everyone looked up at us in surprise.

"Under the circumstances, we feel it to be in the best interest of our relationship to remain together in our approach of this thing," Vance said. He reached over and took my hand. "Using one or the other of us is just too difficult for the person left behind to handle."

There was silence in the room as everyone absorbed what he was saying. I knew this had been a difficult thing for him to do. He felt strongly he should be the bait in this situation, since it was his father we were dealing with. He was doing this for me, to protect my feelings once again, placing me first in front of everything else in his life.

"All right," Dad said after a minute. "We appreciate your openness, and we'll see what we can do when and if the situation arises."

"Thank you," Vance said, pulling me close. "It means a lot to both of us."

Dad turned back to face the rest of the group. "Does anyone else have anything to add?" When no one answered, he continued on. "Very well then, I took the liberty of drawing up some surveillance itineraries. Basically it'll just be more of the same. Watching the warehouse, which I think Juan could easily keep track of for us, and keeping a heavy scrutiny on the house, or possibly tailing Damien if the need arises. Are we all onboard with that?"

Everyone seemed to be in agreement.

"Now obviously we can't afford to spend Vance's entire trust fund renting fishing boats to keep an eye on the place. And after what happened before, I think it would be in our best interest to remain away from the regular marina just in case things aren't as patched up as we hoped they'd be with Enrico and his crew. My suggestion is the purchase of a regular motor boat and a trailer, something small enough that we can pull it into the secured parking lot here during the day and take it out at night when we might need it."

"I think this is a great idea," Vance agreed with Dad. "I'd also have two motors put on it. One more powerful that we can get up some speed out of, and one that'll run quietly so we can maneuver around without making a big distraction if the need arises."

"That's a very good idea," my dad agreed. "I'm also thinking evening surveillances would be our best bet. It was too hard to see into the window during the day last time. Now, I also need to know if anyone is having any pressing matters they need to return home for."

There were several who commented, saying they needed to go back to Sedona for work since their Christmas vacation time was coming to an end.

"I'm going to encourage you to go home and do the things you need to do," Dad said to these individuals. "I have no idea how long we're going to be here. If the situation becomes too desperate for us who'll remain—we can always fly you in if the need arises."

The meeting was finally adjourned after much discussion, and it was decided we would be sending everyone back to Sedona except for me, Vance, Dad, Grandma, Brad and Shelly.

"I'm glad everyone is going back," I said later, when Vance and I were sitting out on the balcony with Brad and Shelly.

"Why?" Shelly asked, looking a little surprised.

"Some of them seem scared. I don't think they wanted to be here anymore."

"I got the same feeling," Vance said.

"Well, we're still here for you," Brad said reaching over to grasp Shelly by the hand, and Vance started laughing at his comment.

"What?" Brad asked, looking a little perplexed.

"I'm not trying to sound stuck up in anyway, but doesn't it seem kind of ironic that the full-fledged witches and warlocks are running home, while the newbies are here sticking things out? You two rock," he said as he smiled genuinely over at them.

"Maybe we're just too dumb to know better," Shelly

suggested with a shrug of her shoulders.

"I don't think that's it," Vance replied, growing somber now. "Brad was on the boat. I promise he remembers everything he saw that night. He knows exactly what we're going up against."

We were all silent as we remembered.

"I wish I'd been there," Shelly said quietly with a dejected sigh, a forlorn look passing across her face.

"No, you don't," I said quickly. "Trust me, Shelly, it was not a pretty thing to see, and I didn't even watch it all."

"You didn't?" she asked, seeming surprised by this little tidbit of volunteered information.

"No. Vance wouldn't let me," I told her honestly. "Even he didn't watch everything that happened, choosing instead to try and help calm me down."

"It wasn't the only reason I didn't watch," Vance said, turning to look at me as he swallowed thickly before he continued. "I couldn't watch them consume the blood. It was too … hard."

It never occurred to me until that moment he might have desired to be a part of the blood lust. That comment did scare me a little.

"Shelly, the things that happened were awful," Brad said, redirecting the subject before I could say anything more to Vance's comment. "If I could burn them from my mind, I would."

"Oh," was all she said.

Dad walked out onto the porch. "Hey, kids. You might want to think about calling it a night. We have a full day of things we need to do tomorrow," he said.

"All right, Dad." I stretched out, a sudden yawn overtaking me. "Thanks. We'll head that way now."

We slowly got up from our chairs and filed back inside.

Vance started pulling me toward his room, but I

stopped him, and he turned to face me with a questioning look in his eyes.

"I'm going to sleep with Shelly tonight," I said, softly, even though there were questions I wanted to ask him.

"Is everything okay?" he asked, looking surprised. "Is this about our argument earlier?"

"No. We're good, I promise," I smiled, squeezing his hand slightly. "I just think Shelly's feeling a little left out again. I want to see if I can help her feel better about things."

"Oh. All right then," he said as he leaned over to kiss me goodnight. "Sleep good," he added, stepping away from me, stretching our clasped hands between us until the connection broke.

"You, too," I replied, watching him go until he entered his bedroom and closed the door. I turned and entered into my room.

"Are you getting your pajamas?" Shelly asked me casually, as she watched me move toward the dresser.

"No. Well, yes, I am, but I meant I'm spending the night in here tonight," I replied.

"Are you and Vance still fighting?" she asked me, sounding really concerned about it.

"No." I smiled at her. "I just wanted to hang out here with you tonight."

"Cool!" she said, brightening instantly.

"Actually, I thought I'd tell you about the night on the boat," I replied watching for her reaction. "If you really think you want to know, that is. It was pretty gruesome."

She thought about it for a moment before she spoke. "It just seems like everyone else knows exactly what happened, and I don't. I know it's a dumb reason, but it's the truth."

"Do you want to know then?" I asked her again.

She nodded. "Yes. I do," she replied firmly, sounding

completely sure of her decision this time.

I began to talk, as I got ready for bed, starting with when we first got on the boat, meeting Enrico and his crew, and then working my way through all the events that occurred throughout the day.

She listened with rapt attention to every word I spoke, rarely even stopping me to ask a question.

When I finally reached the part about the demon kiss and the men who were fed upon by Damien and his followers, I could see a sickened look pass over her face, but I didn't skip a single detail, choosing not to sugar coat it.

I continued on with the story about all the hysteria I caused for the crew with my actions and of rigging the boat to fool the fishermen, trying to keep them in the dark about the magic.

She laughed a little at that part.

"So that's all of it," I said at the end of my narration. "You know everything that happened after that."

"Thank you," she said, looking relieved, like a huge burden had been lifted from her mind. "And I'm really sorry it was so traumatic for all of you." she added sympathetically.

I sighed heavily. "I just wish this was all over. I miss just being a normal person with a normal life."

"You're a witch, Portia," she said as she laughed at me. "You'll never be normal again."

"True," I replied, pondering much longer on her comment than she was even aware.

"So is your mom leaving tomorrow with the others?" Shelly asked, changing the subject.

"Yes. The hospital called and said they need her to come back to work," I explained absently.

"You and I should get up early so we can make something great for breakfast for everyone before they leave."

"That sounds like fun. What should we make?" I asked wondering if she had something specific in mind.

"Let's make strawberry crepes," she said. "We have all the stuff for it. I was with your mom when she bought it."

"It sounds delicious," I replied, as I crawled under the quilt and pulled it up to my chin. "As long as Dad doesn't have any other things he needs us to do, I think it'll be a fine idea."

Shelly used a little of her simulated magic to conjure up enough power to turn out the light.

"I don't think I'll ever get used to this lifestyle," she said, and I could hear the grin in her voice.

"It isn't always what it's cracked up to be." I smiled, thinking back to my life's simpler times, but those had been without Vance, I reminded myself.

"Maybe for you!" she replied, breaking back into my thoughts. "Goodnight, Portia."

"Goodnight, Shelly."

I closed my eyes knowing he was listening. He had been listening to every word since he left me earlier.

"I love you, Vance," I said in my head, happy he was still near enough to talk to.

"I love you, too, baby," he answered back softly into my mind. "You were right to tell her everything."

"Do you think so?"

"I do. She needs to feel like she's a part of everything that's going on around here. After all it was when she'd been isolated from your life before that my mom was able to get to her. We don't want her susceptible to anything like that again."

"Thanks for caring about her," I said, before adding, "I'm sure missing lying next to you tonight."

"You're welcome to come and join me," he replied. "I

miss having you, too."

"I can't." I sighed, really wishing I could. "She'd be hurt if she woke up and I wasn't here."

"I know. But hey, look on the bright side. Breakfast sounds wonderful." He chuckled.

"You might want to hold that comment until you taste it. I've never made crepes before," I warned him. "I'm not sure if Shelly has either. It could turn out to be a disaster."

"I'm sure they'll taste fine," he said, encouraging me.

"You know what I want?" I asked. "I mean really, really want."

"What do you want?" He waited for my answer.

"I want to wake up every morning and make you breakfast," I said, smiling at the thought.

He was quiet for a few moments.

"I would really like that, too." he replied back finally. "Except for one thing, I think."

"What's that?"

"Some mornings I want to be the one to make breakfast for you," he said. "I like doing things for you, too."

I smiled bigger. "That does sound pretty nice."

"Hopefully someday soon," he replied.

"I wish for that, too."

"Get some sleep, baby," he whispered.

"You, too. Goodnight," I said back to him, and I slowly drifted off to sleep.

I woke up some time later while it was still dark. It was still well before sunrise when I wandered out onto the balcony from the sliding glass door in our bedroom. I pulled a chair up close to the wall so Shelly could see me if she woke up and know I hadn't abandoned her.

It was chilly, though, so I wrapped my sweater around myself a little tighter as I burrowed back against the chair, crouching myself into a tiny ball to conserve body heat. I closed my eyes and just sat in the dark listening to the sound of the relentless surf with its relaxing push and pull.

After a little while of dozing on and off, I stood and went over to the rail, looking down, trying to see the water moving beneath me. I could see the beach, as it was dimly lit by light from the grounds of the resort, but the water faded out into the darkness making it difficult to see on this moonless night.

I suddenly felt the urge to go sit by the water and let my mind just be. I needed to let things go.

Slipping back into the bedroom, I fumbled around in the dark until I found where I left my slippers under the bed, sliding my feet into them.

I quietly tiptoed out the door, through the living room and down the hall, pausing for a moment at Vance's door to invite him to come with me. I thought better of it, though, worried about offending Shelly if she woke and found me out with him when I had committed to spend the night with her. I didn't want her to feel left out of things again.

I moved silently out the front door, shutting it softly behind me, before I hurried over to the elevator and pushed the button to go down, waiting impatiently for it to make its way back up from the ground floor to get me.

Soon, I found myself at the steps to the sand, and I ran down to the water's inviting edge. I sat on the ground, much as I had earlier the day before and stared out into the drifting sea. I couldn't see out very far, but I was able to make out the small white caps of the waves as they rolled inward before thy crashed heavily into the shoreline.

It was very soothing to me. The ebb and flow did a lot to calm my turbulent spirit which was churning inside me. I thought of the argument I had been in with Vance, and I could easily see we were both suffering, yet we both desired to be part of the same goals.

I suddenly felt very selfish for fighting with him earlier. He really was trying to make things better for both of us I realized. I needed to apologize and tell him to do whatever it was he felt necessary regarding the situation we were finding ourselves in. I wasn't going to hold him back from doing whatever he felt was right.

Sighing, I felt a huge weight lift off me, and I knew this was the right thing for me to do.

I continued to sit by the water, watching as a pre-dawn fog began to drift in toward the shore.

"What are you doing down there, pretty girl?" I heard Vance's voice in my head, and I jumped at the unexpected sound, being completely unprepared for the intrusion into my thoughts, though it was a welcome one.

Turning slightly, I looked up toward the resort, and I could see him standing out on the balcony at the railing, softly illuminated by the dim lights that were shining on the property.

I stood up and waved my hand, smiling at him, though I didn't know if he could see that at all.

"I've been thinking about a lot of things," I said, through our connection, wanting to share my self-discoveries with him, while also wondering why he had awakened so early.

"Do you feel better?" he asked, as I stood brushing the sand that was sticking to me from my shorts and legs before I began to walk through the mist-shrouded air toward him.

"Much," I said, suddenly worried he might have awakened because he was having trouble from withdrawal again.

"Good." he replied. "I'm glad."

"Actually, I feel better than I have in a long time." I said, turning to look at a movement that caught my eye in the swirling fog.

Fog! The fear streaked through me instantly, my body going on full alert as I looked about in trepidation.

"What is it?" Vance asked, feeling my sudden alarm, and I felt him tense in return.

A figure stepped out of the shadows and walked straight toward me, and I recognized the scene from my nightmares instantly.

"Hello, Portia," Damien Cummings said, as a smile spread across his face. "It's a lovely morning for a walk, isn't it?"

I swung my face back around toward Vance, hoping with every fiber of my being that I was dreaming.

"Vance!" I screamed with all my might, feeling like the word was being dragged slowly from my mouth.

"Run, Portia!" he yelled, reaching out toward me, and I started to run toward him, my legs feeling like they were lined with lead in the sand.

Two very strong arms reached around my waist and lifted me into the air. I saw a fireball shoot out of Vance's outstretched hand, heading at a rapid pace straight for us. I struggled to get away from the iron grip that held me prisoner, fearful we would both be hit by the onslaught of powerful magic shooting out from Vance.

At the last possible second, the fireball was diverted by some unseen magical force, zipping passed us harmlessly, and I saw Vance lift his arm again, ready for another attack.

It was the last thing I remembered as I felt the hard stick of something sharp into the side of my neck.

Then everything went black.

The Demon Kiss

Chapter 20

It was dark. Something was wrong—really wrong, I just couldn't quite place what that something was. I tried to rouse myself some more, but everything in my head seemed so foggy.

I felt the crush then as the physical pain of separation filled my being, signaling that Vance was no longer near me. *Has he left me again?* I thought, confused, and I felt panic rising as my mind sought desperately to fill in the blanks. *Why would he leave me? Hadn't we worked everything out?*

No, I thought, and I had a sinking feeling as I remembered. I left him, or more appropriately, I had been taken from him. The images of my capture on the beach now danced vividly inside my head.

"Is our little girl coming around finally?" a strong voice I never wanted to hear again permeated the air around me, sending a jolt of fear into my cloudy mind. "Open your eyes, Portia. It's a beautiful day today. The sun is shining, everything is going as it should be, and you're missing it."

My eyes opened immediately in response to the request, even though I had no intention of doing so. This was instantly irritating to me, but being able to see what was going on around me could have its advantages. I fought to focus on the fuzzy images that floated in my sight, blinking several times to try and get through the haziness, before my vision finally cleared.

I was restrained in a very comfortable chair, in a small space of some sort. Damien Cummings was sitting across from me, holding a champagne glass which appeared to be partially filled with blood, watching me with great interest it seemed.

We were on an airplane, I soon realized as I began to recognize the whirring sounds of the engine floating in the air around us.

"It's a great day for a flight, don't you agree?" Damien asked me, and he gave a quick glance out the window at his left, as if to survey the world that was zipping by below us.

I resisted the urge to follow his look toward the outside world, wondering whether or not it would yield any clues to my location, choosing instead to keep my attention on my untrustworthy opponent.

A smartly uniformed woman came down the aisle, holding a crystal container which carried some of the same red liquid inside and offered to refill Damien's glass for him. He let her do so, then returned his gaze to me when she turned to walk back in the direction she had come from.

"So I'm guessing you have a lot of questions right now. Feel free to ask me anything," he said as he swirled the macabre drink around in his cup before inhaling the aroma of the contents with a deep sniff.

I didn't say a word, preferring to just sit there and glare at him, wishing I could burn a hole with my vision right through his perfectly coiffed head.

"Not too talkative this morning, are you? No worries. I don't mind doing all the talking." He smiled and gave me a wink, before taking another swallow of the disgusting looking liquid in the glass. He closed his eyes for a moment, rolling the fluid around in his mouth, as if savoring the taste of a fine wine, his face completely enraptured in that second of time, before he opened his eyes and began speaking again. "Do you want to know how I found you?" he asked. "It's a great story. You'd probably really enjoy it."

I just looked at him, trying to have a disinterested expression, but not knowing if I was really pulling it off or not.

"I'm hurt at your rudeness this morning, Portia," he said, feigning a sad expression on his face. "I was under the general impression you've never had any problem whatsoever when it comes to conversing with my son."

"You leave him out of this," I spat, my anger coming swiftly to the surface at his casual reference to Vance. "After all you've done to him, you aren't even worthy to speak his name!"

He smiled widely, looking very pleased with himself and the reaction he had gotten from me.

"There's the little spitfire I've been waiting for," he said with a slight wink in my direction. "That's much better. Now we can have ourselves a nice little conversation together."

I instantly regretted speaking out, falling prey to his game which he was intent on playing with me.

"That boy of mine is something else, isn't he?" Damien continued on, baiting me with his words. "I think I knew he was going to be something fantastic from the moment of his birth."

He took another large swallow of the red liquid, the supreme satisfaction moving across his face once again.

"Where are my manners?" he said suddenly, as if he were completely horrified with himself. He sat up a little straighter, tipping his glass slightly toward me. "Would you like something to drink?"

I stared hotly at him, hoping he could see my anger over the fact that he was offering me the blood of some innocent witch or warlock to drink.

"It's an excellent vintage," he said, swirling the contents. "The best I've ever had, in fact. I like to call it, Le Sangue de Vance."

My face blanched instantly, and I didn't need a translator to know what he had said. He was drinking Vance's blood!

What's happened? Where is Vance? What has he done to him? The thoughts raced frantically through my head, and I felt my panic level begin to rise to the extreme.

"Don't worry," he said, reading my reaction to his comments perfectly. "Your lover boy is safe and sound. As a matter of fact, he's still in residence with your sweet little coven back in Mexico." He looked at the contents of the glass again. "No. This lovely blood was an early gift from my lately departed wife, Krista. I believe you were acquainted with her?"

His eyes bore into mine as he questioned me, but all I could feel was the rush of relief running through me. He didn't have Vance. Vance was safe. He was still with the coven. They would protect him.

"I've been saving this particular bottle for a special occasion, seeing how you destroyed the entire shipment she was going to have sent to me," Damien continued on. "That was very disappointing."

He gave me a look, like that of a father disciplining his child, which I returned to him stare for stare.

"I must say I'm very interested in finding out how you managed to stop his demon conversion, however. That's been quite unheard of before now. Would you care to share?" he asked me.

He lifted an eyebrow.

When I didn't answer, he continued.

"No? Well, maybe later then," he said, with a

nonchalant shrug, as he repeated his previous move of swirling, sniffing and tasting the blood in his glass, making an obvious show of his delight in the mixture.

It made me sick to my stomach to watch him, to know he was devouring a part of Vance in that way. I tried not to let it get to me, since I knew he was deliberately baiting me with it.

He was quiet for several moments while he sat and watched me. Having nothing else better to do, I returned his stare, not wanting to show any weakness. We sat that way for what seemed like ages before he spoke again.

"Imagine my surprise when I was sitting in my home the other night, having just performed a ritual on the most stunning little witch from India, only to look out my window and see the most magnificent surge of magical power rushing through the air, one that put the India witch's powers to shame," he said, never taking his eyes off my face.

I began to have a sinking feeling as he spoke.

"You may not be aware of this, but after a transfer of power is complete, one becomes extremely sensitive to the magic running in the currents around them. It's quite an exhilarating feeling," he explained as he watched me carefully. "But I'm diverting from the subject."

He paused to take another swallow from the glass, and I watched as his Adam's apple bobbed in his throat with the action, feeling nauseous at the sight.

"I looked out my window to see a beautiful burst of color in the sky over a small fishing boat out in the bay," he was saying, as he waved his arm in a circle over his head. "It captured my interest instantly. I grabbed my telescope and looked out only to discover this wonderful girl all lit up on the deck of this particular tiny watercraft. Certainly you must imagine my surprise as the vessel turned in the water and went out, not only to rescue my earlier guest from certain death, but to see my own son crawl out of the water with her."

I was going to vomit. It was entirely my fault. My magical display had alerted him to our presence.

"I was very excited, of course!" he continued, as a devious light began to dance over his face. "I began to plan my family reunion immediately. Of course, it occurred to me my boy might not come to me alone, of his own free will—even if I invited him, so I made a new plan. I decided I'd invite a guest I knew he'd have to come see."

I was bait. He was going to use me to draw Vance to him.

He smiled, and he looked positively evil, his features taking on cunning light. I couldn't help the little shiver of fear that danced down my spine.

"I kept watch, looking for a time when I might be able to catch you alone. I have to give a little credit to that son of mine. He doesn't let you wander too far away from his side, does he?"

He looked me up and down, as if he were judging a piece of meat in a contest. His perusal revolted my senses.

"Not that I blame him. You look like you might be quite a tasty little treat. I'm sure he was enjoying you quite regularly," he said suggestively, cheapening our very relationship with his words.

I looked away from him, toward the window, not wanting to give his lewd comments the dignity of my response.

"No?" He laughed as he continued to look me over provocatively. "I must admit I'm surprised. The kid must have morals of steel. He probably got those from his mother—you know, before she woke up and realized what I really had to offer her."

"You're a very sick man," I said quietly, wondering why I suddenly was wishing I could reason with him somehow.

"Really?" he replied, perking right up at my response. "Please, my dear. Enlighten me."

"You had everything in your life that's worth anything. A beautiful, loving wife, a wonderful son, and still you threw it all away." I paused. "Vance is the most perfect individual I've ever known. He's good to the very center of his being. Why would you want to destroy all that?" I asked, wishing in that moment I could understand his sense of reasoning and what was driving him.

He laughed. "Don't worry, my dear Portia. You'll come to understand. I'm glad to see you love him so much, because I have plans for both of you. All these warm and fuzzy feelings the two of you have for each other will make things work out even better."

"Please leave him alone!" I begged him. "Do whatever you want with me—just please let him live his life."

He placed his glass down and started clapping his hands together in slow rhythm.

"Bravo, Portia! Acting as the martyr!" He laughed at my pain, his cynical smile moving across his face. "You never cease to surprise me this morning! Here I thought I'd end up with a crying, cowardly girl and have instead found you to be a delightful little witch. And, of course, I mean that with the deepest respect. I may even think some more of my son at the moment. Apparently he's pretty smart, falling for someone like you. He does have some taste for the finer things in life." He smiled as he reached out and picked up his glass, holding it out toward me.

I looked at him in disgust.

"Cheers!" he said, before he downed the entire contents, drinking every last drop.

It made me sick to watch him. I turned to look out the

window as we flew over the desert landscape below.

"Where are we going?" I asked, deciding to try to get some more information out of him.

He shook his finger back and forth at me. "No, no," he replied, looking at me with a patronizing expression. "That's a surprise for later."

"Whatever." I closed my eyes, silently wishing I would never have to look at him again.

"Don't worry. You won't be disappointed. I promise," he added, his voice thick with amusement.

I opened my eyes, allowing them to flash angrily over at him. "I don't care where it is, I won't be there long. I'm positive Vance and the other members of the coven are on their way to find me right now!"

"Oh touché," he replied, watching me curiously. "But I wouldn't count on seeing your family any time soon."

"What have you done?" Fear rose into my throat, tasting just like bile, as a million maniacal plans he could have implemented began dancing in my head.

He laughed again. "Me?" he asked innocently, lifting a hand and placing it upon his chest. "I haven't done anything to anyone. I just happened to leave Vance a little message behind, where I was sure he'd find it."

"What message?" I asked, a nervous feeling beginning to float through my body.

"When he goes to storm my house looking for you, he'll find a little note from daddy explaining if he doesn't come to me alone, he'll never see you alive again. I was very careful to tell him if I see one person from the disgusting, measly, little coven of yours in the same city we're in, I'll kill you on the spot. Trust me—I'm positive he'll be coming by himself." His eyes flashed at me.

I knew he was right. There was no way Vance would risk putting me in any more danger than I already was. If he had to magically contain the entire coven to keep them from following him, he would.

I felt a sick, sinking feeling in the pit of my stomach. It was going to be just the two of us against him now.

"He might not come," I bluffed, with a very slight shrug. "He doesn't know where we are."

"Don't worry about that." He smiled at me. "I've been sure to leave an appropriate trail of bread crumbs for him to follow. It may take him a while to get to us, but he'll find his way. I promise."

I tried changing my tactics then, needing to throw him off his game somehow. Plus I wanted to knock some of the self-assuredness off his face.

"So what's so great about this demon kiss?" I asked, trying to appear nonchalant while completely switching gears.

He grinned widely at my question. "You surprise me again, Portia! Now you're changing tactics to gain information. I'm impressed!"

"Well?" I replied, not bothering to deny it.

He stared at me for a moment as if weighing whether or not to tell me what I was asking for.

"First of all, I prefer to call it an exchange, not a demon kiss," he said, making a face as if the very words put some sort of distaste into his mouth. "The exchange is a most exhilarating experience. The power moves into you and heightens your senses to an unheard of extreme. Magic flows in the very currents around you, and everything twists together into something like this great soup of power. It flows through your being, racing as it sings. The only problem is it doesn't last more than a few hours. Sure, you get to retain most of the individual witch or warlock's powers permanently, but the rush leaves much too quickly."

I laughed as I stared at him. "So you're just a glorified

junkie! You're destroying all these people so you can get high!" I exclaimed.

He lost his cool demeanor at that remark, leaning forward to grab me at the collar of my shirt. He yanked me toward him—his eyes turning the all too familiar bloodshot red as his teeth sharpened into fangs in front of me.

"Watch your mouth, you little witch, or I'll kill you right here, right now," he threatened in a menacing voice, and I knew he meant it.

"Go right ahead," I spat back at him vehemently, not backing down one inch.

He let go of me suddenly and leaned back in his chair while pointing a finger slowly at me. He smiled then as if he had just figured out something that he had missed before.

"You're linked to him, aren't you?" he said, suddenly making the connection. "What did he do? A binding spell perhaps?"

I closed my eyes, knowing he had gained too much information, mentally kicking myself for giving too much away.

"You want me to kill you so he'll know you're dead. You don't want him to come, but you know he's following that link," he added.

He laughed then, and I opened my eyes to watch him again.

"It's priceless really," he said. "No matter where I could take you in the world, he'd eventually find his way there. I guess you'll just have to live, at least for the time being, until he shows up."

"I hate you!" I spewed out at him in frustration, wanting to attack him somehow but only having words to do it with.

"Hate, now there's an emotion I can work with." He smiled, as his features cooled and morphed back into his human look.

"Screw you," I said as I looked away from him.

"Come on now, Portia. Don't be that way," he replied, toying with me. "It'll be fun. You'll see."

He left me alone after that, choosing not to speak, instead just staring at me with his unnerving gaze.

I turned to glance back out the window, watching the terrain moving below as we flew quickly overhead.

The flight attendant returned with more blood for him after a little while, and I watched him as he tasted it.

"Not as good as Vance's, but nice," he said, taking another swallow as he tested it out.

I shook my head, not rising to take the bait this time, and turned back toward the window.

I needed to start looking for an opportunity to escape. If I could get away and back to Vance, everything would work better for us. I started to run possible scenarios through my head, trying to figure something out.

We would have to land at an airport somewhere. If I could keep him from drugging me again, maybe I could get away from him there. Maybe I could somehow get someone's attention.

I sighed in frustration.

Who was I kidding? There was no way Damien was going to allow any kind of opportunity like that to present itself, and even if it did, he had the magic capacity to stop anyone who could try to help. I had to think of something else.

I tried pushing against the magical barrier restraining me to my seat. When I saw I couldn't move physically, I tried using magic to break through. My powers, however, just arced back at me, which resulted in me shocking myself with a very hard jolt.

I cried out a little, in pain.

Damien chuckled to himself as he watched me.

"Trying to escape right in front of me?" he asked, lifting an eyebrow in question. "You aren't afraid of anything, are you?"

I was afraid all right, just not so much for myself. I couldn't let him hurt Vance.

"I can see that life with you is going to be very interesting over the next little while." He looked amused.

"Not if I can help it," I mumbled under my breath, and he laughed at me again. I found myself wishing I could punch my fist clear down his throat to stop the sound of it.

"Portia, my dear," he began, and I hated the very sound of my name dripping from his voice. "Every second I spend with you helps me to see why Vance is so attracted to you. You're absolutely precious!" He gave me a little wink for emphasis.

I made up my mind right then and there to kill him as soon as I had the chance. I wanted to show him exactly how precious I could be.

A voice crackled over the cabin speaker.

"Sir, we'll be beginning our descent shortly," an unseen male voice said, and I assumed it was the pilot's.

"It's time to buckle up!" Damien said with a smile as he reached down to lift his belt, strapping himself into the seat easily. "Would you like me to help you with yours?" he taunted, leaning forward slightly as he stretched out his hands toward me in a helpful manner.

"I'm fine thanks," I said, sardonically, considering the fact that his powers were keeping me from being able to even move an inch, plus I would rather court death than let him touch me.

"Suit yourself," he replied with a shrug of indifference, and he eased back into his chair, still continuing with his unsettling stare.

I watched out the window, and I could see we appeared

to be approaching a large metropolitan area.

The plane slowly began to get lower in the air as we traveled along, and I could finally make out the large runways at the airport we were approaching. It looked to be one of major size, perhaps an international one.

The closer we got, the better I was able to make out shapes of buildings in the surrounding area of the airport. I concentrated on them hard, trying to make out anything which might give me some sort of clue as to where I was.

Suddenly some of the distinctly shaped structures caught my attention, and I realized right away that I recognized them. They were lines of casinos, running side by side down a long strip of road, as well as more than a few others that dotted the landscape spreading out around them.

I knew exactly where I was.

"Welcome to Las Vegas!" Damien said, with a smile.

We were in Nevada.

The Demon Kiss

Chapter 21

The small aircraft touched down easily, not even making a bump, as the wheels came in contact with the solid ground beneath us. We taxied down the runway until we turned off on another access road and moved toward a large row of hangars off on the far side of the massive space.

We passed by several of the large buildings, all of them closed, before I finally saw one that was standing open in the middle of the long row. The plane glided into it easily, and the large doors were closed behind us.

I sat quietly with Damien while the engine was shut down. The pilot made an appearance to visit with Damien and find out if the flight had been to his satisfaction, while the attendant brought him a briefcase.

When they were finished speaking with Damien, the two of them went over to the door, opened it and lowered the stairs down to the hangar floor.

At this point, a couple of men in dark suits boarded the plane.

"It's time to go," Damien said, looking over at me, and suddenly I was released from my magical holdings.

I had been waiting for the possibility of this moment, and the instant I felt myself freed I flung my arm out him, sending several ice shards in a row speeding out toward him.

He quickly waved his hand to the side, and the weapons

were redirected away from him, landing in the chest of one of the men who had just boarded.

The man gave a grunt of surprise, looking down at the group of shards protruding from his chest and fell over dead.

Damien shook his head at me, as if completely dismayed by my behavior.

"Portia, Portia," he said in that patronizing voice of his, "look what you've done! You've killed poor Michael. What did he ever do to you?" He made a clicking sound with his tongue while shaking his finger at me.

"I didn't do anything to him," I replied, standing from the chair that had been my previous prison, to confront him. "You did."

"Well, if that's the way you need to see it so you can feel better about yourself ...," he said trailing off in mock horror, as he got to his feet across from me.

It was the first time I noticed he was actually a little taller than Vance, by at least a couple of inches, which just served to make him look all the more imposing.

"Take her," Damien said, ordering the one man still standing next to his dead accomplice.

"Don't touch me!" I shouted as he approached, raising my hand threateningly, and he paused slightly to look over at Damien with a questioning glance.

"If you'd just come easily and quit provoking everyone, he wouldn't have to touch you," Damien said in exasperation, as if this were the most apparent thing in the world for anyone to understand. "You have to know I'm completely prepared for you. There's no way I would've allowed you from your restraints otherwise. Now be a good girl and get a move on!" He jerked his head curtly in the direction of the door.

I looked at him, weighing the situation, wishing I could wipe his smug, self-assured look off his face, before giving a sigh of defeat and brushing passed him to exit the plane. I noticed the waiting black limousine immediately when I stepped through the doorway. Its windows were tinted so darkly there was no hope of anyone seeing me inside, even if I were to lean up against the glass and pound on it. I paused, as I looked at the sleek car, knowing I was just being transferred, moving from one prison to another.

The driver was standing, smartly uniformed, and ramrod straight at the door, holding it open, waiting for us to enter the vehicle.

"Move along," Damien said from behind me, prodding me forward with the sound of his voice at my back, and I continued to make my way down the steps toward the waiting vehicle.

I stopped at the bottom of the stairs just to be annoying, pretending I didn't know where to go, and I looked around with a perplexed gaze.

"Get in the car, Portia," Damien said brusquely, not appreciating or even remotely falling for my little act.

I gave a frustrated sigh and walked over to the vehicle to climb into it. Under any other circumstance, I probably would have enjoyed going for a ride in a stretch limousine. Today was not one of those days.

Damien followed me in, along with the other suited man, while the driver closed the door and hurried back around to the front of the vehicle.

I scooted to the opposite seat that ran down the side of the limousine so I wasn't sitting next to either of them, earning myself an irritated glance from Damien in the process. I gave him a little half sneer in return, just to goad him a little bit more, knowing it wasn't the wisest course of action, but unable to keep myself from doing so.

"Is everything ready?" Damien asked, turning to the man sitting next to him, once the car was in motion.

"Yes, sir," the man replied, nodding. "Things are just as you requested."

"Good," Damien said, and his gaze returned back to me, the self-satisfactory look moving back into place.

"So where, pray tell, are we off to now?" I asked, trying not to sound too curious, but feeling it was important to try and gain as much information as I could about where he might be taking me.

"Why, to my place, of course," he responded.

The limo moved out of the hangar, driving into the bright desert sunshine outside.

"Just how many 'places' do you have exactly?" I asked, thinking back to the big spacious house he had recently occupied in Mexico.

"Several," he replied, casually. "I like to have the comforts of home when I travel."

This comment confirmed what I already had decided. He must have huge monetary resources. The fact that Vance's trust fund had been so large when his mom had run with him suggested Damien had a lot of money. He could probably buy anyone or anything he wanted.

That certainly wasn't going to help the odds against Vance and me at all. Lots of people could be persuaded to turn a blind eye toward things for the right amount of cash. Money could definitely talk.

I closed my eyes, trying to relax, as I searched my mind for any mental connection to Vance. I didn't really think I would find one, but I needed to look for him. I was feeling completely alone and vulnerable at the moment. There was nothing, of course, just as I expected.

The car moved out onto the surface streets, and I noticed we were beginning to make our way over toward the strip of hotels and casinos Las Vegas was so famous for.

At this point the suited man moved over to sit next to

me. I leaned away from him cautiously as he popped open the briefcase I'd seen Damien carry off the plane with him.

"I'm sorry, Portia, but it's time to go back to sleep now," Damien said, and I looked back at him for a moment in confusion, just before turning back to see the large hypodermic needle in the hand of the man next to me.

I didn't have time to react as I felt the sting in my neck again and all went dark once more.

When I awoke several hours later, it was to find myself lying comfortably on an extremely luxurious bed, the likes of which I had never lain on in my life.

I shifted against the soft fabrics as I looked around and tried to get my fuzzy brain to connect with its surroundings.

There was a large wooden canopy overhead with sheer curtain panels that hung down the sides. A beautiful imported silk duvet covered the bed, which was loaded with massive amounts of throw pillows of all sizes and varieties.

Sitting up slowly, I examined the Edwardian styled room with its rich custom-made furnishings. Everything was in a soothing pallet, decorated in shades of cream and gold.

My gaze ran over the fancy lamp at the bedside as I turned to look at the nightstand.

No phone. Not that I was really surprised about that.

Throwing my legs over the edge of the bed, I crawled down onto the floor, so I could look under the end table, searching for a phone connection. Even the actual phone jack had been removed, leaving a bare spot in the wall where it had previously been.

Damien is thorough at least, I thought.

Getting up from the floor, I looked around the room, my eyes resting on a closed door on the other side of the bed. I went and opened it, revealing a huge walk-in closet that contained many articles of clothing. Upon closer perusal of things, I discovered everything here was my exact size. While I found it a little creepy that all these items had been placed here for my use, I figured it was probably a good thing since it meant Damien must be planning on keeping me around for a while, versus the possible alternative.

I walked out of the closet and over to another door, not far from the one I just left. This one led to a large bathroom, complete with a giant whirlpool tub.

The vanity had been fully stocked also. There was a complete cosmetic line in the shades appropriate for my skin tone, as well as lotions, deodorants, shampoos, and all other hair care products a girl could possibly need. It could have almost been exciting to see all this, if one didn't know they were vacationing with their own personal Satan in the middle of Hell.

Leaving the bathroom, I walked over to the large picture window in the far wall and pulled the shades back so I could look out.

I wasn't familiar enough with the strip to know exactly which hotel we were in, but I could easily tell we must be in the penthouse suite, since I was looking at the highest possible point of the building.

The strip glittered like a many faceted jewel below me. It was now dark and all the exterior lights were on. I could see cars and people moving about on the street below, though I doubted I'd be able to get anyone's attention from this staggering height.

There was, however, a large balcony outside a set of double french doors. Perhaps I might be able to get someone to notice me from out there. I went to the doors and tried to open them, but I couldn't get out. They were firmly secured, completely unmovable, almost as if they'd been welded shut.

I tried magically forcing the lock, but it didn't budge an inch. I gave up after a few moments. It wasn't actually realistic to think I would be getting any help from that direction anyway. Even if I did get someone's attention, Damien would hear me and whisk me away before anyone would be able to find me.

I turned back to the room and rummaged through drawers in the desk, dressers, and nightstands, looking for anything that could help me out, or be used as a weapon of some sort, in case I needed it. I even went over and rubbed my hands over the marble fireplace mantel to see if I could find any good places to hide something if the need were to arise.

Of course, the fireplace was gas, so that ruled out a chimney as a possible means of escape.

I was getting up off my hands and knees when I heard a slight rattling sound at the door to my room. I whipped around quickly, bracing myself to react to whatever might be coming through it.

The door swung open, and a maid clad in full uniform entered the room, carrying a large tray of food which smelled absolutely delicious. I realized in that moment—I was starving. I'd had nothing to eat all day.

My appetite was soon dampened, however, as Damien followed into the room shortly behind her. He was dressed to the nines, which was the only way I'd ever seen him dressed, now that I thought about it. If it weren't for the hardness that glinted off the planes of his face, he would have been good looking.

The maid didn't even glance at me as she carried the tray over to the sitting area and placed it down on the beautiful cherry wood coffee table, which was flanked by two chairs.

Damien moved across the room and sat down in one of

the chairs, making himself comfortable, as he looked over at me.

"This is Darcy," he said, motioning to the pretty, petite woman. "She's been told that you're a guest who'll be staying here with us for a while. If you ever need anything at all, she's been instructed to see to your every need. All you have to do is ask."

"Perfect!" I replied, clasping my hands together in exaggerated enthusiasm over his remarks. I stepped up in front the maid, my tone turning serious. "Darcy, could you have the car sent around, please?" I asked very politely. "I need to catch a flight to Phoenix as soon as possible. If you could call ahead while I'm on my way to the airport, I'd appreciate it. Just make sure I get a good seat on the plane. First class would be preferable, if you don't mind. It shouldn't be too hard as it appears Damien can afford it."

Darcy looked confused at first and then swung her head to look back toward Damien, as if she wasn't exactly sure about what she should do with my peculiar request.

Damien started laughing, as he shook his head slightly from side to side at the perplexed maid.

"You're dismissed, Darcy," he said, waving his hand at her without taking his gaze away from me.

Darcy gave him a curt nod of her head and left the room, closing the door behind her.

"Maybe I should amend my statement," he replied. "She's to see to your every wish that doesn't interfere with any of mine. You might want to know—Darcy is a demon witch. I supply her with all of her blood, so there's no chance she'll be persuaded to assist you with anything that goes against my designs. She would sooner be persuaded to kill you than to help you get away," he said, as he watched me. "But, before you get any bright ideas about that, let me assure you that she's been threatened with her own demise if she were to even touch you in any way which might bring you harm."

I just stared at him, not replying, wishing he couldn't read my thoughts as easily as he did.

"Come have a seat," he said in an almost friendly sounding tone as he gestured to the chair next to him.

I eyed him for a moment before I walked over and sat down—trying to show bravado I didn't really feel.

"So, how do you like your accommodations?" he asked me with a smile, his gaze never leaving my face, making me feel nervous about how he was always watching me so closely.

"Looks like a prison cell to me," I replied as I glanced about, feigning disinterest for the fabulous suite.

He was every bit the actor I was, as he then pretended to be completely distraught over my answer. "Portia, you have no idea how that offends me! I've gone to every length to make your stay here as comfortable as possible. After all, you're my future daughter-in-law," he replied, his gaze dropping obviously to the diamond ring that graced my finger.

I didn't say anything, feeling a little sick over the whole daughter-in-law comment, realizing it was completely true and this monster would indeed be my father-in-law if Vance and I were to marry as we planned.

"We're like family, you and I," he continued, his voice sickeningly sweet, as it dripped in eloquent tones through that patronizing smile of his. He continued on. "I've made arrangements for you to have run of the entire penthouse. You may go anywhere you choose, and your every need will be catered to." He waved a hand like a magician at the food on the table.

"Well, that's good to know, because I *need* to go home," I said.

"You know I can't do that. And even if I could, I'm not sure I'd want to. I'm finding your companionship quite enjoyable." He smiled at me as he crossed his legs, placing his hands in his lap, and continuing his unnerving stare, purposely trying to make me feel uncomfortable.

"In that case would you care to join me for dinner? Or is it specially poisoned for my particular pallet?" I asked sarcastically, glancing toward the food on the silver serving tray in front of us.

"I would never poison your food," he replied, reaching out to take a grape off the tray and pop it into his mouth. "I pay a lot for my famous chef. I wouldn't dream of defiling his food."

"And which famous chef would that be?" I asked, wondering how one might go about finding someone who caters for demons.

"No one you're familiar with," he replied in dismissal of my question. "But I'm sure you'll enjoy his creations just the same."

"I don't know," I said skeptically. "I tend to be more of a peanut butter and jelly kind of girl."

"I understand completely. It's so easy to find a taste which one tends to prefer over all else." He agreed with a nod. "However, my tastes tend to run more to the liquid variety."

His eyes flashed red for a second as he smiled at me, emphasizing his meaning, before fading back to their natural color.

"Whatever floats your boat," I said, rolling my eyes at him. I reached for a cold cut slice of meat and stuffed it all into my mouth at once; trying not to let him think his little display had affected me at all.

I chewed it slowly, making a face of delight, as if it were the greatest thing I had ever tasted in the world. When I finished swallowing, I purposely licked every one of my fingers, just to be annoying to his perfect set of manners.

He laughed at me before reaching over to pick up a fork, sticking it into another piece of meat, and holding it over to me.

I eyed him for a second, through narrow eyes, before I decided to trust him and take it from him. I was starving.

"Eat up," he said, reaching over to pat me on the knee with his hand, in a familiar gesture.

I yanked my leg away, cringing at his touch, and he laughed as he stood to walk out of the room.

"When you're finished with your dinner, Portia, you may want to get cleaned up. Just set your tray outside the door, and I'll see to it you aren't disturbed for the rest of the evening, that is unless you want to come spend the evening with me," he added over his shoulder as he paused at the door.

"Not likely," I said rudely, over a mouthful of food, not even taking my gaze away from the plate.

"Suit yourself," he said with a shrug. "I should warn you, though—I'll be having a few … guests … over for dinner."

I didn't miss the hidden meaning of his words.

"Get out of my room, you sick pig," I said, trying to annoy him and not think at all about his little dinner soirée.

He smiled at me with an almost charming smile. "As you wish, my dear." He bowed curtly and left the room, closing the door behind him.

"Freaking psycho," I muttered to myself under my breath after he was gone, feeling relieved at his absence.

I continued eating until I polished off every crumb of food available, before lifting the tray and taking it to the door. I only opened it a crack, not wanting to witness any gross or disgusting thing which might be going on outside it.

I slid the tray straight out the opening, not even risking a glance to the space beyond, and hurriedly closed the door behind it.

I locked it afterward, placing my own magical reinforcement to the lock, just as some added protection. If I had to be a prisoner, I was going to reinforce my own prison space to keep unwanted people out of it. I didn't want anyone being able to sneak up on me while I was unaware.

Wandering back into the large closet, I began rummaging through all the clothing there, trying to find a decent pair of pajamas to wear that didn't look like something straight out of a lingerie shop.

After digging through half the closet, I finally had to settle on a short, silky, white nightdress which had spaghetti straps, and was slit up to my hips. It was the most modest thing I could find. Thankfully it had a matching robe to go with it, even though it was short, too.

I rummaged through the drawers, holding up the lacy under things I found in there with a questioning look. I wasn't finding anything that looked too appealing, let alone comfortable. Suddenly I found myself wishing for a pair of my boxer shorts and one of Vance's t-shirts. I gave up and just grabbed something before turning to head into the bathroom.

After magically reinforcing this door, I turned to the large bathtub and began to fill it. I poured an obscenely excessive amount of the sweet smelling bubble bath into the water, watching it foam up, before undressing and sliding into the deliciously hot water.

I flipped the jets on and closed my eyes. I knew the tub was overflowing with bubbles onto the floor, but I didn't care. Just because I was being forced to be a "guest" here didn't mean I was going to be an easy one. Maybe I would flood the room beneath me, and someone would have to call maintenance up here. *I bet that would upset him,* I thought with a chuckle.

Tired of thinking about my captor, I tried to calm my racing thoughts and center my feelings onto Vance.

"Vance," I whispered into the air, my chest tightening at the thought of him. "Where are you?"

There was no reply, but then I'd expected that. I sighed and continued speaking to him anyway.

"I'm okay. He hasn't hurt me," I said, even though I knew he couldn't hear me. "I love you," I added after a moment.

I let the dam I'd been holding in break then, and the tears streamed freely down my face.

He was probably frantic with worry right now. I knew exactly what he was experiencing. I felt it all before when he had gone missing after the explosion. I hated being the reason he was in pain.

Taking a deep breath, I tried to clear my head. I needed to think rationally and come up with some type of plan instead of sitting here like a crying silly ninny.

I needed to venture out at some point and survey the rest of the penthouse. In order to devise a good game plan, I should to know what the playing field looked like and what resources were available to me.

Tomorrow would probably be the best day for that, I decided, as I had absolutely no desire to run into Damien's dinner party this evening.

After soaking for over an hour and making sure I was completely pruned beyond recognition, I climbed out of the tub and got dressed. I was surprised to find the silky clothing I chose to be very comfortable as it was made from very high quality material.

How ironic is it that the nightgown from my captor is

probably more expensive than my entire wardrobe at home? I thought. Life could certainly be funny that way.

I wandered back into the bedroom, leaving my massive mess of water and bubbles all over the floor in the bathroom, and plopped into one of the chairs in front of the fireplace. I picked up the remote on the side table and pushed the button to make the flames in the grate jump to life. I sat in the dark, watching the fire burn as I ran one hand through my damp tangled hair.

My thoughts drifted back to Vance once again, and I wondered where he was and what he was doing.

Reaching up to finger the locket hanging next to the amulet at my neck, I gently opened the silver heart and looked at the tiny remnants of his hair that lay inside it.

I remembered the day I cut these trimmings from Vance's thick locks. We had done it in a desperate attempt to ease some of the physical discomfort we felt when we were separated from each other, so we could always have part of each other with us at all times.

I reached into the locket, placing the tip of my finger against the soft fibers. I couldn't believe how good it felt just to touch a piece of him.

After a few minutes, I gently closed it again; afraid of losing the only physical thing I had of him right now.

Leaving the fireplace burning, I went over to the bed, removing some of the many pillows so I could actually reach the top of the quilt. I pulled it back and crawled under the covers.

I closed my eyes and let sleep claim me.

Chapter 22

I allowed myself to lie in bed for hours after the normal time for me to get up passed. I didn't see any reason to rush into this new day, and I certainly did *not* want to spend any of my time visiting with Damien.

Finally, I decided I couldn't stay there for another moment. My stomach was growling viciously at me, and I was beginning to feel sick from lack of food.

Glancing over at the door, I realized apparently my little magical lock had held, since no tray of breakfast arrived with Darcy this morning. Of course, the downside to my little plan had left me very hungry now.

I climbed out of the bed, walked over to remove my reinforcement spell from the door, and opened it.

Since I didn't really give much care to what anyone thought here, I strode out into the hallway, in my nightgown, with my messy hair tangled about me, to have a look around the place.

My eyes were not prepared for what awaited me, and I had to purposely stop my chin from dropping in amazement at the sight I beheld.

I was standing in the second story of an opulently designed penthouse. A large rotunda was over my head, made entirely of stained glass, which accented the giant wood and wrought iron curving staircase that twisted down to the floor beneath.

The flooring was made entirely of marble, and the walls were covered in thick moldings and large paintings, depicting many scenes of magic and mayhem throughout several periods of time. A gigantic crystal chandelier hung from the center of the ceiling and down into the circle of the winding staircase.

I noticed another set of carved double doors just down the curved hall from mine and wondered if it led to Damien's room. I shivered at the thought of him sleeping so close to my quarters, but I certainly wasn't going to go exploring there to find out if I was correct.

Turning away, I walked across the hallway and placed a hand on the smooth, thick railing. Quietly, I tiptoed down to the first floor, my bare feet not making a sound against the cool stone as I moved along.

The bottom of the staircase revealed a plush sitting room to my right, which was decorated with many antiques, and a large dining room which was adjacent, with a table that could probably seat twenty, to my left.

I turned in the direction of the dining room, assuming the door beyond it must lead to the kitchen. I was not disappointed.

I entered the room through a swinging door and found myself in an immaculate kitchen that was fully equipped with the latest appliances and luxuries. Any chef would have truly been proud to work in this space.

It was then I noticed Damien sitting at a small table over in the kitchen nook with a newspaper in his hands. A glass filled with blood sat on the surface in front of him.

He looked up casually as I entered. "Ah! You finally decided to grace us with your presence this morning. How delightful!" he said, as he eyed my bedraggled appearance, shaking out a wrinkle in the paper as he spoke.

I pretended he didn't exist as I walked over to the

refrigerator and opened it, moving past without looking at him.

"I have good news," he continued, ignoring my attempt at rudeness. "Vance left Rocky Point this morning and is on his way back to Sedona."

This did perk my interest, but I didn't want to rise to his bait, so I kept my mouth shut, even though it was difficult.

Damien folded the paper and placed it back on the table in front of him, while he continued to watch me.

I kept looking through the fridge, trying not to notice the heat of his stare upon my back.

"Yes, my little spies say he's quite frantic right now," he went on. "Apparently, there's been a lot of arguing between him and your father over how to properly handle the situation."

I worked hard not to show any emotions, actually biting the side of my mouth a little, trying to keep from speaking out.

Locating a pitcher with orange juice in it, I pulled it out and set it on the granite island. I walked over to the cupboards and began searching for a glass to pour it into.

"Vance would have made a good boy scout," Damien continued, and I could feel him looking at me still, though I didn't return his gaze. "He's following the bread crumb trail quite nicely, I think."

I finished pouring the juice into the glass and set the pitcher back on the counter. I walked right up to Damien, picking an apple out of the fruit bowl in front of him, before turning to walk out of the room.

My knees were shaking by the time I made it through the swinging door, and I paused for a moment to lean up against the wall for support, breathing a little heavily since I'd been holding my breath unknowingly.

My emotions raced through me. Vance was on his way,

a little bit closer to me. He was coming. Somehow he would find me. I was both thrilled and terrified all in the same moment.

Pushing away from the wall, I quickly walked back up the stairs to my room. I shut and sealed the door behind me, before walking back over to the enormous bed.

I placed the juice and the apple on the nightstand, feeling unable to eat or drink at this moment due to the sudden churning in my stomach. I climbed back into the bed, pulled the covers up to my chin, and began to sob.

Conflicting thoughts rushed through my head. I was so torn. I wanted him to come for me, and I wanted him to run as far away as he could possibly get, never looking back.

"It's a tricky little situation, isn't it, Portia?" Damien's voice came from the direction of the doorway.

I jumped and turned toward the sound finding him leaning casually against the frame, the door wide open next to him.

"How did you ...?" I trailed off in surprise.

"You need to remember this is my house," he said as he pushed away from the wall and came to sit next to me on the edge of the bed. "Everything in here responds first to my powers, not yours. I'm sorry if it bothers you," he said, apologetically. He reached a hand out and placed it gently on my knee, squeezing it slightly as if he were trying to comfort me.

This time I shoved his hand off me and scooted away from him, up against the headboard.

"Don't touch me!" I glared at him, revolted.

"And why not?" he asked. The light of humor, and something much darker, flashed in his eyes. "Where do you think the very flesh you crave a touch from so much came from? If it weren't for me, your precious love wouldn't even exist."

"He's nothing like you," I spat back, feeling my insides begin to shake uncontrollably.

"Au contraire, he's everything like me, which is something I intend on proving to you when the time comes," he stated flatly.

"Why do you want him so badly?" I asked, staring straight at him, locking my gaze against his. "Aren't your precious minions enough for you? Why must you take him, too?"

He looked at me hard for a moment as if considering whether or not to answer me, before he spoke again.

"Because it isn't right for the son to be more powerful than the father," he replied, as he stood and paced out into the floor.

"What are you talking about?" I asked, exasperated. "You've sucked the powers out of how many witches? What could Vance possibly have that you don't, besides some common sense, that is?" I added, hoping he would be offended by my remarks.

He laughed an irritated laugh. "He doesn't even know his own power—it's wasted on him," he replied, with a slight sneer.

"Sorry, I'm not following," I said, confused.

"You really want to know?" he said turning to look at me. "Then I'll tell you. He replenishes!"

I looked at him with a blank stare, not comprehending what it was that he was trying to tell me.

"His magic is unstoppable," he continued. "I could perform an exchange on him a thousand times, and his powers would regenerate themselves every single time. He has an endless supply of magic that will never run out."

I felt sick as I wondered if this were really true. "How could you possibly know that for sure?" I asked. "There's been no way for you to even test your theory."

"When he was a child, I used to drink from him constantly," Damien stated. "He never became weak or ever lost any of the control over his powers. I assumed it was the same with all witches and warlocks. But then I started drinking from others, and it wasn't the same. Their blood was thinner, plainer. I had to drink a gallon from someone else to get even remotely close to the power that half a pint of Vance's blood generated. I knew then he was something special, but before I could do any testing on him, Krista ran with him. I began searching everywhere for him, desperately wanting to get him back. In all my travels the world over, I've never met one magical creature who had even a quarter of Vance's power."

It all made sense to me. "You want to turn him into a demon, to serve you and keep replenishing all your powers, don't you?" I asked.

He shrugged. "That's part of my plan," he said with a small smile. "All you really need to know is he will become one of the most magnificent warlocks the world has ever known, and he'll be second only to me. I can teach him everything I know, and together we could literally rule the world with an unspeakable, not to mention unstoppable, power."

I covered my mouth with my hand, feeling like I was going to vomit at the idea. Then another frightening thought occurred to me.

"Why are you telling me all this?" I asked. I slowly removed my hand from my face, watching him carefully.

"Because you're the brilliant pawn in all this." He smiled as he stalked back toward me. "You're the only thing Vance really wants in this world, and I'll be the one to give it to him."

"What do you mean?" I asked, tasting the fear in the back of my throat as I swallowed hard.

"It's simple really," he replied, sitting back on the bed next to me. "If he agrees to let me finish his conversion, then you get to live. If not, he loses you forever, and I'll turn him anyway."

"He'll never agree to it," I said shaking my head as my eyes began to water, knowing in my heart Vance would indeed do whatever he felt he had to in order to protect me.

"Yes, he will," Damien said, looking very sure of himself. He leaned in closer to my face. "Because if he refuses, I'll be the one who takes you away from him, in every way he can imagine."

He grabbed me by both arms and pulled me to him roughly. His lips smashed into my face, kissing me full on the mouth.

I fought against him ineffectively. He had me pinned tight in between the headboard and his body. The harder I struggled against him, the harder he pushed against me, and I sensed he seemed to be enjoying it.

I gagged, feeling the bile rise up in the back of my throat as I felt him thrust his tongue in my mouth. I used the only weapon I had, my teeth, and bit him as hard as I could.

He jerked away from me with a small yelp, and I saw I had injured him. A trickle of blood welled up in his mouth and ran down his lower lip. He lifted his finger to touch the spot gently, pulling his hand away as he examined it, before pulling out a handkerchief and dabbing the blood away.

He looked at me without any emotion now, his expression like ice for a moment, and I wondered if he might kill me right now after all.

"Like father, like son, eh, Portia?" he said, with a sudden laugh as he stood up and walked to the door, pausing to turn and look at me. "Who'd have thought you'd be the one to stir up the lust in both of us?"

He turned and smiled a purely evil smile before he

walked out, closing the door behind him.

I jumped from the bed and ran into the bathroom, slipping to my knees on the wet floor I forgot I left behind the night before, sliding precariously across the tile. I crawled the rest of the way over to the toilet and heaved the contents of my already empty stomach over and over again, uncontrollably.

When I was finally able to stop retching, I stood up and shakily made my way over to the glass shower. I opened the door, hugging the wall as I climbed inside, clothing and all.

I turned the water on as hot as I could stand it and sat on the seat, sobbing in horrible spasms, as I took a bar of soap and scrubbed at my skin, clothing, everything I could reach, wanting desperately to get the feel and the taste of him off my body and out of my mouth.

"Vance! Where are you? I need you!" I called out in my mind, wishing desperately he could hear me, but knowing he was much too far away for that to be possible.

"Portia? I'm here!" his voice came back, and I jumped against the glass before sliding into the bottom of the shower in shock at the sound.

I must be dreaming, or worse I was starting to hallucinate. "Vance?" I called out again, holding my breath in fear that he wouldn't answer—that my brain was playing some horrible trick on me.

"I'm here, Portia!" he called back to me again, and I could hear the desperation in his voice. "I'm on an airplane just coming into Las Vegas from Phoenix! I didn't think I was close enough for you to hear me yet."

Phoenix! Apparently Damien's spies had been wrong. Either that or he lied to me, which was always a very real possibility.

"Hurry, Vance!" I sobbed, this time in relief, knowing he really was on his way.

"Portia, are you okay? Has he harmed you?" his frantic voice asked me, and I could feel his great concern over my wellbeing.

"He kissed me ... hard. He tried to ... tried to ...." I began sobbing even harder, my tears mixing in with shower water as it ran down my face.

The anger burst immediately through him, and I could feel it strongly. It was a rage that burned more powerfully than anything I ever felt or experienced in my life.

"I'll kill him!" he yelled, his emotions coursing through me as they ran wildly through him, and I knew he meant every word.

"I'm all right," I hiccupped, trying to explain, knowing I needed him to be thinking calmly and rationally right now. "He didn't ... hurt me ... he only threatened to. I bit him, and he stopped, but he says if you don't join him willingly, he'll take me away from you in every way possible."

This perhaps was not the best thing I could be telling him right now. I could feel his fury as it seethed through every cell of his being, like little flames igniting every particle in him until he was a giant firework, ready to explode.

"Portia, where are you?" he asked, and I felt dizzy as his anger and hatred toward his father began to overpower me.

"I don't know," I replied, trying to steel my own body against his emotions. "We're somewhere on the strip in a really big penthouse."

"Can you look out the window?" he asked me.

"Yes."

"I want you to go to the window and look out, Portia. Start describing everything you can see. I'll need some landmarks so I can find out where you are."

I climbed out of the shower, running carefully this time as I dripped across the wet floor, and out to stand at the french doors that led to the balcony, moving the curtains back so I could look out.

"I can see a lot of the big-name hotels down the road."

"Which ones?"

"Um, Mandalay Bay, New York, New York, and Excalibur; they're on the opposite side of the street. I can see a lot of limos pulling in at the base of this hotel also. I'm in a white tower on the very top. There's a large balcony off my room, but he's sealed the door somehow so I can't get out onto it."

"I'll find it," he said. "We're coming in for landing now. I'll be over as soon as I can get there."

"He has set this all up for your benefit," I reminded as a flash of fear for him streaked through my veins. "You're the one he really wants. You'll be running straight into his trap."

"No. I'm going to attempt a rescue first."

"How can you possibly do that without alerting him to your presence?" I asked, my anxiety level reaching an all-time high.

"Leave that to me," he replied, his voice thick with emotion. "If he comes to you again, try not to antagonize him anymore. I just want you to do your best to stay locked in your room right now and wait for me to come."

"I will," I said, my mind racing with things I wanted to tell him in this very moment. "Vance, he says you have powers you aren't aware of. He says you can replenish yourself and you would never be in danger of losing all your powers. He says he could perform a demon kiss on you repeatedly and you'd never be human. That's why he wants you so badly. He hasn't ever been able to find anyone else as powerful as you in his life. The transfer is like a drug to him. He's addicted to it. He wants to change you so the two of you can rule over everyone in the world, like some demon empire."

"He told you all this?"

I could hear the worry laced in his voice. "Yes. He figured out we must be linked, but he doesn't know I can speak to you mentally. Otherwise, I'm sure he would've never said anything."

"Either that, or he intends to kill you no matter what," Vance said, and I could feel the hot surge of his anger flash again.

"I'm more concerned about what he intends to do to you. I love you, Vance. Please be careful!" I wished there was something else I could do to help him.

"Portia, do whatever you need to do to get ready to leave with me," he ordered. "If I can get in there, we're going to need to leave in a hurry, so make sure you're dressed appropriately."

"I will, but where will we go? He'll hunt us both down." I ran into the closet to look for something to change into, my dripping clothes leaving a trail of water on the carpet behind me.

"I have no intention of letting him live long enough to do that," he replied angrily. "But you're my first priority; I can deal with him later. I just want to get you out of there right now. I'll take care of him when you're safely deposited back with your family."

"Where's the rest of the coven?" I rummaged through the clothes in the closet looking for something suitable to wear, finally settling on a designer tracksuit I found toward the back of the rack.

"They're in Sedona by now probably. I hopped the first flight I could get on in Phoenix."

"How did you know where to go?" I asked, truly amazed he'd gotten here so quickly.

"After we searched the beach house for you and found the note he left behind, we went to the local airport. I found out a flight for Las Vegas had left the airport in Rocky

Point. It was the only flight that had gone out. I took a chance, and it paid off."

"So Damien thinks you're just barely in Sedona then?" I smiled. "He has no idea that you'd get here this quickly!"

"Taxi! Taxi!" I heard him shouting and knew he was calling for a cab outside the airport.

He must have run through the entire facility, I realized, wondering how he had been able to get off the plane so fast.

"Take me to the strip, please," I heard him tell the driver, and I assumed he must have handed the driver a significant wad of cash when he spoke again. "All this is yours if you can get me there with as much speed as possible."

There was a quick pause before he spoke again. "I'm on my way, Portia. Are you getting ready to leave?"

"Yes." I went into the bathroom to comb through my wet tangled hair and pull it back into a ponytail.

"All right, I'm going to make a stop to purchase some rope and binoculars," he explained. "I'm going to try to get to the balcony off your bedroom from the roof of your hotel after I find it, okay?"

"Please be careful." I came back into the bedroom and sat down to put a pair of running shoes on. "I imagine he probably has people watching for you all over the hotel."

"I'm hoping that won't be the case, since I'm earlier than expected, but I'll come in through one of the service entrances to try and avoid detection," he replied, trying to reassure me.

The door to my room opened suddenly, and I severed the mental connection with Vance just in case Damien could see it.

It was Darcy, though, not Damien, carrying a tray of food for lunch.

She placed it on the table without looking at me, then turned and left the room again, this time only to step out into the hall before returning with supplies to clean up the bedroom and bathroom.

I thought I was going to die as she moved about the rooms, taking her time cleaning up my messes.

She made the bed, fluffing it up all proper, before she marched into the bathroom. She emerged a short minute later with a glare on her face after she discovered the flood in there.

To her credit, she didn't speak a word to me, and it was all I could do to not pace the floor in agony as she mopped at the water-sopped area. I finally made myself go sit in a chair in front of the fireplace and click it on so I could stare into the dancing flames as a distraction. It seemed like hours passed before she went back out with all her cleaning gear.

"I'm okay," I said as soon as she shut the door behind her.

"What happened?" Vance asked, and I could hear the nervousness along with relief in his voice.

"The maid came in. I thought Damien might be coming into the room also. I was worried he'd be able to see our mental connection somehow."

"I don't think he can," Vance replied. "Otherwise, he'd have known about it that night on the beach when he took you."

"That's true," I said, remembering that awful night, kicking myself one more time for being so careless as to have gone to the beach by myself. "How close are you?" I felt very impatient as I paced the floor.

"I'm riding in the taxi up and down the strip trying to find a hotel matching your description. Portia, do you have something that's brightly colored you can put up to the glass in your window? I'm going to be searching for your room with the binoculars now."

I looked quickly around the room before deciding I'd have better luck in the closet.

I found a long neon green scarf folded in one of the drawers. I yanked it out and ran back into the other room where I hung it from the rod over the window, pushing it against the curtain from behind so it would drape closer down the glass pane.

"It's a long fluorescent green neck scarf," I told him.

"Okay. Give me a minute," he said, and I heard him give some more instructions to the driver.

It turned out to be about five minutes of pure agony on my part before he spoke up excitedly.

"I see it! It's a green scarf hanging in the window next to the balcony, correct?"

"Yes! That's it!" I pushed the curtains to the side and pressed myself to the window to look for him.

I saw a cab pull up into the parking lot far below, and a figure I would recognize anywhere emerged from it.

"I'm here, baby! Just hang on! I'm coming!" he mentally called out to me.

Chapter 23

I paced the room anxiously as I waited, every second seeming like an hour passed as the clock ticked away.

He wasn't speaking to me as he traveled through the hotel, being extra cautious to avoid any kind of magical detection.

I was terrified for both of us.

"I'm on the roof," he finally said in my head. "Give me a minute to secure this rope to a good spot and then I'll be down to get you."

"Okay." I felt the breath I had been holding release slowly. I looked around to make sure we were still undetected from this side of things.

Long excruciating minutes passed before I saw the rope hit the balcony in front of the glass windowed doors. Then he suddenly slid into my view, stepping away from the rope to move toward me.

He took my breath away, just standing there in front of me. Even clad in a black t-shirt and blue jeans, he was still the most wonderful thing I had ever seen. I didn't even want to blink because I was afraid he would disappear before my very eyes. I didn't think I could possibly ever love him more than I did in this very moment.

I placed my hands up on the square glass panes as I looked out at him.

He raised a finger to his lips, and I nodded in

understanding. I wouldn't make a sound.

He grabbed the knob to the door, and I watched as his hand turned a bright red color. The knob on my side of the door began to glow right in front of me, and the fixture began to melt in his grasp until it was molten liquid running down the frame. Then he reached his hand into the latch and melted it also.

When he was finished, I heard a little popping sound and the door swung open easily as he pushed on it. I rushed out to him, throwing my arms gratefully around his neck.

He grabbed me to him and kissed me with a force I had never experienced. If the situation still hadn't been so desperate, I would've never let go.

"We need to leave, Portia!" he whispered as he pulled my arms from around him. "Do you remember our lesson in levitation?"

"Yes." My thoughts bounced back to the night he had taken me to the high school to show me what we could do.

"We're going to use those powers to climb back up the rope to the roof. You ready?"

"Yes," I answered. He placed the scratchy rope into my hands, and I gripped it tightly.

"You go first this time," Vance said with encouragement in his voice. "I'll be right behind you."

In essence it was as if we were rappelling up the wall. We would bounce off with one step and take a couple up into the air before bouncing off again, using the rope as a guide as we ran up the exterior of the building.

We had almost cleared the wall when Damien suddenly burst out onto the balcony, leaning back to look up at us.

"Stop!" he yelled, and he lifted a hand toward us to fire some sort of magical burst of power through the air.

"Run!" Vance said, pushing me the rest of the way over the ledge. He jumped over right behind me.

The two of us took off in a fast sprint over the roof until we reached the edge. We levitated in a leap across from one tower over to another, hitting the roof lightly with our feet, until we reached the stairwell that led back down into this building.

Vance grabbed my hand as we tore down the stairs together. We pushed through a set of double doors and out into a large hallway.

Two men in dark suits turned to look at us as we entered.

"There they are!" one of them shouted, lowering the handheld radio he had up to his ear.

Vance shot a fireball at them, not waiting to see if he hit his mark, pulling me back through the doors we had just run through.

We scrambled down two more flights of stairs before we tried going through another door.

This hallway was empty, and we turned left and raced down the carpeted path stretched before us.

Vance stopped abruptly when we passed a door marked as the entrance to the service area. He turned quickly, pulling me back in this direction, and we raced through it.

"Where are we going?" I gasped, my lungs feeling like they were about to explode from our sprint.

"I'm trying to get us out of the building right now!" he explained, sounding as out of breath as I was, as he dragged me through a noisy laundry area filled with many workers.

He used magic to slide full laundry carts into the path behind us, not caring that there were confused workers standing all over the room shouting at us as we ran through the area.

We turned the corner, ran down another hallway, turned once again, and found ourselves in a huge vacant loading bay. We ran toward the open delivery door.

"Almost there!" Vance said, and I felt the surge of hope shoot through me. We raced to the exit only to have all hope dashed in the next second. Damien stepped around the corner in front of us.

We slid to a halt, and Vance grabbed me up to him as I lost my footing.

Damien slowly walked toward us, a large smile spread over his face. "Welcome home, son," he said, with a nod toward Vance. "It's good to see my boy again."

"You've lost the right to call me that," Vance said, and I noticed the red flames had shot instantly back into his eyes.

"What, no kiss for Daddy?" Damien asked in feigned shock, placing a hand over his heart as if he were mortally wounded by this. "Portia was kind enough to give me one, weren't you, baby?" he added, inadvertently using Vance's pet name for me as he winked at me.

I felt Vance's temper flare, and he pushed me behind him, shielding me from Damien. I also noticed the two men who had been chasing us in the hallway had finally caught up and were closing in on us from the rear.

I placed my back against Vance's as I watched them approach, never taking my eyes off of them, watching as their demon masks slipped into place.

"You got those two covered?" Vance asked into my mind, as he continued to face Damien.

"Yes. You take care of your dad," I replied back into his head, not wanting him to be distracted.

Damien continued forward, goading Vance as he walked. "I must applaud you on your taste in women, son," he said. "She certainly is a delicious little thing. I quite enjoyed the little taste I had of her."

"You won't ever touch her again," Vance replied, his voice sounding furious and deadly.

Though I could feel his emotions boiling to a whole new

extreme, I chose this moment to attack. I threw my hands out right, shooting from my palms and catching both guards in the chest with stakes of ice.

The two of them registered a look of shock before falling to the floor, writhing in pain as they clutched at the ice, their shirts quickly becoming stained with the blood they were losing.

I turned back to face Damien.

"I'll let her live if you'll join me, son," Damien said.

Vance snorted. "Why, so you can have her? I don't think so, *Damien*." He sneered. "I don't want her to be anywhere around you."

The three of us slowly circled around each other. "Forget the girl then," Damien said trying a different approach. "There's a whole magical world out there, just waiting for us to take control of it. We could rule it together. Think of all the power we could have."

"You mean all the power Vance would have. The ones you'd try to steal from him, right?" I spoke up, clarifying what he had said to me earlier.

"Shut up, you little witch!" Damien said glaring at me as his face transformed into his demon features.

He took a step toward me, raising his hand into the air, and Vance threw a fireball straight at him.

Damien pivoted and waved his hand, deflecting the fireball away from him and moving it toward me with a burst of magic. I had to duck quickly to prevent being hit by it.

"Portia!" Vance called out to me, and I knew he hit his boiling point.

I saw his eyes flare with a strength I'd never seen before as he turned back to face Damien.

Vance raised his arm and shot out a continuous arc of flame at his father this time, stepping toward him ominously.

I had to move several steps backward, raising my hands involuntarily into the air to protect myself from the wave of heat that washed over me.

Damien raised his hand, and a force field shot up in front of him, deflecting the fire harmlessly around him.

Vance continued to send the flames toward him, this time raising his other hand, throwing flame from it as well, and I could see Damien was slowly being forced backward, as he tried to maintain his field of protection.

Warily they circled, neither one giving in to the other, and I scooted silently back away from the intense heat, moving farther across the floor.

I didn't consciously realize how close Damien had gotten to me, until suddenly I could see he was standing between Vance and me, and I realized I hadn't been paying enough attention to my own position. I tried to run, but I felt a sudden magical restraint take hold of me, and I was unable to move. Damien's arm snaked out and grabbed me, pulling me up against his body.

He dropped the magical restraint that contained me, diverting the bulk of his power back to the shield that was protecting him. I pushed against his chest as I struggled to get away.

"I'll kill her!" Damien shouted out, and Vance immediately dropped the flame, taking a step back away from him.

"Let her go!" he shouted, his chest heaving, as they continued to face off against each other.

"I can't do that." Damien smiled shaking his head. "She's the only leverage I have."

He yanked my head roughly to the side and sank his sharpened teeth into my neck, and I screamed loudly.

"No!" Vance yelled and ran toward us, fear tearing

across his face as he approached.

Damien threw his hand up, sending out a burst of power that sent Vance soaring across the room, slamming him up against the opposite wall.

Struggling against the horrible pain of the bite, I tried desperately to pull away from him. Damien yanked me harder against his chest in an iron grip. I could feel the weakness starting as he drank from me, my knees threatening to give a little under the onslaught.

Slowly, I lifted my hand to cover his heart, and summoning all the energy I could muster, I slammed a giant ice shard right through his chest.

I felt the gurgle as he let go and fell away from me to the floor, releasing me so suddenly I stumbled backwards, grasping at my neck in an effort to try to stop the bleeding.

I watched for one second as Damien struggled for breath, crawling away toward the doorway, gasping as he moved. Then I turned and ran haphazardly over toward Vance, who was slowly regaining his feet. I tripped and fell into him heavily, leaning on him for support.

"How bad is it?" he asked, pulling my hand away from my wound so he could check it.

Instantly I realized this was a mistake, and I felt the craving as it leapt through him when he saw the blood running from my neck.

He let go of me, like I'd burned him with a hot poker, and he stepped back from me.

This is not good, I thought, as I saw the yearning for a taste pass over his face, his longing very evident.

Vance eyed me warily, his expression a mask of both desire and despair as he watched me, and I could tell he was struggling with a decision.

A loud grunting sound came from across the room and made us both turn away from each other to look in that direction.

I was horrified to see Damien slowly stand up, and the ice shard I shoved into him began to push backward out of his chest, until it fell out, shattering into a million pieces on the floor.

We both watched in amazement as the hole in his chest closed and he was completely whole once again, as if he had never been touched.

A low laugh escaped his lips as he took in our expressions, and he began walking toward us slowly.

"Let's finish this, son," he said seductively, calling out to Vance, enticing him with the call for blood. "I can see the desire ripe in your eyes. You want her badly. Do it! She's yours for the taking. Nothing can stop you now."

I looked at Vance, and I could feel the emotions warring inside him. I began to taste a bit of fear in my mouth.

There were two forces here, and I was caught between them. If Vance turned against me, then all was lost. There was no way possible for me to survive this without him. I couldn't fight them both.

I placed my hand back over my neck, trying to protect myself as he watched me, and began to back away, until I realized I was moving away from him and toward Damien. I stopped, not knowing what to do.

"Take her, son! Now!" Damien yelled at Vance.

Vance reached out and grabbed me, pulling me hard up against his body, and I felt desire shoot through him.

"Do you trust me?" his voice shot through my head, thick with some unseen emotion.

I hesitated only a second. "Yes," I replied back to him.

He yanked my hand away from my neck and covered the wound with his mouth, sucking hard as the blood flowed freely into him.

I grabbed at his shirt with both hands trying to keep

myself standing, feeling the weakness enter my limbs almost instantly. He was drinking in earnest now, both of his arms wrapped tightly around me, and I could feel his body singing against me as he drank my blood.

"Yes, son!" Damien cheered with an evil laugh, as he walked up next to us. "Yes!"

He watched as Vance continued to feed on me. "Now let me perform the kiss, son, before she's too far gone," he instructed him. "We can take all of her powers, too."

Vance let go of me so suddenly I slumped to the floor. "You want a kiss? Then go ahead! Take it!"

Damien hesitated for a moment, in perplexed surprise, as he looked at me on the floor in front of him. I saw Vance reach behind his back to pull an athame out of the holder on his belt.

Vance raised the weapon up, shooting his hand out and yanking Damien to him. He moved so quickly I hardly registered the sight of the knife slitting Damien across the throat.

Damien grabbed at his neck with both hands as the blood started to pump out.

Vance dropped the athame and grappled Damien by the collar, pulling him right up next to his face, dropping his jaw.

I watched in horror as I realized it was Vance who was performing the kiss on his father, not the other way around.

Damien tried to scream, but couldn't with his throat being cut, instead making a horrible gurgling sound.

I found I couldn't look away, and I watched Damien convulse, his blood spraying as all his powers drifted up out of his body and into Vance's.

Vance's veins began to glow, and Damien became weaker, until it was only Vance's brute strength that was keeping Damien standing.

Vance began to tremble as his body was trying to

absorb the massive amount of power it was receiving.

He dropped Damien to the floor and took two steps backward before he started to shake violently.

The veins in his neck and arms were protruding, and his face was beaded in droplets of sweat. He dropped to his knees, falling forward slightly, unable to keep standing with the force of everything.

"Vance!" I cried out hoarsely, reaching for him.

"Don't touch me, Portia!" he hollered with great effort, as the magical currents continued to fight in his body.

He gave a loud yell as he arched his back, flinging his arms out away from his body, and sparks shot out the ends of his fingers, followed by little bursts of flame. It was almost as if he were being electrocuted, as wave after wave of shocks rolled through him.

I cried as I watched him being wracked with pain.

He convulsed that way for several moments, and then he finally fell to the floor in exhaustion as the effects of the exchange subsided. He collapsed in a heap right next to Damien's body.

I crawled over to his side, passing by Damien, who was still and pale, lying in a puddle of his own blood. I could tell by the flat vacant stare he was really dead this time.

"Vance!" I called out as I slouched next to his limp form, placing my hand on his blood-splattered face. "Vance! Please answer me!"

His eyes opened into tiny slits, just large enough for me to see the clear, blue eyes there, which surprised me.

"I'm okay," he breathed heavily, as he looked at me. "What about you?"

"Well, I feel better than I did the last time you did this to me," I replied as I continued to hold my wounded neck.

"I'm sorry about that," he whispered, as he lifted his blood-covered hand to rub down the side of my face, then thinking better of it.

"It's fine," I said as the tears dripped from my face and onto him leaving wet spots to mingle with the blood on his shirt.

He slowly began to sit up on his own, reaching over to pull me into his embrace, cradling me tightly to his chest.

"Are you sure you're all right?" I asked, searching him over for any damage I might have missed.

"I think so," he replied, as he ripped off a part of his t-shirt at the hem, folding it into a thick square and placing it against my neck and applying pressure there. "That was quite a trip."

"How did you know to even try that?" I asked, with an incredulous look upon my face.

"It was something you'd said," he explained, holding the tight pressure against my skin. "You said I had more powers than I was aware of. I just had the thought that he always wanted me so he could perform that stupid demon kiss. I suddenly realized maybe that was the power he was after specifically. I figured if I strengthened myself with your blood, then maybe there was enough demon in me to try it myself."

"You took a huge risk, Vance! What if it hadn't worked?"

"I still had a big knife." He smiled and gave me a wink.

He stood then and pulled me to my feet after him, wrapping his arms around me and pulling me into his embrace. He tilted his head a little to observe the bleeding at my throat.

"I need to heal this, Portia. But I'm not sure if my powers might be adversely affected." He sighed, seeming concerned about it.

"Just do it, Vance. I trust you."

"Are you sure? I don't like taking risks when it comes to

you," he replied, his eyes flitting over my face.

"So bleeding to death isn't a risk?" I asked him with a small laugh.

"I see your point," he smiled. I felt a warm heat pass through me as he cupped my neck in between his strong hands. "Kiss me," he said when he was finished, looking down at me tenderly.

"Why? So you can steal my powers now?" I teased back, albeit badly.

"No, just your heart," he replied, seriously.

"You can't steal what already belongs to you," I reminded him. I wrapped my arms around his neck and kissed him with every intense emotion I had, until he finally had to pull away.

He held me tightly for several moments, and we finally turned back to survey the damage in the room. We looked at the three dead bodies lying on the floor, drenched in their own blood.

"It's finally over, isn't it?" I said looking up at him, having a hard time believing the two of us were responsible for the gruesome scene in front of us.

"Almost," he replied, with a nod.

"What do you mean?" I asked, looking up in confusion, wondering what I might have missed.

"Now it's time to clean house," he said.

Chapter 24

Vance checked us in to another hotel and placed a call to my family in Sedona, letting them know he had found me. He explained everything that had happened, and everyone was greatly relieved to hear we were both safe.

The coven came to Las Vegas to assist in the cleaning up of loose ends, as Vance had called it.

We spent a lot of time in Damien's penthouse, going through files and personal items trying to trace all the other members of his coven, so they could be destroyed also.

Every time we found a lead, we organized a strike team to go and take care of the threat. Soon we had found everyone except for Darcy, the maid from the penthouse who had been instructed to take care of me.

I watched Vance in amazement as he handled things with great efficiency. It was almost as if he had assumed the role of leader in our coven, though he politely deferred to my dad and Grandma in every aspect of decision-making.

I also noticed his powers were significantly stronger than they had been before. I could feel it when I was standing next to him, pulsating through his veins, but it was even more obvious as he destroyed every demon we encountered, fighting like nothing I'd ever seen before.

The strange thing in all this was he seemed to have suffered no ill effects in performing the demon kiss. In fact, it seemed to have just the opposite effect, as he no longer suffered from the awful withdrawal he had experienced before, and I had yet to see the red eyes reappear. We finally decided the exchange must have completed something in the cycle he had been going through. Vance and Dad had also been going through all of Damien's holdings, which proved to be vast indeed. Vance decided to liquidate all the properties, which were located all over the world, stating he certainly did not have a need for so many places of residence. He told my dad to use the money from those sales to give to the witches and warlocks Damien had stolen powers from. It wasn't magic, but Vance felt they should be compensated somehow for their losses.

Even with all his generosity, Vance was still going to easily be a multi-millionaire. Damien had been a very rich man with a lot invested in many lucrative pots that were still accruing money hand over fist. Dad assured us Vance would be extremely well off for the rest of his days.

That evening, Vance and I were getting ready to walk down to Freemont Street on the strip. It was New Year's Eve, and there was a lot of celebrating going on in the city.

Vance had asked me out on a date, to go see the light show and watch the fireworks. I was very excited about it. We had been through so much lately, I was ready for some relaxation and celebration.

We walked hand in hand as we strolled down the sidewalk, watching the people passing us by, and reading the bright signs that were advertising all the A-list headliners for the evening.

"How are you feeling?" Vance asked as he looked at me.

"I'm a lot better," I replied, knowing he was referring to the weakness I felt after being fed on by both him and his father. "Thanks for healing my neck."

"No problem," he said as he squeezed my hand. "I'm just sorry you were placed back into that situation."

"It wasn't your fault. I was just the means to an end."

"Don't talk like that," he said turning to look at me.

"Like what?"

"You're so much more than a means to an end," he said, staring at me with eyes full of love. "You're my life! I couldn't live without you."

I smiled and gave him a quick hug before we continued on down the strip, until we reached Freemont Street.

The light show there was fantastic, as we stood shoulder to shoulder with hundreds of other people packed into the place to watch the spectacle.

As the colored images flashed down the roof in many patterns, I suddenly spotted a face in the crowd I recognized.

I nudged Vance hard.

"What is it?" he said loudly over the music, and he leaned toward me so he could hear me.

"It's Darcy!" I shouted back, pointing over to where she was standing several feet away.

He followed my finger with his gaze, his eyes searching the crowd.

"She's the one in the red jacket with the fur around the hood," I described as I continued to point at her.

It was as if she heard us, for she turned right then to look at us. Fear instantly crept over her face, and she ran away through the crowd, shoving people out of her way.

Vance instantly took off after her, and I started running after him.

Several people protested loudly as we pushed and stumbled through the throngs, trying to move after her through the crush of bodies.

Ahead, I could see Darcy reached the edge and moved to run down a darker alley, just as we came to the outer rim of the masses.

Vance took off after her with a sudden burst of speed, and I found I had a hard time keeping up with him, his enhanced powers becoming more evident with each passing day. Darcy rounded the corner onto another side street, then across traffic to go into another alley.

Vance and I danced through the traffic as we crossed the street behind her, causing several people to slam on their brakes and honk their horns angrily at us.

As we entered the alley, we could see Darcy running ahead of us down at the far end. Vance threw a burst of magic at her, hitting her and causing her to trip and fall forward onto her hands and knees.

Vance was easily upon her after that, picking her up none too gently and dragging her to her feet.

"Please don't kill me," she gasped in fear as her face transformed into her demon mask.

"Give me one good reason why I shouldn't," he replied roughly, jerking her and lifting her cleanly off her feet, so she was dangling in the air in front of him.

She hesitated for only a second. "Because I know where your mother is," she huffed, her eyes looking wildly about.

"Sorry. Try again. My mom is already dead," he growled back at her. "I killed her myself."

Darcy shook her head. "No, she isn't," she replied, her red eyes never leaving his face, though her lower lip quivered as she spoke.

"What are you talking about?" Vance asked, shaking her like a rag doll.

"Damien sent a shape shifter to get you. He was toying with you," Darcy answered him.

"Liar! That isn't possible!" he yelled, but I saw a flicker of doubt cross his face.

"Yes, it is," Darcy pleaded with him. "Krista was his prisoner, but he never turned her. He needed her for something else."

Vance pondered this for only a second. "Where is she?" Vance said, pulling Darcy within an inch of his face, his sculpted features hardening into a sudden deadly calm.

"Scotland," she cried out desperately. "She's in Scotland with Damien's parents ... your grandparents!"

Vance released her in shock, taking a step backward.

Darcy took full advantage of the release and ran as fast as she could down the alley, rounding the corner out of sight.

The fireworks began shooting off overhead as Vance turned to look at me in disbelief, his face a mask of complete shock.

Krista Mangum was still alive!

The Demon Kiss

About the Author

Lacey Weatherford has always had a love of books. She wanted to become a writer after reading her first novel at the age of eight.

Lacey resides in Arizona, where she lives with her husband and six children, one son-in-law and their energetic schnauzer, Sophie. When she's not supporting her kids at their music/sporting events she spends her time writing, reading, and blogging.

Visit the official websites at:
http://www.ofwitchesandwarlocks.com
http://www.laceyweatherfordbooks.com
Follow Lacey on Twitter at:
http://twitter.com/LMWeatherford

The Demon Kiss

Lacey Weatherford

Also From

Moonstruck Media:

Nominee for
Best YA Romance
of 2010!
~The Romance Reviews

Blood
of the
White Witch
of Witches and Warlocks

Lacey
Weatherford

"I have never cried or shouted so much at a book in my life!"
Susan Mann, Susan K Mann Reviews

When love came knocking on the door of novice witch, Portia Mullins, in the form of handsome bad boy, Vance Mangum, she had no idea how quickly the attraction between them would escalate. Now she finds her relationship with Vance taken to a whole new level, in a way she had never dreamed possible at this point and time of her life. Yet even as the personal connection between them explodes, the two quickly find themselves in a world of shifting balances. While searching for Vance's missing mother, they realize they are suddenly unsure of who to trust, learning that sometimes things are not always as they appear. When Vance's demon characteristics abruptly begin to resurface again without warning, the horrible truth comes out, crashing down upon them and shattering some of their most precious dreams. Once the deadly plan is uncovered, Portia and Vance find themselves hastily rushing against the hands of time in an attempt to stop an ancient ritual from being performed. But will they be successful before fate reaches out to twist them cruelly, possibly separating them and changing magic forever? Passion, loyalties, powers, and family ties, will all be tested when dangerous adventures abound in this third installment in the ...*Of Witches and Warlocks* series, *Blood of the White Witch*.

"Each book keeps getting better and better, I didn't know it was even possible. I have never cried or shouted so much at a book in my life. This is one rollercoaster of a ride, full of ups and downs." ~*Susan, Susan K Mann Reviews*

HAIL TO THE
QUEEN OF
HEARTS.
Lacey Weatherford
BOOKS

Made in the USA
Lexington, KY
10 September 2012